PENGUIN BOOKS

WALTER

David Cook was 'born into a working-class Lancashire family in
1940. He failed Grammar School Entrance at eleven, was sent to a
Secondary Modern School, and left at fifteen, unable to spell and
with no aptitude for arithmetic. As an adolescent, he held a variety of
dead-end jobs in quick succession: in the storeroom of a slipper
factory, unloading lorries for Woolworths and making bricks at a
brick works'. At the age of eighteen he was accepted by the Royal
Academy of Dramatic Art in London. After his training he played
leading parts with the Bristol Old Vic and various repertory
companies throughout Britain. He created the part of Trevor in John
Bowen's *Little Boxes* in the West End; and spent a year as the host of
a children's television programme, as the side-kick of a bear.

David Cook began writing in 1969, and has published three other
novels, *Albert's Memorial*, *Happy Endings*, which won the E. M.
Forster Award, 1977, and *Winter Doves* (Penguin, 1981) a sequel to
Walter. He has also written several scripts for television, including
'Willy' and 'Jenny Can't Work Any Faster', both of which were
nominated for awards. *Walter* received the Hawthornden Prize for
1978.

He lives in London and near Stratford-on-Avon, and does his
writing in both homes and sometimes at the local Public Library.

DAVID COOK

WALTER

A KING PENGUIN
PUBLISHED BY
PENGUIN BOOKS

Penguin Books Ltd, Harmondsworth, Middlesex, England
Penguin Books, 625 Madison Avenue, New York, New York 10022, U.S.A.
Penguin Books Australia Ltd, Ringwood, Victoria, Australia
Penguin Books Canada Ltd, 2801 John Street, Markham, Ontario, Canada L3R 1B4
Penguin Books (N.Z.) Ltd, 182–190 Wairau Road, Auckland 10, New Zealand

First published by The Alison Press/Martin Secker & Warburg Ltd 1978
Published in Penguin Books 1980
Reprinted 1980
Reprinted in King Penguin 1982

Set, printed and bound in Great Britain by
Cox & Wyman Ltd, Reading
Set in Monotype Ehrhardt

For my sisters, Kathleen and Carole

Part One

His Parentage and Birth

I

If you let a man get his way with you, you'll live to regret it

SHE wanted a child.

First she had wanted to be married. To be married first, and then to have children. That was what women did, if they were to have respect. If they remained unmarried and childless, they became Old Maids, and lacked respect. If they had children without first becoming married, they became Fallen Women, and had no respect at all. It was proper and it was natural for a woman to marry, and thereafter to have a child.

The fact that her own mother had been married and had given birth to a child – to her, Sarah – and had hated both experiences did not deter her. Her mother had merely added fear as an element to the mixture of mainly pleasurable and exciting emotions with which Sarah looked forward to marriage and motherhood. Hips, it seemed, were the problem. Sarah's mother had the narrowest of narrow hips. Consequently Sarah's arrival into the world had been achieved only after the most painful of all deliveries. Sarah's mother spoke with authority for all women who had ever had babies. The hips of none of them had been as narrow as Sarah's mother's hips, the delivery of no baby more painful than the delivery of Sarah. At fifteen, Sarah did not question her mother's authority on the subject of hips.

'You've got them too. You get them from me. You think twice, Sarah, before you let a man go too far. Least done, soonest mended. One moment of pleasure is certainly not worth the pain I went through, giving birth to you.'

Sarah's mother went on to say that there were many ways to satisfy a man's desire without permitting actual penetration. 'They've talked to you about it at school, I suppose?' Sarah shook her head. 'They' never meant the other girls, always the teachers, none of whom had ever spoken to the fifteen-year-old Sarah of the ways by which male lust might be satisfied without permitting actual penetration. This was clearly a shortcoming of the educational system, but part of Sarah feared that to admit it would bring forth all the gory details from her mother. Another part of her – the lower part – wished to be enlightened on what to do, and how far it was polite to go.

'You mean, they haven't told you anything?' Again Sarah shook her head. 'Well, I'll be – ' but she was never to find out what her mother would be, since a second thought came quick on the heels of the first. 'What about the other girls? They must have talked about it.'

Sarah wasn't sure how to answer this. Then she said, 'Only in a dirty way.'

Mother looked at daughter in a manner that suggested that she was not sure they were related. She could not remember that she had ever put on such airs, though if airs were to be put on at all, she supposed that this was the age for them.

'What's dirty about your body?'

The question did not even seem simple, and was bound to be less simple than it seemed. It would be one of her mother's trick questions, designed to find out exactly how much she knew, and then, having found it, her mother would condemn it all as filth. 'Nothing I hope.' She would not be tricked.

'So should I.' Sarah's mother waited, watching for a flicker of guilt on her daughter's face. 'Do you really mean to tell me you don't know anything?'

'I'm not sure what you're getting at.'

'When and if you get married, there are certain things you have to know about. There's nothing dirty about the way babies are born. Dirt of that kind is all in the mind. But if, as in your case, you'll want to avoid having children, you should be put straight on ways of being fair to your husband, and yet not finding yourself as I did, Sarah, screaming to the Lord for forgiveness because I couldn't bear the pain you were causing me. And don't you expect help from those Sisters of Mercy at the hospital, because they only slap your backside, and call you a ninny. The one who did that to me had never taken a man into her bed in all her life, and she had hips like barn doors. She could have given birth to a wheelbarrow, provided it arrived wheel first.' Sarah closed her eyes. Her mother's imagination was fertile, but seldom expressed as crudely as this.

The silence which followed this speech seemed to be as important as the words of which the speech consisted. Sarah did not know which was worse, to fill the silence or to let it go on for ever. Meanwhile her mother moved around the room, setting the table for tea, refusing to make eye-contact with her daughter, her every movement indicating a continuation of the fury which her daughter had done nothing to provoke. Clearly the silence must be filled. Sarah said, 'I'm sorry.'

Her mother sniffed, and asked her what she felt sorry about.

'About causing you such pain.'

Her mother laid a knife down slowly at the wrong side of a plate, and remained looking down at it for what seemed like an eternity.

Then she spoke in a slow controlled way, measuring her words out carefully as she stared at the knife. 'If you let a man get his way with you, you'll live to regret it. It's sad, because we're both women, and giving men pleasure is what we're made for, but if God makes you too narrow, you'd be better off becoming a nun. Be God's wife. *He* won't force his way into you, without a by-your-leave. I'd been warned about my narrow hips, but I was weak against your father. But he was a big man, you see. And we were married. He said he had every right; it was his right to . . .' Sarah's mother considered the various forms of circumlocution open to her, and chose one '. . . to do it properly. I begged him to allow me to accept him in other ways, but he wouldn't; I think he was puritanical really. Then, when he had forced his way in, I begged him again to be careful. We were fighting. Like animals, I remember. He was what they call "on heat"; he thought it proper for me to fight him, but I was in earnest; I was too frightened for pleasure. Lord! he was a big man. Then there was blood, me being a virgin. I thought he'd damaged me inside for good. I didn't know then that there would be blood, you see. Like you, I hadn't been told. I kept pleading with him to be careful, and withdraw. We were both sweating so much, the sheets were wet with it. Soaking.'

She stopped talking, and remained still; the memory of that pain was still painful. Sarah was crying silently, her throat and chest near bursting with the effort not to make a noise. When she could speak, she said 'What happened?'

'You did. You're what happened.' Her mother looked away towards the window. 'He was up inside me so far, there was no way his seed could escape. My only hope was that the seed might be inferior, and not bear fruit, but that was not to be; the seed was fruitful.' Her mother sank slowly into a chair, and continued speaking. 'He came out almost as painfully as he had entered me, and then he slept. I didn't. The sheets were so cold by then, with the sweat cooling off. I thought a lot of funny things as I lay there, with my eyes open all night. I hated him so much. I even thought of creeping downstairs to get my dressmaking scissors. He was sleeping so heavily, I could easily have cut it off, and stopped him wanting me ever again. One snip! He would have bled like a pig, I shouldn't wonder. That seemed fair, when I had already bled for him. I thought a lot about that. I also thought that I was beginning to go mad, with the shock. Nothing seemed real any longer. Not him, pushing and pumping inside me, not his anger because I didn't want to, not his sweat dripping into my face. All unreal.'

She stopped again, this time to remember. It was important to try to be accurate, since this was the first time she had talked about it to anybody.

'I was so completely his property. Pinned down by his arms and his chest. I . . . I lost myself, the moment he took my virginity. It's important, that. You must feel that.'

Sarah nodded.

'I treasured my virginity. It made me feel as if I was somebody.' She looked out of the window at the lawn and the rockery with the different kinds of heather she had planted. 'And his brute strength bled it to death in just a few seconds.' She looked round at Sarah. 'Also he'd been with lots of women before me. He swore he hadn't, of course, but I could tell by the way he handled me. He knew what to do. I could tell at once by the way he pulled me apart. He'd lied to me; he'd said there were no others, but he couldn't have that knowledge without the knowledge of others; he couldn't have the confidence. After that, as long as he went elsewhere for that sort of thing, I kept house for him, and concentrated on you. When the war came, I was glad. Do you know, he never wrote to me once, or I to him. I got the usual telegram when his ship went down, and that was that.'

There was a long pause. Then Sarah said, 'Have you never wanted another man? More gentle.'

Sarah's mother smiled. 'Of course I have. I'm not unnatural. I've teased quite a few in my time, just teased, you know.' She smiled again, and wiped her eyes with the back of her hand. Then she stood. 'Well, there we are. I wasn't expecting to tell you all that. They should teach you at school about all that sort of thing.'

2

We've been and gone and done it, then?

THEY were going to Southport. She sat opposite him in the train, and thought, 'What have I done?'

The object which prompted this question to enter Sarah's mind was Eric's neck. As they sat down in the compartment, which they had managed to get all to themselves, Eric had removed his scarf, and Sarah had realized that she had never before seen him without one. His neck was so thin and scrawny that she couldn't take her eyes off it.

Here they were, with the train rattling along, taking them to a honeymoon in Southport, and all she could think about was how thin his neck was. He hadn't worn a scarf during the wedding ceremony; he couldn't have; her reason told her that she must have seen Eric's neck before. Yet here it was, naked in the compartment, and she was looking at it as if she were seeing it for the first time.

Eric's mouth was dry. He couldn't stop swallowing, and his Adam's apple shot up and down. Even a sip of alcohol, even a sniff of the cork, went straight to his head, and, feeling that he was no longer in control of himself, he became frightened. Therefore he had not sipped, he had not sniffed the sweet sherry which had been given to him at the small reception held at Sarah's mother's house. He had held a glass in his hand, and pretended to drink from it. The church service had made his mouth dry, since it was important to get it right and to do nothing, say nothing which was not in order and always said. He had hoped that he would find an appropriate moment to go to the bathroom, and drink from the tap. Unfortunately, from the moment he had placed the cheap wedding-ring on Sarah's finger, he had been watched, talked to, joked with; there had been no moment to himself, no opportunity to slip away without making much of it. If he had asked for a non-alcoholic drink, he would have been an object of hilarity to all the men present. His soul thirsted for ginger beer, for squash or Tizer, and they had given him sweet sherry, which he knew better than to touch. None of these men were friends of his. Even the Best Man had been provided by Sarah's mother. He knew no one except the farmer for whom he worked, and who had been unable to attend the wedding because (Eric being away) he had to do the feeding himself. And resented it. He had disapproved strongly that Eric should take a week off work for something as irrelevant as a honeymoon.

He did not understand why, when both he and Sarah were chapel, Sarah's mother had insisted on a church wedding. Sarah had worn white, and an organ had played. There was no organ at the chapel, but white could have been worn there. He would have been less nervous in a more familiar place.

Sarah watched Eric's Adam's apple shooting up and down, and wondered if he were going to be sick. He had behaved strangely all day. He was nervous, of course, but so was she.

'Are you alright, Eric?'

He nodded.

Fascinated by the thinness of his neck, and the way it made his head seem much too large, she began to count the number of times he swallowed, and having started, had to make a positive effort to stop and to look out of the window.

As she watched the countryside move past, she thought how little they knew about each other. They had been for walks, mostly on Sundays after chapel. They had held hands. She knew that he worked on a farm, that he had told her he had been brought up in an orphanage, that he was quiet. He was a quiet man. They had taught him to be quiet at the orphanage. He had never even tried to kiss her. She had thought this odd, but remembering her mother's experience, had put down this apparent lack of passion as a mark in his favour. He certainly wasn't big and muscular as her own father had been. He would never force his attentions where and when they were not wanted. He would be worried about their first night together, more worried than she. She looked again at the stiff white collar around his sunburned neck. She could see the veins standing out, purple on the red neck, squeezed into that solidly starched band of white. And the Adam's apple. No, he would not be difficult to control; he had pulled no one apart; she would be in charge. They had been sitting in the train for half an hour, and all he had found to say in that time was, 'We've been and gone and done it, then?' and all she had said was, 'Yes.' They both looked out of the window. He would be unlike her father; he would not handle her roughly.

They walked from the railway station to the hotel. Eric insisted on carrying both their suitcases, so that he had to stop and change hands every three minutes. On arrival at the entrance hall, Sarah waited for him to go over to the desk and ring the bell, but he stood there, looking around like a puppy which has lost its mother. Sarah rang the bell, and a young girl asked them to sign the register, and then showed them to a large room with a double bed.

Eric put both suitcases on the bed, and began to unpack his own. Sarah noticed that, right at the top, he had packed seven or eight comics. Children's comics! Sarah laughed out loud at the idea of children's comics on a honeymoon, but when Eric turned to find out why she was laughing, his expression was of a child who has discovered that there is no Father Christmas. Both fell silent. Their silence was total. Eric left the comics inside the case, locked it, and placed it on top of the large Victorian double wardrobe. The comics remained there, and were not mentioned.

It was not yet dark, but there seemed to be nothing to do but to go to bed. They undressed, with their backs to each other. Sarah slid into bed first, and kept her back to Eric, who was taking longer to undress, even though he remained in his underwear.

Two hours later, it was dark, and both were still awake. Neither had spoken or moved. They lay side by side with their eyes open, staring into the blackness, each waiting for the other to make a move.

Finally Sarah reached out a hand to find his hand. Almost immediately, her hand was full of a sticky substance. Eric said, 'I'm sorry.' Sarah placed the sticky substance where she thought it should go, and in doing so, found a way of exciting herself.

She was to need that discovery a great deal, later on. 'Sorry' became the word she would fall asleep hearing quite often.

3

A young couple who have just remembered a previous appointment

WHEN Sarah woke the next morning, she saw Eric, already fully dressed, standing by the window, looking out.

She watched him for a long time before he sensed that he was being watched, and turned round. Then they both said, 'Good morning!' in a rather formal way, as one might say it to the newsagent or the postman, and Eric turned back to look out of the window.

The people in the streets below moved mainly in the same direction, like evacuees from a threatened city, carrying with them their most precious possessions, buckets and spades, striped towels, rubber balls and bathing costumes. Prams containing small ill-tempered babies were pushed by women whose thick overcoats announced their belief that the weather would change before lunch.

Eric said, 'We have to be downstairs by quarter past nine, if you want breakfast. I don't mind. I'm not hungry.' They had paid for breakfast; they would eat breakfast. Sarah began to get out of bed, and Eric turned back to look out of the window again, respecting her modesty.

She dressed in silence. Three times Eric cleared his throat, as if about to speak. Finally he did speak, and what he said was, 'Shall we go home?'

He was standing with his face pressed against the window, which was clouded by the steam of his breath. Only the back of his head was towards her. Sarah said, 'Why?'

'I thought if you wanted to, we could. They might not charge us for the whole week. I could start back at work tomorrow. It would mean a bit more money for . . .' He stopped to consider what the extra money might be used for. 'Mr Davies wasn't keen on me having the whole week off. We could put the money towards furniture.' His voice trailed away. He was exhausted at the length of his speech, and embarrassed at having made such a demand on someone else's attention.

'What would people think?'

'What people?' He had no friends; there would be no one to scoff. Mr Davies would actually be pleased.

'The people at the hotel. All the people who came to the wedding and gave us presents. How would we face them?'

'I'm sorry. I hadn't thought.'

'No.' Even if there were no one else to consider, her mother would have to be faced, if they were to return home after one night of their honeymoon. She might say Eric had been taken ill, but that would not be believed, if he were to begin work again at once. It was not possible. They must stick it out, for the sake of appearances.

They left the bedroom together, he following her. Over breakfast they sat alone in silence, and the waitress who asked them whether they wanted porridge or cornflakes smirked as if the question had a dirtier significance. When the waitress returned to the kitchen, the sound of giggling could be heard from behind the serving-hatch.

They stayed at the hotel the full week. She made no further attempt to touch him, and he slept beside her with what seemed to be as little interest as if they had been married forty years. Sarah told herself that things might improve once they were home again.

Every morning she asked him what he would like to do that day, and every morning he replied that he didn't mind. One day, they went on a coach-trip. It was a Mystery Tour, which passed through Bootle. During the other days, they sat side by side in deckchairs, looking out to sea, each wrapped in separate thoughts, each longing to know what the other was thinking, and neither daring to ask.

One evening was spent at the Concert Party on the Pier. The audience around them roared with laughter at the comedian's jokes, while Sarah and Eric sat in silence, wanting the show to end. The comedian made two jokes about honeymoon couples, at which the audience laughed even louder than before. Sarah began to sweat, and then to tremble. 'Darling, you've curdled my wee-wee,' the comedian said, and the middle-aged woman in front of them went into a paroxysm of hilarious coughing and was thumped as hilariously on the back by her companion. Sarah found that she had become very frightened; she did not know why. She grabbed Eric by the arm, and pulled him to his feet and along the row of seats, past laughing faces. The comedian noticed two youngish people leaving in the middle of his act, and capitalized on the insult by bringing them to the attention of the rest of the audience. 'There's a young couple, folks, who've just remembered a previous appointment.' Those in front turned to look. Eric closed his eyes, and allowed himself to be led. As they walked up the centre aisle, every face in the audience was turned towards them, and as they reached the back of the auditorium, the audience began to applaud.

'Well, I've often felt like a bit myself, you know, but I can't say I've been that desperate.' A roar of laughter. There was a lighted sign, which read, 'EXIT', and Sarah willed herself towards it, dragging Eric behind her.

'As my missus always says – always, and this is the truth – "Just keep it on ice for me, Bernard; the waiting's more than half the pleasure."' Laughter. 'Just like the Eskimo, who was engaged to be married. Kept it on ice, but his fiancee broke it off.' Laughter and applause. 'You can't be too careful.' They were through the swing doors and into the foyer.

As the comedian signalled to the pianist that he was ready to go into his 'Getting off' song, he contemplated the advantages there might be in planting two young members of the stage staff to do every night what Sarah and Eric had just done.

For the rest of the week, Sarah and Eric spent their evenings sitting in the lounge of the hotel. Sarah read the back copies of *Punch* and *Woman's Own* which lay about there, and Eric, since his comics remained locked in his suitcase upstairs, looked at the photographs in *The Field*.

On returning home they were to stay with Sarah's mother, until such time as Eric could find a job as a farm labourer which had a tied cottage that went with it.

Sarah's mother met them at the door, wearing a new pink blouse and more make-up than Sarah remembered ever having seen on her mother's face before. She was also wearing ear-rings, the very ornaments which she had once told Sarah that only women of the very lowest character wore. If the Lord had intended women to wear such things, He would, she had told her daughter, have supplied small cup-hooks on their ears. Those had been her words. Now, as she leaned forward to kiss her new son-in-law, miniature replicas of Blackpool Tower were swinging at each side of her face.

'Hello, love!' was all she said to her daughter, but to her son-in-law she said, 'I expect you'd like a nice cup of tea.' Eric nodded.

'Are you sweet enough, or do you take sugar? I like lemon with mine, when I can get them. Such a refreshing taste!' She guided Eric by the shoulders, and lowered him into the most comfortable chair. 'We've got to make him feel at home, haven't we? Start as we mean to go on.' After a sideways glance at Sarah, who stood dumbfounded at this totally new aspect of her mother's character, she added, 'Well, we'll do our best, we hope,' and disappeared into the kitchen.

Sarah looked across at Eric, who was swallowing almost as quickly and as often as he had in the train on the way to Southport, and thought, 'If only she knew!' All that talk! The warnings to keep her legs crossed, and not allow him to go too far. The vivid and detailed accounts of the manifestations of her father's lust. His size. His experience of other women. If only she knew how her daughter had spent this past week! But she would not know. Nobody would be allowed to know.

Sarah's mother made her entrance carrying a tray of tea and cakes, and wearing an apron with frills on it. She said, 'Well, then, how was the weather? Have you had a nice romantic week? You must tell me everything – everything that won't make me blush, that is,' at which Sarah laughed, loudly and suddenly, and found herself unable to stop.

She laughed and laughed, like Little Audrey, while her mother and Eric sat looking at her. Finally she placed the fingers of one hand between her teeth and bit down on them, so as to force herself to stop. Eric's face wore the same expression as when she had laughed at his comics. Her mother would want an explanation, and continue to want it until the want was satisfied. An explanation came to her. She said, 'Mother, what have you got on? That's not Blackpool Tower hanging down from your ear, is it?'

There was a silence before her mother removed both ear-rings from her ears, with a deliberation intended to demonstrate that she was hurt and offended. Then, handing them to her daughter for inspection, she said, 'They're replicas of the Eiffel Tower in Paris, if you must know. They were a present from a very old and dear friend; they're diamanté. But you're quite right, Sarah, as always; they are too dressy for the daytime. I simply wished to please my friend by wearing them when I wanted to put on a bit of a show for your homecoming.' She glanced at Eric, who was studying the pattern of the hearth-rug, with the air of someone who has lost a battle and won the war.

The next two months were the most difficult Sarah had ever endured. Her only refuge was at her work in the drapery shop in town, where she had liking and had respect, from the owner for her pleasant appearance and punctuality, and from the customers for her cheerfulness and civility. She in turn liked her job. It didn't require all the potential which she was sure she had, but because of that she found it relaxing, and it gave her time to think. Now her thoughts and daydreams were no longer of wedded bliss and a cottage, with lupins in the garden and roses round the door, of meals she would cook for her strong but gentle husband, and the attractive and well-mannered children who, with her encouragement and love, would grow and progress from Grammar School to college and on to secure jobs with the Midland Bank and as learned professors – perhaps higher? who knew? – and would in their turn marry, and give her grandchildren swaddled in silk and in cashmere.

Her daydreams now were nightmares, her thoughts of loneliness, of growing too old to have children, of ways to support a jobless husband, of remaining for ever as a lodger in her mother's house, of the impossibility of divorce, which only the upper classes could afford, and of the shame and scandal which would be caused by the only grounds she had for it, non-consumation, since Eric would not, *could* not, be adulterous. Also she thought of death, her own, Eric's, her mother's.

At home, her mother took every opportunity to corner her. Whenever and wherever they were alone together, her mother would close the door and whisper questions about Eric. Asking what he was like, meaning, what was he like in bed? Asking if she were being careful. Reminding her of the narrowness of her hips. Complaining that Eric spoke so little. Didn't Eric like her? What could she have done to offend him? Yet she had noticed how little he spoke to Sarah, his own wife. Was everything alright between them? Was he resentful at what Sarah was quite rightly denying him? Did Eric blame *her* for this? She knew she shouldn't mention it, but she had to mention it: when Eric came home, the smell of pigs and of cattle on his clothes was impossible to remove from the house. She was not complaining, but the neighbours had inquired whether she were keeping livestock. She wanted Sarah to know that the reason she had stopped buying belly of pork, or pork of any kind, was that the smell on Eric's wellingtons had so strong a relation to the smell of that same animal, and that the associations of that smell had affected the animal's taste to Sarah's mother, so that pork was a meat she could no longer stomach.

Sarah countered all the questions and complaints as best she could. She said that Eric was gentle in bed, that there was no fear as yet of her getting pregnant, and that, as for the smells, Eric was lucky to have a job at all, with so much unemployment about. As for the fresh eggs Eric smuggled home in his pockets, she would like to suggest, without wishing to appear at all rude, that her mother found nothing distasteful about *them*.

To Eric's face, Sarah's mother flirted with him, like a small girl in her first party frock. His lack of response to her attentions was the cause of many of her questions to her daughter.

The other place, besides the drapery shop, where Sarah had time and solitude to think about the future, and what, if anything, she could do to shape it, was in bed with her husband, when, as happened every night, he had turned away from her, squeezed himself into a foetal position, and said, in a very quiet and sad voice, 'Goodnight.'

Two months and three days after their return home from their honeymoon, Sarah decided to take matters into her own hands, so to speak. She had spent many hours at work thinking about it, and had planned, and then replanned, what she intended to do.

The light had been switched off. Eric had rolled himself up, and said his quiet, 'Goodnight.' Gently but firmly, using as much strength as was necessary for the work but no more so as not to alarm him, she pulled his right arm, so that he turned, still in the foetal position, with his knees stuck up in the air to form a tent of the bedclothes. Sarah held each side of his face with her hands, and kissed him firmly on the lips, forcing her tongue into his mouth. Then, still holding his face between her hands, she lifted her face away from his, and said, 'We have to talk about this.'

Her hair hung down on each side of her face, so close to him that he could smell it. He closed his eyes, then lowered his knees, so that for the first time he lay there beneath her, unguarded and passive. From beneath his left eyelid, a tear trickled to the top of his nose, and ran down the side of it. A moment later, his right eye shed water too. Sarah kissed him gently on the tip of his nose, then pressed her lips gently on to each of his eyelids.

'There must be something we can do about it.' She spoke softly, with optimism and tenderness, encouraging a child to take its first step.

He lay still, with his eyes closed. Then his lips began to tremble, and without sound, he mouthed the words, 'I'm sorry. I'm so very sorry.'

The feelings, like floating weeds, which had grown in the base of his stomach, and had accumulated and tied themselves up into the kind of knot one can't undo, now suddenly broke free, and came rushing up into his throat to find release. The corners of his mouth turned down, as he bit hard on his lower lip to stop the feelings escaping, but the force of emotion was too powerful, and first he began to sob, grabbing Sarah's hands and pulling them down so that he was able to turn his face to one side, and then gradually between the sobs there were words, fragmented, some swallowed as they were uttered, some cried out, some whispered, some incoherent, some half-finished. So his feelings poured from him, as his head jerked from side to side as if he were in a fever. His eyes were still closed as tight as he could close them, but the tears still flowed.

'Can't help . . . Help me . . . Takes me . . . by surprise. I do . . . do want ... do love. Can't ... control it ... No warning ... Me ... not you ... My fault ...' and suddenly, loudly, 'IT'S SO BLOODY UN-FAIR', swearing in Sarah's presence for the first time, uttering for what must surely be the first time the clear statement of an unalterable belief, which was that this not so much premature as instantaneous ejaculation was unfair, a trick played on him by some bloody-minded Creator, determined to ensure that the one thing any man could do, he, Eric, would do wrongly, and to no effect but sorrow and embarrass-ment. He could not believe that it would happen, and yet it happened every time, and every time the surprise and disbelief and shame was as strong as before. Sarah, aware that her mother might already have her ear to the wall, listening for the sound of bed-springs, touched his lips lightly with her forefinger to indicate that he should keep his voice low. She whispered, 'We have to try together. If you turn away from me, I can't help you. It doesn't matter if it takes a long time for you to get better, as long as we keep trying. If we keep touching each other, per-haps you'll get used to me.' Thus, in the year 1923, many years before Masters and Johnson had begun their work among the premature ejaculators of the United States, Sarah's intuition took her towards what was to become an essential principle of Marriage Guidance. The world is full of humble people who have anticipated the discoveries which have made others rich, and died without even a *Times* obituary.

Eric said, 'Hate ... not being ... like other ... They can ... able ... I have duties ... as a husband.' He cleared his throat, and his Adam's apple, Sarah knew, would be bobbing up and down in agonies of embarrassment. She stroked the side of his sunburnt neck with the backs of her fingers. He was not unattractive to her; he did not repel her, as her father had created in her mother feelings of repulsion. 'Should have ... have told ... told when ... Thought ... Couldn't ... Talking dirty to mention ... Telling you ... dirty talk ... Not on a Sunday.' They had met, had conducted their courting, had been at least for country walks together, on Sundays. Even if Eric could have brought himself to introduce the topic at all, Sunday would clearly not have been the day for it.

Sarah said, 'How could you know before? Before we were married. How ...?' But her voice trailed away. If he had tried with other women, and failed, she was not sure she wanted to know about it. If other women knew his secret, then it would be known in the town; there would have been secret sniggers at the wedding. Anyway, she did not want details of that sort from Eric; they did not help her plan. But Eric covered his face with both his hands, and spoke. Once he had begun, he had to tell it all.

He spoke so quietly that she could only hear by putting her ear very close to his mouth, and this tickled, but she bore it. There had been no experience with local women. It had been at the Orphanage. He had told her he had been brought up at an orphanage. He didn't want to offend her; he didn't want it to sound dirty; he hoped she wouldn't laugh at him; he had to tell her. Sarah shook her head, so that her hair brushed against the backs of his hands. She would not laugh at him. He took her hair in his hand, and held it against his face.

There had been a woman at the Orphanage. She was the one who would go round the dormitory at night, tucking everybody up, saying, 'Good night. Sleep well.' But for some of the older boys, she did more than tuck them up. She used to put her hand under the blankets, and touch the secret parts of some of the older boys, and play with them, and she would stand close by the side of the bed, and allow them to put their hands up inside her skirt and into her secret parts. But she had laughed at Eric. Because when she touched Eric's secret parts, or if Eric should first put *his* hand up under her skirt, then at once ... immediately ... just as it still was ... always ... every time. And she laughed. There was no excitement, no enjoyment, just surprise and shame. He had thought it was because he was so young, and he had asked the other boys, and they had told him that they had kept their hands within her secret parts for many minutes, in some cases very many, and what it was like up there, inside her, their fingers inside her, how she had become open and wet inside, and had wriggled, and ... and even at the telling, often, at the mere account of it, Eric had experienced the same strange and shameful orgasm, which he did not know was an orgasm, or even what an orgasm was, but only knew that he could not control it or hide the effect. 'It had to be a secret. Otherwise they would have sent her away from the Orphanage. She never told the others about me. But they guessed.'

He stopped, let go of Sarah's hair, buried his face in the pillow, and was biting it. So much regret, and anger, and deep shame. Sarah leaned over him, thinking of all the girls at school who had 'talked dirty', and of all those who, unlike herself, had cried at their first period. She had not cried; she had suddenly felt much older, a woman, and almost of the world. Eric had small golden hairs on the back of his neck, she knew. She put out a hand in the darkness, and touched them. She was a woman, he only a boy who had outgrown his strength. But she had strength, she must use it.

Slowly, while her husband sobbed soundlessly into his pillow, Sarah got to her knees on the bed, and removed the nightdress she was wearing. Then she took one of Eric's hands in hers, and led it around the contour of her body. Using her own fingers to spread out his, she moved his hand over and under and around each of her breasts in turn, down the front of her stomach, then sideways over the curve of her hip, down the outside of her thigh and up the inside to between her legs. As his finger touched her pubic hair, his hand tightened, and he tried to withdraw it, but she held the hand firmly, and refused to let it go. As she lowered herself on to his fingers, she said, 'Don't worry about what happens now. It really doesn't matter,' and forced his fingers inside her, brushing her vulva with one of them.

'We have to love one another, Eric. Because we promised God that we would.' And she thought to herself, 'One day! I can wait. One day he will give me a baby.'

She kissed the back of his schoolboy neck, and, with her fingers intertwined with his and her right arm over him, they both fell asleep.

4

Everything cost a penny or less, and the eyebrows of the salesgirls were of little importance

ON the twenty-first of April, 1926, Princess Elizabeth, later to become Queen of Great Britain, was born. Sarah and Eric had been married three years, and still they were childless.

Sarah had remained at her job with Tyson's Drapery and was now the manageress. To young women of a romantic nature, she sold brightly coloured garters from a card at sixpence each. Such young women must have too much money for their own good. Sixpence would buy a pound of stewing-steak which, cooked with a cow-heel, allowed to cool in a basin, and turned upside down when the jelly of brawn had set, would be meat for a family for four days. Sarah disapproved the extravagance, but sold the ribbons anyway.

She took great pride in her display booth, in which she set ribbons and cottons, laces and rolls of netting. Thrifty women came to the shop with their daughters to purchase trimmings with which to refurbish a handed-down frock so that it could pass for new. Some of them would bring the frock in with them so as to get Sarah's advice on how to go about it. She did not sell such customers more than they could afford or needed; her advice was good.

Most of Sarah's customers came to her for Vedonis Egyptian cotton underpants and vests, and for socks of various sorts – bed-socks, hiking-socks, ankle-socks, or grey socks for school with red and black patterns of diamonds at the tops, which turned over. The pure silk stockings, at three shillings and threepence, were seldom sold, but remained, wrapped up like treasure, on the shelves behind the counter. Those women, whose pride would not allow them to go bare-legged to chapel or to work, bought imitation silk at one shilling or seconds at ninepence. White French knickers with lace edges were stocked, and sold for weddings and the honeymoons which followed, sometimes for christenings, seldom for funerals. Sarah herself wore French knickers and imitation silk stockings, below a sensible blouse and skirt, for she had a discount on all goods she bought for herself, and was expected to look her best when serving.

She and Eric now lived in a tied cottage at the end of a row of one-up-and-one-down similar cottages, though theirs had the advantage of a small extra room at the back, in which there was a stone boiler, which had a heavy round wooden lid and an iron grate below it, in which wood or coal could be burned to heat the water. This boiler took up a quarter of the room. The smoke from it was supposed to go out through a pipe at the side of the cottage, but in practice it usually blew back into the room, stinging the eyes of any occupants, and blackening any laundry which had been hung up there to dry. In wet weather, Sarah's blouses for work, which were always crisp and clean, had to be kept away from the boiler, and ironed dry with a flat-iron heated over the fire.

Life at her mother's house had been far more comfortable, but the cottage gave them privacy. Also it was something which Eric himself had acquired by his own work, and this, Sarah hoped, might increase his confidence, and some of that increased self-confidence might find its way into their cold but private bedroom.

The summer passed. Eric worked longer hours at the farm than in winter, and was correspondingly more tired when he got home, so that their love-making, which had improved, regressed again. Sarah found that she was irritable, and less concentrated at work. Her manner was sometimes offhand, and occasional customers complained. She sacked a young girl who had until then shown promise of becoming an efficient saleslady, simply because the girl arrived for work one day with her eyebrows drawn on with a burnt matchstick. It was not the use of the matchstick to which Sarah had objected. This, like top-of-the-milk as face-cream, and soot or salt as toothpowder, might be thought a praise-worthy economy. But the girl had done it so badly, first by not following the natural line of her eyebrows, then by allowing the matchstick line to get smudged, so that she looked like someone who had (for some private reason) pushed her head up the chimney just before leaving the house.

The girl was sacked. It was a mistake. The girl cried, and said what was most likely true, that she would be unable to find another job. Sarah became angry at what she considered to be blackmail, and stood her ground, feeling that if she were to give way, with the other girls looking on, she would no longer be able to control them. So the girl left, and was difficult to replace, none of the many other applicants for her job being even half as competent. Sarah's exasperation was not lessened by hearing that the sacked girl did find another job, with

Cohen's Bazaar in Preston, where everything cost a penny or less, and the eyebrows of the salesgirls, whether drawn on properly or not, were of very little importance.

Harvest Festival came and went at the chapel. Flowers and fruit were arranged in various decorative ways to the greater glory of God, before being transferred to the Cottage Hospital, there to be consumed by the patients, but Sarah's womb had borne neither flower nor fruit. She fitted white ankle-socks on to the feet of infants and grey three-quarter-length stockings on to the legs of schoolboys with bruised and blistered knees, but bore no child of her own on which to fit socks of any length or colour. She undressed and re-dressed only her display window, and with less flair and interest than once she had shown, carrying out the task because, if it were not done, the goods there faded or grew dusty and had to be marked down.

Three years more, three more fertile springs, three ripening summers, three Harvest Festivals, three bleak winters, one thousand and ninety-five nights of trial and error. Sarah was now thirty-two years old, Eric thirty-four. Slowly their love-making had improved. Gradually she had brought him to the state in which he took her almost as powerfully as her father had once taken her mother, and as she had laid there, encouraging him to go higher and deeper into her, she had imagined her own father, whom she had never seen, breaking into her mother with his brute force and callous determination, and always it was that image which prompted her orgasm.

One day, in the late spring of 1930, the doctor confirmed that she was pregnant.

By Harvest Festival, she would be round and ripe as the fruit arranged so tastefully about the altar by Mrs Grant and Mrs Williams: she would be as heavy-laden as the sheaves (more usually the sheaf) placed against the pulpit by Miss Burton. But her fruit would not be taken to the Cottage Hospital or feed the old, the sick, and the poor. It was at the Cottage Hospital that her fruit would be delivered, and would be brought forth from there, to grow and thrive; it would see Harvest Festivals long after the Grim Reaper had gathered Sarah and Eric to Him. It would see Christmas as she herself had seen it, as a child (Eric would tell her little about Christmas at the Orphanage), and it would wonder and tremble with excitement at the carol-singing, and the cribs, the home-made mangers, the creches with their Holy Family and all the animals cut out of cardboard and the cottonwool snow and the tinsel, all lighted by real candles. Later it would play in the cold white magic sent down by God in tiny individual flakes especially for children.

It would love her, and show its love for her. No matter what pain she suffered to give it life; that would be of no account. It would be hers; it would give meaning to her existence. Its future would be her responsibility.

Eric received the news with amazement. Since their marriage, his world had been centred around Sarah and her body. She had shown him how to attain and sustain a prolonged erection, as other men did; he adored her. She had excited him to orgasm, yet it was an orgasm without guilt; it was a release both desired and expected, not an humiliating and guilty surprise. He had sown his seed in a fertile furrow, and his seed had germinated. He was to become a father.

That night Sarah couldn't sleep. Her mind was racing with plans. Nothing must ever go wrong now. She would work out her notice at the shop, and then rest until the baby was born. She was no longer young; there might not be another chance; she must contain her excitement, and keep calm. The Lord had heard her prayers at last. She had said 'Thank You' to Him a thousand times under her breath when in company, aloud when alone. It was not enough; she must make her life a continuous 'Thank You' at least until after the baby's birth, so that He might have no occasion for changing His mind.

Eric lay awake beside her, thinking his own thoughts. Summer was nearly upon them. The hours of work would be longer. There would be haymaking, backbreaking to endure. He remembered the cutting, the turning, the raking, working full out while the weather lasted. Because he did it well, he would again be given the job of standing on top of the horse-drawn cart, and receiving forkfuls of hay from the temporary workers, to stack and make a load that wouldn't fall halfway back to the barn. He had been stabbed twice last year by casual labour, boys from the local Reformatory, hired cheaply. The stabbings had not been intentional, but out of stupidity and boredom and irritation at blistered hands; the boys had had no experience of heaving hay up into the cart with a fork, and had spiked him. He was not looking forward to the summer.

But the news of the baby had made Sarah so happy. He leaned over, and kissed her on the forehead. He moved his hand, just as she had taught him, over and around her breasts and down the centre of her belly, over the curve of her hip, down the outside of her thigh, and then on the inside upwards. But as his hand slid upwards, stroking the inside of her thighs, and just as he was about to move her legs apart as she had shown him, suddenly she squeezed her thighs together, crossed her legs, and then took his hand away, and placed it on the sheet between them.

'Please don't do that any more, Eric. I have to be careful now. It's going to be difficult enough, because of the narrowness of my hips. Try to be patient.'

Eric lay on his back, his hands by his sides, looking at the blackness above and around him. His erection, which they had both worked so long and patiently to achieve, now wouldn't go away, but remained like Cleopatra's Needle as a memorial to their mutual achievement. She had encouraged him to be dominant, praised him when he had thought he might be hurting her. Now she had turned on her side, away from him; for the first time in their marriage, she had turned her back on him. He tried thinking of what he most disliked, such as dogs and mice, so as to fill his mind with what repelled him, and undermine the need he so powerfully felt. But the dogs and mice he imagined were all in a state of copulation. Before his marriage, even as a boy at the Orphanage, the sight of one cow abortively attempting to mount another had been enough to provoke from him an unwanted emission, Miss Barnard had whispered to him. 'You're going to have to practise.' Now he had practised. He had practised through many, many nights with his wife, and practice had at last made perfect. Yet now, when he was at last capable of giving pleasure to himself and her, he was no longer to be allowed to do so. Even he knew that some of the groans and exclamations Sarah had made in the early years had been only to encourage him, but not lately. So why? Why now? If penetration would in some way harm the baby, that was not reason enough; they had experimented in other ways. She had taught him to be dominant, and he would be.

He turned on his side, facing her back. He reached his arm over her body, and touched her breasts. She sighed, and took his hand away, placing it near his own genitals. 'Do what men do when they're on their own. Don't make it difficult.'

He lay as still as he could in the darkness. There was no question of his doing what men do when they're on their own; she must know that. He wasn't on his own; he couldn't do it, not here, lying next to her; the toilet was downstairs in the yard. He felt humiliated and lonely. He had not felt loneliness for so long. He was lonely now, numb with it, apathetic and numb. He turned away from her, and lay awake.

Was it a punishment? They had told him, when he left the Orphanage, that he must never have children, that he must take 'precautions', and they had tried to explain those precautions to him, but even to speak of such things had inflamed his imagination, and his embarrassment had precluded close attention to what was said. They had not explained it well; he had not listened well; he knew that he must not have children, but not why, and Sarah's will was stronger than his incomprehension. It had been in some way important that his father ... that his father with his sister had ... that his sister had been sent away ... that Eric had been taken into the Orphanage ... they had told him that his parents were dead, but now ... that it was important; he must remember; he must take precautions; that it was not his fault; he was not to blame; but he must remember.

Was it a punishment? He had not remembered, or at least he had done nothing of what they said. How could he, when it was Sarah who said what they should do? How could he tell her what he himself did not understand, but only knew that it was in some way dirty, because Mr Higgs had looked down at his desk all the time he was talking?

Now he was lonely. Sarah had rejected him. Was it a punishment for not remembering what he had been told before he left the Orphanage?

Two hours later, Eric Williams, the product of an incestuous union, fell asleep. At least he had one secret left.

5

Just about the same time as the R101 was crashing into a field south of Beauvais

AT the beginning of October 1930, Sarah sat up in a hospital bed, feeling pear-shaped, and reading glossy magazines which had been left at the hospital by ladies who could afford such extravagance, with the intention that they should circulate amongst the General Wards to remind the aspiring working classes how they, the other half, lived.

In London, at the Phoenix Theatre, a play called *Private Lives* was to open. The author, Mr Noel Coward, was to appear in one of the two leading roles, Miss Gertrude Lawrence in the other. They would be supported by Miss Adrienne Allen and Mr Laurence Olivier. The play was to be about 'swapping partners', she read, and was bound to be tremendous fun. Advertisements praised the ivory tips of De Reszke cigarettes; Sarah wondered how many people could pronounce the name well enough to ask for a packet at the corner tobacconist's. Mansion Polish was advertised by a peacock in a top hat and spats and a toucan in a shawl; in the glossy magazines even the birds and animals were well turned out. Down below in the hospital yard, a fight had broken out among those members of the unemployed who were queueing for jobs as casual porters or mortuary assistants.

Late on Saturday night of 4 October Sarah entered labour. It was to last until the early hours of Sunday, 5 October. It was not an unduly protracted labour; there was no remarkable excess of pain, brought about by narrow hips. At much the same time as the British airship R101 was crashing in flames into a field not far south of Beauvais, Sarah felt her last pain, and gave birth to a baby boy. They had drunk champagne on the flight-deck and in the passenger lounge of the R101, and toasted the Airship Age. Sarah's child weighed seven pounds, four ounces, and seemed in every way perfectly healthy. Sarah had already decided that he should be called 'Walter', because she fancied the name.

Two weeks after Sarah brought Walter home, the front page of the local paper carried a large photograph of the newly-christened little princess, Margaret, and her mother, the Queen. On an inside page, in much smaller type, and a much more inconspicuous position, it carried the announcement of Walter's birth. The Queen had not been asked to pay the local paper for publishing her daughter's christening photo, but Sarah and Eric had been asked to pay for announcing Walter, and had, after a quarrel about the cost which Sarah won, done so. Sarah said that all the women of the neighbourhood, who had stared at her in chapel so often and for so long and with such interest, should in fairness have their prolonged curiosity satisfied, and know that she was not barren.

Sarah's mother sat in Sarah's kitchen, her hands resting on the boiler for the warmth it gave off, and watched her daughter breast-feeding Walter. An adjustment had been made to the boiler's chimney, so that it was now possible to sit in the kitchen without being choked by smoke.

She had brought with her two bags of pot-herbs, and a sheep's head, to be boiled into a broth. The sheep's tongue would be left to cook, and then sliced and eaten with mustard.

It was a day in January. Sarah's mother kept her coat on, and Sarah wore a grey army blanket over her shoulders. The cottage was cold and damp, Sarah's mother said, after the warmth of her own house. If Sarah wished Walter to live through the winter, she had better rub his chest with goose-grease and keep him well wrapped up. 'Sounds a bit wheezy to me.' She looked upwards and sighed at the damp patches on the walls, after which she tut-tutted at the thinness of the curtains and the general lack of furnishings. Sarah's mother made these noises and exclamations every winter, but this January they were louder for Walter.

'And you never screamed?'

'I don't remember. I expect I did. Nobody slapped me, or called me a ninny. They were very considerate.'

'I expect you were drugged, dear. They have these new drugs, to help you bear the pain.'

'If I'd been offered a drug, mother, I'd have refused it. It could have done harm to Baby. Anyway, they didn't offer. No drugs were needed. There was nothing out of the ordinary in my case.'

'There are young girls in our street, as have taken to wearing berets, and chewing gum. You see them every day. There's no respect.' A pause. 'How are you going to manage on one wage?'

'The way others do.'

'Is he alright to you now?'

'I don't know what you mean.'

'I mean what I say. Eric. Is he alright to you?'

'You've not heard me complain.'

'Not recently, no. But then, you don't both sleep in the next room to mine any more. I heard enough in those days to make my hair curl.'

Sarah wanted to reply, 'Eavesdroppers never hear good of themselves,' but it hardly seemed appropriate, so she contented herself with, 'Curly hair would go well with those Eiffel Tower ear-rings your so-called friend gave you.' It was the first time her mother had admitted having listened to what went on between Eric and Sarah in bed. 'You know what they say about nosey-parkers.'

'There's these women in Hungary been poisoning their husbands with arsenic. Fifty, at least. They got it off the midwife. She started up a poison factory, and they went to her for it. Well, nobody would suspect, would they, a midwife; she deals in drugs. Arsenic. They dug the husbands up, and found it in them. It was on the wireless this morning.'

Sarah lifted Walter up to her shoulder, and rubbed his back. He burped, as if in agreement with her opinion of nosey-parkers. 'Good Boy!' Her mother was still wearing the expression of hurt indignation, which Sarah knew so well. 'Anyway, it's what turns out in the end that matters, isn't it?'

Eric's face appeared at the window, before the question could be answered. He smiled, and held up close to the glass something he was clutching between his two hands.

'What's he got?'

'Looks like a bird. Don't let him come in until I've got this blanket round Walter.' Sarah's mother stood with her shoulder to the back door, while Eric rattled at the latch, and Sarah hastily covered Walter against the cold. Then she gave the signal, and her mother opened the door.

'What you lock the door for?'

'She was wrapping the child up, so's he wouldn't catch his death. Not that he mightn't do that any road, considering that there's moss growing on those walls.' Sarah's mother no longer flirted with her son-in-law as she had while he had lived in her house. On the contrary, she now treated him as a person to whom one makes complaints, particularly about his own shortcomings. 'And what's that supposed to be?'

'A racing pigeon.'

'Isn't it going to get left behind, sitting there?'

'There's something wrong with it. Can't seem to fly.'

33

Sarah looked at the grey bird her husband was clasping, and said, 'Don't you bring it near this child. It might have a disease.' She pressed Walter against her side, and adjusted his blanket.

'I thought he might like to see it.'

'He's sleeping. Take it outside.' Eric turned slowly, and lifted the doorlatch with his elbow. He wished she wouldn't talk to him that way in front of her mother.

The pigeon had landed at the farm where Eric worked, and had showed no sign of wanting to finish whatever race it was engaged in. It had followed him around the yard, and he had stolen a handful of grain to feed it. Once fed, wherever he went, it went. It looked up at him, its head on one side and its bright eyes watching his every move. When his work was over, he had picked it up and brought it home with him.

Eric placed the pigeon in the coalshed next to the outside toilet, leaving it with more stolen grain which he had brought home in his pocket, and a shallow dish of water from which to drink. The pigeon walked steadily to the top of the small pile of coal, and blinked at Eric as he closed the door.

Sarah's mother stood; she would not outstay her welcome. As she buttoned her coat, she nodded towards Walter, and said, 'Are you going to go in for any more, then? Now that Eric's found out how to do it?'

Part Two

Scenes from his Childhood

I

A good boy eats with a knife and fork, and not with a spoon

WHEN, in a later life, he was asked what was his first memory, that was a question which required thought. They had asked him other questions which did not require thought, and they had asked him questions which he could not answer, but this was a question he could answer, except that it required thought.

His first memory was of a girl's face. The girl was giggling, covering her mouth with one hand, and pointing at Walter's face with the other. He was standing beside his mother, leaning against her legs, his arms wrapped round them, holding her skirt. It was his first day at school. He was crying. His mother was trying to explain to the teacher that special allowances had to be made for him, because he was different; he was a late developer, and unable to form words properly. He could identify some objects, but not others.

The teacher told the little girl to go away, but she didn't; she just stood there, laughing. Nevertheless, though she was unable to control her laughter, she continued to keep her mouth covered, because she knew that to laugh at an ugly person is wrong.

All this Walter remembered when they asked him. But he was unable to find words with which to express this memory, so in the end, he said he did not know.

He had been five-and-a-half years old on that first day at school, and his baggy grey trousers, two sizes too big, had revealed that beneath them he still wore nappies and plastic pants. The teacher had noticed this, but had found herself unable to mention it to Walter's mother. His mother herself had intended to inform the teacher that she had not yet been successful in training Walter to give her proper warning when he felt the need to go to the lavatory. Later Walter was to be given the nickname of 'Shitty Pants', and made to sit on his own at the back of the classroom, as far away from the teacher as possible. This placing was a kindness to Walter, for it was at the nearest desk to the door; he was told that he might run out of the class whenever he felt the urge, without raising his hand first to ask permission. The desks in front of him and to his left were kept vacant, and that was a kindness to the other children, Walter's classmates. Whenever unkindness was felt to be necessary for any of those children, by way of punishment, they would be made to sit at one of those two desks. Often, when a child was bored or could think of nothing better to do, he would turn round towards the solitary Walter, squeezing his nose between a thumb and forefinger.

It became clear to the teacher that Walter was unable to concentrate his mind upon even the simplest of sums and that both reading and writing were arts which would be for many years beyond him. So Walter was given a large sheet of what was called sugar-paper – usually dark blue and of a rough texture – and told to draw whatever he wished. Walter drew. He was never asked to stand beside the teacher, and read aloud. He had no idea how letters could be put together to form sounds and how those sounds, alone and in concert, represented words, and words would come together to form sentences, to form speech, conversation, what was said and written by human beings to each other. Walter's vocabulary consisted of five words which he had learned from his mother, after laborious effort on both their parts.

After a year, it had become clear to many people at the school that Walter was 'different'. The headmistress called Walter to her room, to try to ascertain how different he was.

The interview began by the headmistress asking Walter what day it was. Walter did not know. What had Walter eaten for lunch? Walter could not remember. She pointed to the picture of a cow. What was that? Walter knew what the picture represented; he had seen cows before, but did not know what they were called. Shyly he offered 'Moo.'

This was distinctly encouraging to the headmistress, being at least half the right answer. 'Moo what, Walter?' She waited. Walter was silent. The woman wanted more from him. After a while, it came to him what more he could give. 'Moo Moo,' he said. Now he was making a close approximation to the noise a cow makes. 'Moo Moo Moo.'

'Yes. It's a moo-cow, isn't it?'

Walter was tired now. His imitation of a cow had exhausted him. He looked towards the window, at the sky outside, trying to assess by the amount of light how long it would be before his mother came to collect him.

'Try to pay attention, Walter, when I'm talking.' Walter blinked, and yawned without remembering to cover his mouth. 'Are you tired?'

'Tired' was not one of the five words included in Walter's vocabulary, but he had a fair idea of what it meant, so he nodded without turning to look at the headmistress.

'What I have to decide, Walter, is – ' The headmistress had second thoughts. 'Do you understand the word "decide"?' Walter looked at the sky outside. 'I mean, do you know what "decide" means?' The clouds moved. They came together, and moved apart; they made big patches of white against the blue and split into smaller bits; sometimes the white was all thick and piled together, and sometimes it was so thin, you could see the blue through it. Walter made no sign of understanding or even hearing the headmistress.

'What people are going to want to know from me, Walter, is this. Are you a backward boy, who doesn't understand, or are you a boy who has decided to be naughty?'

The only word out of all that which had any meaning for Walter was the word 'naughty', which was one of the words in his vocabulary. On hearing it, he turned on the surprised headmistress, and screamed at the top of his voice, 'Not naughty! Not naughty!' Thereafter his face crumpled into a silent sobbing. Screwed up like this, it was even more disturbing than it was in repose.

'Alright now. That's quite enough. I don't want any of that, Walter. Do you hear me?' His tiny hands were rubbing his eyes, and his mouth was wide open in silent anguish. 'I'm sure you're not naughty really. It's just that I have to know what you can and can't do.' What he was doing at the moment was making her feel extremely uncomfortable. 'We have to know what to do with you, Walter. I mean, where to put you. Nobody's going to harm you. Perhaps you might be better off in a different school; you might be happier there. We only want your happiness. Please, Walter, don't cry like that. It's very unsettling to watch, you know.'

So far Walter had made no sound; this was his own particular way of crying. But the expression on his face and the liberal flow of tears from his eyes had frightened the headmistress. Was he holding his breath? Might he at any moment faint? Was he about to have an epileptic fit? She hoped desperately that someone would come into the room, which was not likely, since she had left instructions that she should not be disturbed. What did one do in case of fits? Her mind flew back to her Girl Guide training many years before. The patient's tongue must be held, she remembered, to prevent its being swallowed. Had Walter perhaps swallowed his tongue already? That might explain the lack of noise. Clearly she was dealing with a highly disturbed child. First his lack of concentration, and now this frightening silent anguish; it was most disconcerting. She attempted to smile, and found that it set on her face. She must take some action, and she would.

'Alright now, Walter, let's play a guessing game. What have I got in here, do you think?' The headmistress unlocked a drawer in her desk, and opened it. From it she took a circular tin box, and pushing it across her desk towards Walter, she said, 'Now, then. You guess what I've got in here. Can you?' With the flourish of a magician performing the final trick in an act which had so far gone almost entirely wrong, she removed the lid from the tin, to reveal an assortment of rather old boiled sweets.

'Which colour would you like?'

Slowly Walter lifted his arm as if it weighed a ton, and flopped his hand down into the middle of the tin of sweets. The motion of his fingers was like that of an excavating-machine on a building-site. They dug down into the sweets, and, having secured as many as his hand would hold, lifted them from the tin. Walter ceased his silent crying, and studied the colours and twists of cellophane wrapping protruding from between his fingers, while the headmistress quickly replaced the lid on the tin, and the tin in the drawer, and made a mental note to buy more boiled sweets. There had been nothing about them in the Guides' First-Aid Manual, but they seemed to be efficacious in dealing with fits.

'Well, there, then! That's better, isn't it? I'll have a talk with your mother, when she comes to collect you, and we'll see what we can do. Alright, then, Walter. No need to go back to your classroom now. The bell's just about to ring for playtime. Why not run along, and find someone nice to play with? Off you go.'

Walter stood, holding the sweets as carefully as one might carry a piece of cut-glass. Slowly he left the room, and behind him the smell of stale pee.

Walter moved around the playground slowly, his arms held up in front of his face, with elbows bent. They were his only protection from the arms, legs, heads and bodies of the other children, who ran and shouted, waving their arms, who might bump into him from the front or the side, or even back into him as they backed away from some pursuer. He had begun by attempting just to stand with his back to a wall, taking no part in the play, but only watching, squinting and blinking his eyes as one child made accidental contact with another. But he had been noticed by an older boy, who had made it his business to patrol the boundaries of the playground, so as to make sure that all newcomers joined in the fun. Any newcomers who declined to join the fun would be challenged by this older boy to a fight. The older boy's name was Addison. His territorial behaviour was the reason why many would-be watchers, many more than Walter, became participant in the exercises of the playground and familiar with the texture of its asphalt surface.

Walter kept to the centre of the playground. Nobody had ever told him of the calm in the eye of the storm, but the same instinct which had kept him to the extreme edge until he was hounded from it by Addison now drove him to the centre, which was not, in fact, calm. He tried to look as if he were joining in the fun; in fact he looked like a blind man moving in fear among a field of cattle. There were fifteen minutes of morning break, fifteen in the afternoon, and a period of free time after Dinner. These periods exhausted Walter more than lessons did or could. When, at the end of each such period, a teacher came into the yard with a handbell, and rang it to signal the end of play, Walter would freeze to the spot, arms up, protecting his face, while the other children darted about, to stand behind each other in neat lines, ready for class, and Walter himself would first be called to, and then fetched by one of the older children, to be placed at the back of his line.

So it was on this day. The old boiled sweets were soon knocked to the ground from his tightly clenched fist, and the other children pushed, and fought, and trod on each other's hands to secure one for themselves. Walter watched this scrabbling without emotion. Something had told him that the possession of sweets put him into physical danger. The loss of them so soon after they had been given was not a disappointment to him, but the assurance of safety.

'Your child needs special help, Mrs Williams. We can't give it to him here. We have tried, but the case is beyond us. To take a single instance, he still wears nappies under his trousers, and sometimes fouls them while he's here at school. That's not right, for a lad over six years old. It shows no sign of changing. Children can be very cruel; they notice such things. I suggest that you keep Walter at home for his own sake until I've had a chance to consult with the Education Department. Then they'll write to you with the name of a Special School. You'll get a letter from County Hall.'

'He can't undo his buttons yet; that's all.' Walter's mother turned away from the headmistress. Through the window she could see other children being collected by other mothers – girls with ringlets bouncing as they rushed forward in greeting, boys swinging school satchels, boys with ties and long socks, held up by garters, beneath short trousers which showed the shapes of their clean little bottoms. In the satchels, there would be exercise-books, with sums all ticked and words copied in small neat writing. The short trousers would have buttons in the front, and the small boys would be capable of handling those buttons, undoing them and doing them up again whenever Nature called. Her own son's trousers had to be two sizes too big to accommodate the nappy and plastic knickers beneath them.

'He just won't thrive here.'

The faces of the children at the school gate resembled their mothers' faces. They were small round clear-skinned faces, portraits in miniature of their parents. They expressed interest and pleasure. Walter sat slouched in the chair in which he had been interviewed, his eyes staring into the middle distance; he was loudly sucking at sweets she had brought him.

'It's only his buttons he can't handle.'

She was pleading. The headmistress was embarrassed, and looked at the floor. 'I know he's not a bright child, but he's not . . .' The headmistress had used a word to describe Walter. The word stuck in Sarah's throat, and would not be said.

'It's not a nice word, I know, Mrs Williams, but it has a meaning and we have to face facts. I'm not saying that Walter might not just be a late developer. If a child does well enough at a Special School, then of course he's sent back to an ordinary school. There's always that possibility.'

Four boys in the playground were playing a game which involved the twisting of ears.

'Will he ever catch up?'

The headmistress noticed that multi-coloured saliva was dripping from Walter's chin on to a rug beside her desk. 'Well, I really couldn't . . . I mean, it's impossible to predict. I don't think one should raise your hopes too high.' Sarah's hopes were not high at all, and might have benefited from being raised. 'I do think Walter will always have problems – problems of what we call "communication". He has a peculiar way of crying, had you noticed? I do think it might be more than an educational problem; I think your doctor should be consulted. I was quite upset by him this afternoon. I simply mentioned the word – ' She realized too late that to mention the word again might be to risk a repetition of Walter's peculiar way of crying, so she put one hand up to her mouth and whispered the word 'naughty' in quite a friendly way to this woman, Mrs Williams, the boy's mother, before continuing, 'Frankly I wasn't sure what to do. It's a word which is bound to crop up in any school from time to time. I'm sure that gives you an indication of the kind of problem we're facing.'

Outside a boy of six and a girl of seven were holding hands and whispering secrets to each other.

'And now, if you'll excuse me, I do have a Guide Meeting this evening.' Sarah moved away from the window of the headmistress's study, and took Walter's hand into her own. He stood up, and choked on the sweet he was sucking, and then, after his mother had patted him hard on the back, coughed it out on to the rug, already wet with saliva. His mother bent down to retrieve the sweet.

'No, please don't bother. I'll scrape it up with some waste paper. Please don't get your hands all sticky.'

The large oak door of the school was closed behind them, and they walked together across the playground. Sarah looked back at the door. She had been to school here, many years ago. The oak door, with its Norman arch and its heavy iron hinges, was the same. She remembered having to use both hands to turn the large iron handle. She remembered the fear, the excitement, the reverence she had felt then towards this school, the childhood crushes, the fascination of growing older and wiser, the security and comfort of having friends and being liked. She had been pretty; she had been popular. Nothing in her adulthood had matched the excitement of those children's games.

They reached the wrought-iron railings, the tops of which looked like arrowheads, and passed through the gate. The head of a small boy appeared round the corner of the school wall, its features contorted into a small boy's idea of a village idiot. 'Hey! Shitty Pants! Give us a sweet!' Walter's hand went automatically to the trouser pocket in which he had hidden the sweets his mother had given him, and brought out a mauve boiled sweet. Sarah snatched the sweet from his hand, and threw it over to the other side of the street.

Walter looked up at his mother's face, his eyes squinting at the light of the sky. He saw that she was crying without a sound. Her lips turned down at the corners, and were trembling as she tried to keep the lower lip still by biting it. For Sarah did not wish to be seen weeping in the street, and was determined to take herself in hand.

Walter's grip on his mother's hand tightened, and warned her of the danger of tears. She could sense the anxiety swelling up inside him. Once in a moment of anger she had threatened to give him away to the gypsies whom they had seen camped at the side of the road. He had looked at the large piebald horses, and screamed in terror. He feared all animals, and had nightmares about horses.

His head drooped. He looked down at the stones of the pavement, and they seemed to move towards him. He looked at his school boots, the laces of which he could not tie. (The gypsies' children had bare feet.) His boots moved forward, one overtaking the other. It seemed to him that they were not his boots, the feet inside them not his feet. The feet inside the boots moved, and he did not feel them. If only he could feel them, they would be his, and the boots would be his. He squeezed his toes together (they were certainly his toes), and was reassured by the sharpness of a nail inside the left boot. He had felt that nail before, after his father had put new leather on the soles of the boots. He placed his middle toe over the reassuring nail, and pressed down. He felt the sharp point cut into his toe, and pressed harder until he could feel sticky blood inside his sock. Yes, these were his boots. This was his mother holding his hand. His. The boots, the hand belonged to Walter. This was he. He was Walter. He was here. He was walking. Walter was him. He was Walter.

Now he hardly noticed the cracks between the paving-stones and the bits of silver paper and toffee wrappers. These were his boots moving with his feet inside them. Feet, legs, knees, all belonged to him; he could do what he liked with them. That he should own his whole body both pleased and worried him. His mother had told him that he should take pride in himself, not soil himself or scratch or pick at his skin. *His* skin. Walter began to feel fear again. His whole body belonged to him. It was frightening to be in charge of such a thing. And was he really in charge? He had felt pain sometimes, and had not wished for it. He had experienced being sick, more than once. When that had happened, he had thought, 'What is happening to me? What is inside me that wants to get out? He had seen the producer of his pain. It had rushed out of him, causing him terrifying spasms and retching. This pain-producer was sudden, liquid, acid-tasting, brown in colour, having some resemblance to the vegetable soup he had eaten earlier. It did not belong to him. It lived in his insides, and caused them to hurt, and then rushed out and fell about the room.

So that had been in his body, and he had not controlled it in any way. And there was something behind his forehead also, something that worried him, made him cry, and frightened him. It must be his, since it was inside him, but he couldn't switch it off. Sometimes it gave him headaches. It was like . . . He did not know what it was like; it was like fishes; it was like a bowl, with fishes, too many, which darted about swimming and slithering about – thoughts and half-thoughts and dis-connected parts of thoughts, never joining up, but always swimming and darting about like fish, catching the light for a moment, then gone, never waiting long enough in any place to be clear and apprehended. He could never follow one to see where it went, because the others

44

confused him, taking its place and then, in their turn, twisting away from him, glittering thoughts too slippery for him to hold.

Sometimes, when he rolled his eyes up towards the ceiling and stared hard at that to stop the goldfish from darting about behind his forehead, Walter would be slapped by his mother and, told that he was dreaming again, and that he mustn't look in that funny way because people would think he was simple. He would burst into tears, but that was no answer, because the goldfish only returned, and the same people who would think him simple would say, his mother told him, he was a cry-baby if they saw him weeping. And Walter would rub his eyelids with the back of his hand, trying to chase away the goldfish, or at least to catch one and make it keep still.

'Please, Walter, be a good boy,' and Walter would reply, 'Want to. Want to.' A good boy was one without goldfish in his head. A good boy smiled, and sat quietly; he used the potty, and cleaned himself afterwards. A good boy ate with a knife and fork, and not with a spoon, but whenever Walter attempted this, his hands shook, and the food dropped back on his plate, or splashed into his lap or on the tablecloth. With a dish and a spoon held close to his face, he could manage quite well, but this was how a baby feeds itself, and Walter was nearly seven years old.

2

A vet with a pill or an injection, administered while she protested love and kindness, could free her

THE fire in the grate meant security. The red embers said, 'Continue. We do. Day after day, we are here. We comfort you. Grey and cold in the morning, yet we shall be red again by tea-time.' The flames flickered and reached up. They said, 'Hope. Tomorrow and tomorrow; there is always something. Tomorrow is another day.'

Walter looked at the fire, felt the warmth from it, wondered at how it worked, and was glad his mother got such pleasure from it. What she felt, he felt; it was as simple as that. He was safe when she was happy, unsafe when she was sad. Between those two extremes, there was an infinite variety of moods his mother might feel. At such times, he was uncertain.

Sarah saw Walter watching her, looking up from his place on the rug at her feet. Her awareness of his dependence weighed heavy. If she were to smile, he would smile back, but he would watch her still. And smiling once wasn't enough; she could not smile all the time. To see her worries, fears and doubts reflected back in his face tired her. She felt guilty, like a small child, who has been tormenting an animal, but with none of the pleasure such a child might feel in exercising its power to inflict pain. Walter was like a puppy, licking her hand for approval, like a stray dog at the Dogs' Home, who, if she did not take him home, would be put down, whose tongue, eyes, damp nose, every line of his body, said, 'Please! Please show me I am loved and the world a good place. Reassure me. I only live through you. I can only operate with your good opinion, your approval. Roll me over; tickle my stomach; stroke my head; it is in these ways God's favour is shown. My head is so full of disquiet; smooth it away. Please!'

If only Walter had been born a dog and not a human child, how easy it would be to end her sense of responsibility. A vet with a pill or an injection, administered while she protested love and kindness, could free her. And what then? She was not prepared to consider, 'What then?' Sap bubbled out of a log on the fire, hissing and spitting as it proclaimed its greenness, its life, its unreadiness to burn, its indignation at having been wrongly classified and placed with dead wood. Planted in the earth, it might have sprouted new branches, and grown into a tree. Now its life-juice was being turned rapidly into vapour, and by morning it would be ash, to be sprinkled on the garden to assist other plants to grow.

What if they were weeds, what if it were to assist only weeds?

Walter listened to the noise the green log made, and watched the sap bubbling out. He frowned as he watched, and wished the log to be quiet. To him, it was truly alive; anything which made a noise like that was living. He had watched spiders and woodlice crawl out of logs placed on the fire. He had watched them panic, running upwards to the highest point of the fire to avoid the flames and heat, and then he had seen them taken by the fire, shrivelling up into bits of black and dropping into the flames, where they cracked and hissed. He looked up at his mother, hoping that she would rescue the log before all the sap had gone. Instead she picked up the poker, and pushed the green log further down into the grate. When that log had burned, she would go to bed. She would lie and think about all the tomorrows stretching ahead of her. If Walter had been a dog, avenues which were now closed to her would open. There would be choices to make about her future. Now there was only one choice, which was either to put up with the situation and be as happy as God would allow, or to bemoan her luck and make a virtue of unhappiness.

Her husband did not enter either into the choice she must make as matters were or into the many choices which might open before her had Walter been born a dog.

The red embers glowed, and the weak blue and yellow flames teased the young sapling, as her own mother had teased all the men she had known, once her virginity had been taken by force. 'Tomorrow is another day,' said the mendacious flames, 'Hope!' Tomorrow would be another day just like today, and so onwards. She screwed up her eyes at the thought of it, and then remembered to smile a reassuring smile at the pathetically mournful face of her son. There was no good to be gained in upsetting him before bedtime. Get him to bed, and then cry, if she must. Not in front of him. Don't give him nightmares. There would be time enough, between putting her son to bed and the return of her husband from work, for Sarah to cry.

'Tomorrow is another day.' She would not cry now; she would cry later. 'Tomorrow is another test by God of your love for Him. Are you going to fail that test, and be punished at the last by fire?' The flames licked the log, and took it. 'Glory in God's favours now. Come to Him, and bend your knees in prayer. No one is without sin, none without the need to be forgiven. Place your life before Him. Offer the gift of your self to Him who gave selfhood itself to you. Feel His power, His strength surge up inside you, as you come forward today, glowing with His goodness.' She would cry later, as she prepared Eric's tea. There would be no meat; he could not expect meat in the middle of the week, but it would be hot. 'I can feel the presence of Jesus inside you.' She could feel the presence of Jesus inside her; He was inside her. 'You have true riches, beyond wealth. You have happiness. Am I right?' Yes, He was right. 'Did you ever doubt Him?' Yes, she had doubted Him. 'Are you sure now?' Yes, she was sure. 'Can you feel Him inside you? Can you feel His glory inside you, making you glow?' Yes. 'I see that glow, my sister. I am proud of that glow, my sister. I am proud you have found today, the true, the only love of your life. Stand up before the people, sister. Let the people see you glowing?'

Yes, she was glowing, radiating true happiness, which is expressed in tears, weeping the tears of true happiness, fulfilled and made whole by Him who was so deep within her. 'It is your choice, my brothers and sisters. Only you can make the first step towards Him. He calls, and we come.' He called. She came. 'We give ourselves to Him as Sister Sarah has today. I feel good today, brothers and sisters. One more soul for Jesus. Those tears she weeps are tears of joy. There is a new Sister Sarah walking amongst you from today. Look! Look! They are tears of holy joy.'

Walter was frowning, and holding his breath. He had observed the tears of joy; they would give him nightmares. Sarah looked at what Jesus had placed inside her – with such help, with such patient and enduring help from Sarah herself – at what Jesus had placed inside her for nine months. She looked at what Jesus had then drawn forth from within her narrow hips. She held out her hand, and he came and sat on her knee. She cuddled him to her, rocking and weeping. She said, 'I never felt Jesus inside me; you're not a child from Him. I didn't cry for joy. I cried for loneliness; I cried for myself and my wicked thought. I tried to seem a different person afterwards. It was all a pretence. I wanted to be accepted by everyone at the chapel. Chapel people. Respectable people. I wanted marriage, and a house on Shear's Brow, overlooking the town. But nobody rushed forward to make a proposal. I waited, teaching Sunday School, and walking home alone. And then . . . And then . . .'

As she talked in a low soothing voice, trying to undo the damage her tears had caused, she became aware that Walter had fallen asleep, and that he was heavy. Then there was a third thought, unconnected as far as she could tell to the others, but it frightened her, and wouldn't go away. The word 'accident' kept pushing its way into her mind. It danced before her, and with it danced Harlequin, with mask and sword. She found that she could not replace these images with any other, no matter how hard she tried. 'Accident.' 'Painless accident.' Children had them every day; the papers were full of them.

'Oh God, what am I thinking about?'

As she asked herself the question, it was answered, though not by God. She knew the answer. She was thinking of herself, of freedom, of tomorrow and all the tomorrows which would follow it, the to-morrows which must follow it. Unless she were careful, and acted now.

3

The most they could do would be to accuse her of being careless

EVERY day they walked through the streets, hand in hand. She paraded her misfortune. The people who stopped and talked to her always put their heads to one side when they looked down at Walter. Very few of them mentioned him, or talked to him. They assumed that Sarah would rather they ignored him. She felt their pity and their curiosity. She saw their faces, and watched their expressions of relief when the conversation had come to a natural end, or when they had thought of a way of ending it, and were able to move on without impoliteness. She also knew that their seeing her and Walter made them more contented with their own lives.

Other women of her age might have husbands who drank, or looked at, or even chased other women. They might have husbands who had simply grown tired of them, even disliked them, husbands with whom they shared the same house, and that was all. But none of these women was Walter's mother. Her misfortune was their gain.

She had tried staying in the house all day. It was unhealthy. The boredom made her irritable, with herself as well as with Walter. Outside there were things to distract her. At times she was even able to imagine that she was holding the hand of a normal child, the child she had longed for.

At home her awareness of his watching her made her self-conscious. Since no one from County Hall had written to her about a Special School, she tried reading to him, and helping him play with the bricks they had bought for him five years earlier, but she found herself losing her temper too often. If she left one room to go to another, he cried. He seemed happier walking beside her, hand in hand. Sometimes he even seemed interested in the things they saw.

Because of the women she met and the obligatory conversations she did not enjoy, Sarah began taking Walter out into the countryside where they would meet fewer people whom she knew. Sometimes they would get on a bus, and ride to a park where they were not known at all. At other times, they would just start walking away from the houses and into the country.

Walter never seemed to mind how far they walked. He never whined, or asked to be carried. Anyway, he was too heavy to be carried.

One of these walks took them a long way from the houses, down narrow country lanes where no one saw them. They would have to rest before starting back. Sarah settled on a resting-place where a railway line ran under the road. It was not a bridge, for bridges have humps. The road remained flat, but instead of a hedge on either side, there was a brick wall, about four feet high, under which trains passed at full speed.

Sarah was tall enough to see the trains, and just strong enough to lift Walter up on to the wall for him to see them as they rushed into the short tunnel beneath their feet.

She found herself returning more and more often to this place. The speed of the trains, and the smoke which, when a train passed beneath them, enveloped both the brick wall and themselves, fascinated her. It wasn't only that the fast trains suggested freedom and travel and a new and different kind of life. With Walter sitting on the wall, holding both her hands but looking down at the passing train, she felt her freedom to be more than wishful thinking. Here on the bridge it became a definite possibility. All she had to do was to let go of Walter's hands.

Each time they visited the bridge, they spent longer there, and soon they were going there every day. By the end of two weeks Sarah knew at what time a train would pass beneath them. She knew which were the faster trains, and which seemed to gush the most smoke up at them hiding Walter's face from hers. Just a few seconds; she only needed a few seconds. As long as she could not see him, she felt sure, she would be able to release his hands from hers.

The most they could do would be to accuse her of being careless. He was known to be backward, but large for his age. She would say he had heard a train coming, and had run on ahead. She would say she had shouted at him to stop, had run as fast as she could, but that he had climbed the wall, had stood on it, been enveloped in smoke, and had become frightened, and had tried to jump down, choosing in panic the wrong side.

She rehearsed the story over and over again inside her head. The recitation of each small detail excited her. Every one must be plausible. Since nobody had ever seen Walter take the initiative and run off on his own, Sarah bought him a small train to play with, and although he ignored it, she would say that he had become fascinated by trains, and that was why he had run on ahead.

51

Her life would be changed in a very few seconds. There was nothing to keep her with Eric; she need not stay with Eric. She would write away for a post in drapery, somewhere in Manchester, Birmingham or even London. She would rise; she would be at the least a manageress. As for Walter, it was a kindness. How could he ever be happy? If she sighed, he cried; she could not maintain a brave smile all the days of her life. He would be a figure of fun and scorn for the rest of her life, and when she died, they would have no option but to put him away. He would be put away with people who were really mad. Some of them might be violent. It was a kindness.

Day after day for several weeks, they visited the bridge, and each time Walter sat on the wall, holding his mother's hands tightly in his. Sarah closed her eyes when the smoke enveloped them. She moved her fingers inside those of her son, and held her breath. His grip tightened on her hands, as each day she became a little bit braver, and moved her fingers a little more. She tried putting his hands inside hers, but he cried and wanted to get down from the wall. But even with him holding her, she could at any time break free. All it required was a little more strength, a little more determination.

Sarah's strength and determination grew. With every visit to the bridge, she became more positive that her freedom was only a matter of finding the right circumstance, the right moment.

Time passed. Still she had not found circumstance or moment. Every time she helped Walter to jump down from the wall, and they began walking back home, Sarah would feel sadness of an almost overwhelming nature. Every time she would make herself a promise that tomorrow she would be able to pull her hands free from his. With each day that passed, he was growing a little heavier, a little more difficult to lift on to the wall. And his willingness to sit on the wall at all depended on her cheerfulness. Yet the game of pretending that what they were doing was fun, had become harder for her. She had to do it soon.

On a Thursday afternoon, nine weeks after their first visit to the bridge, Sarah was holding Walter's hands, and waiting for the train which gushed the most smoke. While waiting, she talked to him, and patted his hands together. *Pattacake, pattacake, baker's man. We'll bake a cake as fast as we can.* The rhyme distracted him, and the patting of his hands together allowed her to hold his wrists, from which it would be easier to release herself.

They seemed to have been waiting on the bridge for the whole of their lives, and the train wasn't even within hearing distance. She had decided that, whatever happened today, she would never visit the bridge again, unless of course it was necessary to come to explain to those who were making inquiries how the accident had happened. Otherwise she would never stand here again. If she failed today, she never would succeed.

The train was four minutes late. Sarah had run out of rhymes and stories. When she heard the train approaching, she placed an arm round Walter's neck, and kissed him.

She was crying now, telling him that it would be alright, reassuring herself and him that what she was going to do was best for them all. Walter watched with troubled eyes, but did not cry as well, as he would usually have done. He just sat there, and allowed her to squeeze his hands, and stroke his hair.

She was crying with such force, wiping the tears away with her sleeve, talking and crying as the train came closer to the bridge.

'I love you. I don't want to harm you. Be a good boy for Mummy. It's all for the best. I can't make you well. Please help me this time. Please be a good boy.' Her words ran together, between sobs and gulps for breath. She had worked herself up to meet the right moment, and now her plan had to work. It couldn't not work now.

The smoke from the train made her eyes sting. She closed them, and took two steps back, away from the wall. Her hands were free. No one was holding them. She moved the fingers to make sure, then clenched both fists up tight, and crossed her arms across her chest.

The smoke hung over the bridge far longer than it had ever done before. She thought it was never going to clear. Or was it her eyes? Was it the tears and the stinging which clouded her vision? She wiped her eyes again on her sleeve, and could just make out the shape of a figure sitting on the wall.

She moved towards the figure, and grabbed it to her before it fell. Walter's hands were bleeding. He had gripped the edge of the bricks so hard that they had cut into his palms.

He was shaking, and she helped him down. Not only had she released herself from his grip; she had tried to jolt him off balance. She had failed. They would never come to the bridge again.

Sarah wrapped her handkerchief round Walter's left hand, which was the hand he held out for her to hold, and they started to walk home.

On the next day a letter arrived from County Hall, informing her that a Special School had been found for her son Walter.

4

Is your journey really necessary?

IT took forty-three minutes by bus to reach Walter's Special School. Since, as far as Walter knew, it was just another bus-ride, he did not scream until he saw the school, the other children and the teacher into whose care his mother was about to hand him. While Walter screamed on, Sarah spoke to the teacher about her son and his difficulties. And the teacher spoke to Sarah about the importance of what was called 'house-training'. A backward, slow-learning child should be given as much stimulus to learn at home as it was at school. There was a book, which Sarah might be able to borrow from her local Public Library. She wrote the title of the book on a piece of pink paper, rather as if it were a doctor's prescription, and (rather as if it were a prescription) Sarah folded the piece of pink paper, and tucked it into her handbag.

Sarah walked away across the playground, with the sound of Walter's screams echoing inside her head. She had to be back at three thirty to collect him. Considered in terms of the amount of travelling time and the expense, it hardly seemed worthwhile to go home.

She asked, and was directed to the nearest Public Library. She found the book easily, and read it twice, since it was a short book. The necessity for the second reading was that she became sure that she must somehow have misread the first time. Some of the author's suggestions would be likely to send Walter into outright hysterics. There was a section headed, 'Play Wishful Thinking' in which it was suggested that mother and child should act out feelings and thoughts which the child would not otherwise be able to express by giving them to a character in a game. Thus Sarah might pretend that the house was on fire, or that Walter had some dreadful illness which she, as the play-doctor, would cure. Thereby Walter's fear of fire and dreadful illness would be diminished, and also, the author added, with sound practical common sense, 'if it ever does happen, you will both be prepared'.

The most important words for a child to learn were its own name and the word 'Look'. When a child can say its own name, it gains confidence. When it responds to the word 'Look', the world opens up for it. Drawing was good. Sarah must encourage Walter to scribble circles and make straight lines. All children drew houses at some stage of their development and, when Walter drew a house, Sarah must repeatedly ask him the same questions, 'How big are the windows? How small is the door? How much smoke is coming out of the chimney?' (Sarah did not know how one measured the volume of smoke from a chimney, and the book did not tell her.) The question, 'How high is the fence or hedge around the house?' was particularly important, for by the answer might be measured the amount of security felt by the backward child, or – more importantly – lacked.

Later when she asked Walter to draw a house (for he showed no sign of wishing to draw one unasked), he drew a circle, and coloured it red. There were no doors, no windows, no fence, and no smoke. For a long time, Walter's idea of home remained a red circle, and Sarah was left in doubt as to what amount (or lack) of security the red circle signified.

When Walter started at the Special School, he was eight years old, but his mental age was four. Each morning the crying would begin, as Sarah dressed him, ready for the forty-three minute journey to school.

In the bus, he sat next to the window and sobbed, his eyes red and sore, and his nose running. Sarah held his hand in hers, and used her free hand to point out things of interest, using the word 'Look' as often as possible. 'Look! Cows! Look! Sheep!' But the world was not opened up for Walter by that magic word. Nothing interrupted his sobbing.

He would continue to cry, so the teacher told her, for half an hour every morning after Sarah had left him at the school. He would stand, holding on to a coat-hook in the cloakroom, refusing to let anyone remove his navy-blue gaberdine raincoat, and sobbing his heart out.

Left alone, he would become tired, and sleep for an hour on the floor of the cloakroom, still wearing his raincoat, and when he awoke, it would be as if he were a different Walter. He would remove his raincoat leave it on the floor, and join the other children to play. He would play as a four-year-old might play, but since all the children at that school were there because they were backward, the fact that Walter was the size of a well-built eight-year-old was not remarkable.

One day in his third week at the school, Walter just stopped crying. He had cried in the bus, but, instead of clinging to the coat-hook, he went straight into the classroom, and began work with plasticine, allowing a teacher to remove his raincoat as he worked.

After that he no longer cried while being dressed for school, or on the bus.

Plasticine, cutting out pictures with blunt round-ended scissors, counting up to ten and playing in the sandpit at one end of the classroom were Walter's principal activities at the Special School for the next four years. He was then twelve years old, had learned very little, but had been, on balance, considerably more happy than not, and Britain had been at war for almost three years.

As a farm labourer, Eric was in a reserved occupation, helping his employer 'Dig for Britain'; indeed, he did considerably the more digging of the two. He continued to smuggle home fresh eggs, and made and set his own wire snares for rabbits, of which, since they were too bulky to hide in his jacket and must be declared to his employer, he was allowed to keep half; on the many occasions on which only one rabbit was caught, it would be chopped in two by the farmer, and a coin tossed to decide who should have which end. Nevertheless, as far as food went, which was, in those days, never far enough, the Williams family fared better than most.

Sarah continued to work with Walter in the evenings, trying to get him to identify objects in picture-books, but even when it was clear that Walter knew what an object was, he could never be persuaded to pronounce its name. She complained to the Head Teacher at the Special School about Walter's lack of progress, reminding her how much time she, Sarah, had spent in travelling to bring Walter to the school and fetch him home. Forty-three minutes ten times a week, forty school weeks in the year, four years at the school. Had the Head Teacher any idea how much that added up to? The Head Teacher opened her mouth to speak, but Sarah, who had worked out the sum herself on a piece of paper the night before, spared her the pain of mental arithmetic. 'One thousand one hundred and forty-six hours and forty minutes. What do you think of that?'

The Head Teacher did not know what to think of it.

'And just in case it has escaped your notice, three out of the four years I've been bringing him here, there's been a war on. There's been petrol rationing, cuts in the bus service, posters everywhere asking me if my journey is really necessary. Well, frankly, I believe I could have saved myself all that travelling time, to say nothing of bus fares. The space on the buses that Walter and I have taken up could have been used by somebody more directly involved with the War Effort, in my view.'

The Head Teacher was not used to the parents of her pupils talking to her in such a manner. Most of them were only too glad to get their children out of the house, and would cut off their tongues rather than offend the source of their relief. Sarah said, 'I could have achieved far more by keeping him at home and teaching him myself, than what your so-called "Special School" has.'

She had finished. The Head Teacher, who had remained standing while Sarah spoke, unable to break the contact between them, as if mesmerized, turned and moved to the comparative safety of the chair behind her desk. She sat slowly. She did not indicate that Sarah should sit also, but Sarah sat, and discovered that her chair was lower than the Head Teacher's.

The Head Teacher leaned her elbows on her desk, and placed the palms of her hands together. It was a way she had discovered of composing herself.

She began with a silence which was intended to intimidate Sarah, though it did not entirely succeed in making this effect. She said that she did not believe in 'pushing' children. It had been clear from the outset that Walter was only capable of reaching a certain level, and then going no further. She had a great deal of experience with children very like Walter. What was important was that he should be able to mix socially with other children, and at school he did.

Sarah wished to say, 'Yes. With backward children,' but did not.

After the first fortnight, which was always a difficult time, Walter had begun to enjoy coming to school. Sarah must not misunderstand the function of a Special School. It would teach what could be taught to those who could learn, but the Three Rs were not the beginning and end of life in the world; the lives of otherwise restricted and unhappy children might be enriched by Creative Play. The function of a Special School was also to assist parents through a most difficult time. 'We take the strain,' the Head Teacher said, 'We carry a part of the weight. We relax what might otherwise be an intolerable tension, Mrs Williams, in the Home Environment.'

Sarah said she could manage. She had managed before the Special School had been found for Walter, and could again.

'But Walter has to attend school. It's against the law to keep him at home other than for reasons of health. Unfortunately we are the nearest school to your home which is equipped to deal with children like Walter. Please don't think that I don't know what it must be like to have a backward child. I do. All of us here, we all do. But life won't even begin to be easier for you, Mrs Williams, until you accept that backward is what Walter is, and always will be. In two years, he'll be all yours: there'll be nothing more we can do for either of you. It won't be easy for him to find work. Perhaps then you'll wish he were still at school.'

Walter continued to attend the Special School, and Sarah continued to take him there and to collect him, forty-three minutes each way in an unheated bus. The war continued also. Attempts were made to bomb Preston Docks and the Leyland Works nearby, where rubber parts for gas masks were made. Every night, Sarah, Eric and Walter would hear the planes overhead making for Preston, then following the line of the river on to Liverpool and Manchester. They would hear the distant bombing, and see the glow of flames in the sky.

One Sunday, at tea-time, in the small neighbouring village of Lostock Hall, the whole of Ward Street and the houses adjacent were demolished by bombs meant for Leyland. Next day two women arrived at Sarah's door, pushing prams in which they were collecting for the people of Lostock Hall, who had lost everything they had. Sarah gave the women a shilling, Walter's baby clothes (which she had kept in mothballs) and the toys she no longer wished him to play with. Later that day she took him for a walk to see what was left of Ward Street.

Sarah's mother died of cancer of the womb. Neither was a word ever used by Chapel people. The funeral cost twenty-one pounds and fifteen shillings, but since Sarah's mother had been putting twopence a week into the Prudential Insurance Company for much of her adult life in order to meet just such a need, Sarah was well able to pay for it. One hearse and one car to follow it was considered sufficient in time of war, and Sarah had eight pounds of the Insurance money left over.

Sarah inherited her mother's wedding and engagement rings, a string of cultured pearls, and the Eiffel Tower diamanté ear-rings, with various pieces of Victorian furniture, which were moved into the tied cottage, and overcrowded it. She kept the jewellery, but did not wear it; she locked it in a drawer, as her own insurance for a rainy day. She knew that its value would increase. Sometimes she opened the drawer, and looked at the two rings, the necklace and the glittering Eiffel Tower ear-rings lying there. She had something, no matter how little, if freedom came. Or any other emergency.

Nine months later, Walter's Special School was taken over and used to house prisoners of war and their keepers. To meet the needs of the backward children thus displaced, small Remedial Groups were set up in already existing County Schools, one being only six miles from the village, and this was the one Walter now attended. An added advantage was that the school enjoyed the services of a speech therapist, who visited Walter's Remedial Group once a week.

Walter's speech improved, though he was still difficult to understand. He had never seemed to wish to talk before. That he should do so now, seemed to Sarah a major improvement, which might lead anywhere. However, after fifteen months at the school, he became fourteen, and was obliged to leave, so it led nowhere.

Sarah asked if he might stay on, if only for one more year. But she was told that there were too many handicapped children (the word 'backward' had already begun to go out of fashion), too few schools and teachers. She asked the speech therapist whether Walter might have private lessons, but the fees were more than could be afforded. 'Digging For Britain' may have been vital to the War Effort, but the wage of a farm labourer in 1944 was no more than four pounds a week, and to strike was illegal, even if Eric had ever thought of such a thing. As for Sarah herself, she could not go out to work while Walter was at home; he tied her as effectively at the age of fourteen as he had at three. She opened the drawer, and looked at her mother's jewellery, but the time for that was not yet.

The therapist told her that Walter's speech would improve with time and practice, but that, since he had started so late, it would never be perfect. She gave Sarah some useful hints, and Sarah set one hour a day aside to try to improve the way Walter spoke. His concentration-span was no more than ten minutes at the most, so the lessons would end in arguments and tantrums. Sarah stopped the lessons, and simply corrected him whenever he pronounced a word wrongly.

He was fifteen, and still soiled himself on occasions. To speak the King's English perfectly was not of paramount importance.

5

If you kissed me now, I might get pregnant

'A penn'orth of chips to grease your lips, and Out ... Goes ... You!
Ip! Dip! Sky blue! Who's it? Not ... You.
God's words are true. It ... Must ... Be ... You'

Elaine, the eldest of the four girls, was pointing at Walter.

'Oh, no! Not Walter. He never finds us. Do it again.' These words
were spoken by Norma, the smallest of the four girls. Her hair was
ginger, and her face, since this was a fine summer, was covered with
freckles.

'I'm not doing it again. Walter's It. If you don't want to hide, you
can let him catch you. Then you'll be It next time.'

'No fear! I'm not having *that* touch me.'

That was Walter. As Norma said '*that*', she pointed at Walter.
Immediately he covered his mouth with one hand, pointed back at her
and giggled. This was a habit he had acquired at his first school, the
one before the Special School, and it had been reinforced during his
period within a Remedial Group among those who attended the
County School. Any child, confronted with Walter, would point and
giggle. Clearly it was a form of greeting. Therefore Walter did it. Or
perhaps he knew well enough that it was not a greeting, and pointed
and giggled himself to forestall pointing and giggling in others. Any
road, he did it.

'Look at him. He's halfway round the twist. Why do we always have
to play with that?' Walter continued to point. Bent double now, he
acted out the uncontrollable glee and mockery which were usually
directed at him. He was almost nineteen now. Elaine, the oldest girl,
was thirteen.

'How would you like it? He can't help being daft, can he?'

Walter stopped his performance. Elaine was his ally. He looked at
each of the other girls in turn, waiting to hear whether he were to be
allowed to play or not. He composed his face into a tentative smile, and
looked first at Pat, then at Ann, finally at Norma, who looked away.

Sensing that she was outnumbered, Norma said, 'Oh, alright! Come on, then; let's get started. I wouldn't mind if he could count.'

'You shut your face, ginger nut. Come on, Walter. Cover your eyes up.'

Walter obeyed, his long bony fingers cupped over his protruding eyes, and started to count. He could count, as it happened, but only as far as twenty. This he did aloud, and very loud. At twenty-one, he lowered his voice to a whisper, and began again.

All the girls, including the reluctant Norma, were running, and finding places to hide. Norma was chanting,

> 'One! Two! Three!
> Mother's caught a flea.
> Put it in the teapot, to make a pot of tea.
> Flea jumped out.
> Bit her on the snout.
> In came Walter, with his willy hanging out.'

To all but Norma, the game was more interesting when they contrived to make Walter It. He generated such excitement as he darted about, trying to catch them, they allowing him to get close up to them, and then, just as he was about to touch, outwitting him by turning the other way. The closer he got to catching them, the more excited he became. The excitement was shown in the noises he made and in the saliva which dripped liberally from his mouth. On one occasion he had become so excited that he had stopped suddenly in his tracks, and they had stopped running to watch him as he looked down at the front of his trousers in amazement, feeling the warm piss run down his legs and out through the front of his trousers. And they had laughed, and he had left the game, turning at once on his heels, and had gone – half walking, half running, feeling the wet pants against his legs – home.

Elaine was his ally. She would always let him play, and she persuaded the others. She ran away from him, into the bushes. When he caught up with her, she dodged away just enough to excite him, and then she lunged suddenly towards him, pushing him over, and grabbing him in the crotch. Walter lay on the ground, with Elaine lying on top of him, as she rubbed her hands over the front of his trousers, making his willy go hard.

'You have got one, then?'

Walter placed both hands over his face, and began counting again. He had reached fifteen when Elaine slid her fingers between his flybuttons, causing two of them to open. She squeezed and rubbed him, and Walter rolled about with an excitement that he couldn't control, his counting forgotten. Then he gave a frightened yelp. Something was happening to him. The tip of his willy itched, and something was bursting out of it, gushing forth like the contents of a squeezed boil. Unlike a boil, it didn't hurt. Walter couldn't think of a word to describe what he felt. The only word that came into his mind was the word 'nice'. It wasn't the right word, but it was the only one he could think of.

Whatever it was that had burst out of him, was sticky. He felt it on Elaine's hand, and on the inside of his trousers.

Elaine wiped her hand on some dock leaves, and said, 'That's what makes babies, Walter. If you kissed me now, I might get pregnant.'

For weeks afterwards, Walter wouldn't go near the Park. He would walk miles to avoid going even round it. It was not that he didn't want to play with the girls. He wanted to very much, and thought about it constantly. But first Elaine might have told the other girls what had happened, and they might laugh at him, and worse, she might be pregnant. He knew what pregnant was. He had seen women, heavy, with large stomachs, and his mother had told him that those women were pregnant. When he had asked what the word meant, she had said, 'Don't worry. It'll never happen to you. By rights, it only happens after you're married, and that you'll never be.'

He remained confused by what Elaine had done to him, and by what she had said, that if they kissed she might become fat and heavy in front like those women. Elaine was only thirteen. Even Walter knew that was much too young to marry.

6

No one was ever really hurt, no one died,
and the failures always came out on top

WALTER arrived home breathless from having run all the way from the Park. He arrived at the back gate to find his father standing in the back yard, waving a very long bamboo pole at the top of which was a white flag. Walter was told by his father to close the gate quickly, and stand still. He did so, using the gate to lean against, and catch his breath. The substance which Elaine had caused to gush from his willy felt like cold glue. He wondered if it would set hard.

'The buggers are staying out. They won't come sodding home.'

The buggers to which Walter's father referred were Russian High-Flying Pigeons. 'Trust the bloody Russians to be difficult.' Walter looked up, and scanned the sky for any sign of a bird. His father took a referee's whistle from his top pocket, and blew on it as hard as he could. Whereafter Walter heard the sound of a coin being tapped against glass. His mother was standing on the other side of the kitchen window, watching them.

'She's on the bloody warpath, and the sodding buggers won't come down.' Having tapped, Sarah now stood with her arms folded across her chest. 'That's the third time she's done that. Break the bloody window before she's satisfied.'

Sarah was pointing at the Pigeon Loft, which ran the entire length of the back yard. Her meaning was clear. Something would have to be done about those pigeons, if they were to make Eric and Walter late for tea.

The Pigeon Loft was divided into four sections, to house the four different sorts of pigeons which Eric bred, for his interest in pigeons had expanded considerably since his wife and her mother had scorned the solitary racer which had befriended him so long ago. These were not racing pigeons; they were for Show. Consequently it was of the uttermost importance to keep the different sorts of bird apart, so as to control their breeding. The first type of pigeon fancied by Eric were English Long-Faced Tumblers, so named because of their ability to tumble over backwards during flight, or, more strictly, their inability to avoid doing so, since the tumbling which gave entertainment to the onlooker was due to a fault in the inner ears of these birds, which was cultivated by selective breeding. The second type were White-Lace Fantails, which spread out their tails like white lacey fans and inflated their chests so full and high as to make their heads almost disappear. Next were the Turbits, elegantly shaped birds of various colours with inverted necks and tiny bills. Turbits had been inbred until their bills were so tiny that they were unable to feed their own young, which had to be taken from then and fostered, but they were most decorative birds and fit, beholders said, to stand on any mantel – not that they ever would, during their lives, grace a mantel, for, like all pigeons they were prodigious shitters. Last were the Russian High-Fliers, the wayward birds which were causing Eric so much concern at this moment. Because of their ability to stay high in the air, out of sight of the human eye, a long pole with a flag on it was needed to control their flight. A World Record had been set up by a Mr Wilf Wilmer of Staffordshire, who in June 1943 flew a 'kit' of birds for twenty hours. It was stated at the time that the long twilights in England gave him an unfair advantage over his American rival, a Mr Fred Engelberg of Mespeth, New York, who could only manage a flight of seventeen hours, eighteen minutes.

Eric was now fifty-two. He had left the farm, and become a railway porter. Sarah had insisted, the week after their marriage, that they should have their name on the Corporation Housing List, in case Eric ever wished to change his type of work, so that they were no longer able to live in a tied cottage. By 1943, the Williams name had achieved its slow climb to the top of the List, and they had received a letter informing them that if, after all these years, they still wished a Corporation house, there was one to be had.

The decision had not been an easy one. All Eric knew about was farming; he could not envisage doing any other kind of work. Sarah had assisted him to envisage it, by making a list of all the jobs an unskilled man could do. On that list were the words 'Railway Porter'. They were the only words on the list which had got anything akin to a positive response from Eric.

The following day, Sarah had gone to Preston Station, and put their predicament to the Personnel Officer there. He had been sympathetic. 'Right,' he had said, 'I see the problem. Get different job before leaving work on land, and losing roof over heads.' Sarah had said that was it in a nutshell. The Personnel Officer had agreed to interview Eric on the following day, as a result of which interview Eric gave notice to his employer of long standing, and they had moved into a Corporation house in Bamber Bridge. It was not a new house, but it was a better one, and Sarah was pleased.

Eric was not at first overjoyed with his new job. He had to cycle six miles each way to and from Preston, and the shift system caused inconvenience to the pigeons, who had to get used to having their meals and exercise at different times, depending on whether Eric was on the early or the late shift. This confused the pigeons, as it did Eric, but both adapted. Eric discovered that he quite liked wearing a uniform. It gave him confidence. When he talked (which was seldom to anyone but the pigeons or Walter) he talked as the other porters talked, swearing a lot and saying very little. This annoyed Sarah, who would often remark that if she had known what foul language her husband would bring home from Preston Railway Station, she would have stayed and died of pneumonia in the damp of the tied cottage, rather than to have to listen to her God being blasphemed and her son corrupted by the filth that dropped unashamedly from Eric's lips.

Now Eric rested his long pole for a moment, and used both his hands to shake vigorously an old cocoa-tin filled with small pebbles. The pebbles were to represent the sound of grain. Since they made a louder noise than grain, they were necessary this evening, as the Russians were refusing to answer the call to supper.

The referee's whistle was blown in unison with the rattling of pebbles. This brought another tapping on the window by Sarah. She had given up trying to keep Walter and Eric's tea warm. What she was objecting to most of all was the whistle, since by now everybody within hearing distance knew why it was used, and the regularity of its use reminded the neighbours of her husband's incompetence.

'Can't that bloody woman see I'm doing my best?' Eric rattled the tin of pebbles as hard as he could, and shouted up into the birdless sky, 'Come down, you stupid buggers. My tea's getting cold.' Almost immediately a bird was sighted, just the outline, but it was definitely a bird, and not an aeroplane. After a moment, the bird disappeared, and Eric remarked, 'Probably a sodding eagle with its stomach full of my sodding Russians.' The other possibility to be feared was that some neighbouring pigeon fancier had lured the flock to his own loft, either by using a longer pole or a dropper – a dropper being a comparatively low-flying pigeon, sent up to bring the others down by leading them home to food.

'Go and get Freda.' Walter moved slowly towards the long shed, trying to walk as naturally as possible in case his watching mother should suspect that there was something in his trousers that shouldn't be and insist on an inspection. He had never been able to understand why the shed he was about to enter was called a 'loft', when lofts were above the ceiling and this was on the ground in the back yard.

Seeing Walter go towards the Loft, Sarah opened the kitchen window, and hissed at her husband, 'About time too!' His reply was rendered inaudible by the loud noise of the window's being closed again.

Walter opened the door of the Loft very slowly, and slid inside, leaving as little space for any birds to escape as possible. His presence caused a stir, as pigeons flew about his face, pecking at each other for space, and wing-flicking each other for the occupancy of a perch. Feathers flew and dust rose. The disturbed birds were already wondering what had happened to their supper. Walter closed his eyes, and held one arm over his face for protection. He knew exactly where Freda perched, and could find his way there blindfolded, which now in a sense he was.

Freda was an old bird, a White-Lace Fantail, whose breeding days were past. She was no longer capable of producing offspring beautiful enough to be exhibited at the Harrogate Show or even the London Dairy Show (not that Eric would ever be allowed to travel south to the City of Sin). A more scrupulously professional breeder of Show birds would have wrung Freda's neck more than a year ago, and used her perch and the grain she ate to help him breed a possible winner. But Eric's scruples were of another sort. Freda's job as dropper was to circle around as high as she could, but always so as to be seen from the ground, and to flutter her wings so as to attract the Russians' attention and to remind them that there was food waiting below.

Walter passed through Turbits and through Tumblers. He squeezed carefully through the door in the partition which divided Tumblers from Fantails, and found Freda sitting peacefully on her perch. Being old, she had seen it all before, and was not given to the panic and excessive movement of the younger birds. Walter did as his father had taught him, and placed his left hand just above her head for long enough to distract her and so allow him to slide his right hand under her, securing her legs between his two longest fingers, and holding her wings with his thumb on the one side and the tip of his index finger on the other. She was used to being handled in this way, and her only movement as Walter lifted her from the perch was to cock her head to one side, as if she were asking, 'What is it this time?'

'Good lad! She'll bring 'em down. Won't you, Freda love? Didn't want to disturb you tonight.' Of all the birds in Eric's flock, Freda was his favourite. This was because she was the only bird of his ever to have

66

won a prize. In her youth, Freda had won a cup, and so the cup, and Freda's presence, reminded Eric of the one day in his life when he had been successful.

Eric had taken the bird gently from Walter, and was holding her up to his face, her beak touching his lips. Walter saw that his mother was still standing at the kitchen window, her arms folded across her chest. As he looked, she made a gesture of impatience.

'You'll get them down for me, won't you, my little lovely?' Eric lowered Freda so that she could peck up four grains of hemp from his open palm. She removed the hemp seeds so quickly that it reminded Eric of a Keystone Kops film, in which the Kops were forever jumping in and out of moving vehicles. He remembered particularly how one of them clung for dear life to the trailing hosepipe of a fire-engine, being dragged for miles around sharp corners. But they always got up, and brushed down their ill-fitting uniforms. No one was ever really hurt. No one died, not in those days. And the failures always came out on top.

'If only life was like that!' Eric spoke his private thoughts to Freda. Birds couldn't answer back. 'I wish I could flap my arms, and go up there with you.'

Sarah opened the window again, and shouted, 'Are you going to send that bird up, or are you going to talk it to death first?' And closed the window again, like punctuation.

To Freda, the four hemp seeds she had been given seemed small payment for what she was being required to do, but hemp is what pigeons like best, and she had been called upon so often to collect the Russian High-Fliers, and had always been rewarded at the end of each successful mission with a much larger amount of hemp, with the addition of canary seeds, which pigeons also regard as a delicacy. She knew the score. The sooner she was allowed to get on with the job, and get those stupid Russians down, the sooner everybody could eat.

Eric gave Freda a little assistance by throwing her up into the air. Up she flew, heavy and laborious, slapping her wings together behind her back to attract the Russians' attention. She made four complete circles, then started to fly down again, resting her wings and gliding down, using the wind to conserve her precious energy. The 'kit' of High-Flying Russians returned within the next three minutes. They were given food and a severe talking-to by Eric. Freda herself was given a good handful of mixed seed and grain, which included rape, linseed, millet, maple peas, groats and tares, as well as her two favourites, hemp and canary seed. She did not eat the linseed, which is good for pigeons (being a source of oil) but not much liked by them.

Walter and his parents sat down to their delayed tea, and ate dried-up sausages, lukewarm mashed potatoes and cold boiled carrots. His mother could have eaten hers while it was still at its best, but preferred to sit with them in silence – or to be more exact, without speaking, for she did make small noises of disgust with each mouthful, and left at least half the meal uneaten on her plate. Eric finished all of what he was given, then left the table to read the evening paper. Walter also ate the contents of his plate, wondered about seconds (but there were none), then helped his mother to clear the table and wash up, after which he sat beside her on the settee, and was asked to identify certain objects from the pictures in *Woman's Own*.

'What's that?'

'Cardigan.' He wondered if his mother would smell what Elaine had squeezed from his willy with such pleasure. He himself could not smell anything extra, but his mother had a special sensitivity about such matters.

'Good. And that?' Sarah had turned to the Cookery Column.

'Pie.'

'Yes, but what do we say?'

Walter thought for a moment. 'A pie.'

'Good. It's *a* pie. Why? Why do we say "a pie"?'

Walter didn't know. He shook his head.

'Don't shake your head.'

Walter discovered that he was becoming angry. He turned his head away, and began humming to himself, to help to remove the anger and frustration he was feeling.

'Don't you know?'

Walter grunted, and continued to hum.

'Then say, "I don't know, mother."'

Walter made noises which approximated to 'I don't know, mother.'

'I don't want noises either, thank you. You can speak very well when it suits you. We don't only do things that we like in this world, my lad. You'll very quickly find that out, after I'm dead, and he's too old and daft to look after you.' She pointed in the direction of the arm-chair. Eric had placed the evening paper over his face, and was snoring beneath it, so that the Sports Pages rose and fell in time to his breathing. Walter giggled, and pointed to the paper moving up and down.

'Sleep, that's what he's best at. You and him together make a fine pair.' She thought of the evening ahead of her. The emptiness, the pointlessness. The tiny pinpricks behind her eyes warned her of tears. Her mouth quivered. The whole world outside was enjoying its even-

68

ing, and she was here, trapped in a routine of cleaning and cooking, of fouled bedclothes and snoring. She screwed her eyes up tight, defying them to make water and upset her son. She clenched her teeth, and took a deep breath. She took such breaths every day now. Each day was marked out by them. She saw the days ahead, filled with them. She saw herself in a permanent state of 'holding on'. 'One of the three people in this room,' she thought, 'one of us has to die, before this forever holding on and getting through drives me as silly as Walter.'

'Toffee?' He was tugging at her sleeve, saliva running from his mouth to his chin, and then hanging, suspended, before it dropped on to his Fair Isle pullover.

'No, you can't have one. You didn't concentrate at your lessons. Toffees are for when you're good, and you . . . try . . . to . . . CONCEN-TRATE.' She was almost shouting, spelling each word out slowly, as if she were talking to a two-year-old. How she hated the sound of her own voice, loathed the caricature of a disappointed wife she had become! She had moved away, both from her husband and her son, putting as much distance as there was in the small room between herself and the two men. She had reached the door to the stairs, trapped there, not knowing why or what she intended to do. It was too soon to go up to bed, much too soon. She was in a cage with no exit. The man she had married was snoring, hidden by local gossip and the racing results. Soon they would be lying together in the same bed, back to back, not touching, not speaking, the space between them never to be filled. And the child to whom she had given birth, whom she had reared for nearly nineteen years, was staring at her, wide-eyed and dribbling for toffees. They were on the dresser in a glass bowl. They were given as rewards for good behaviour, enticements to quietness and calm. Her only weapon was to withhold what had already rotted his protruding and uneven teeth. She looked at Walter. As always, he was watching her; whenever they were together, he never took his eyes from her. At eighteen as at seven, he could scream if he sensed fear or even uncertainty in her. And the uncertainty was there. His face was already showing signs of apprehension. It was her own quivering face which looked back at her, horribly distorted as in a fairground mirror. She must go, must get out, if only for an hour, must walk to the Park, scream into the darkness, then look up at the sky and count the stars until she was tired.

Her coat was hanging behind the door. She reached for it, and tried to control herself enough to say, 'I'm going out.' Walter's mouth trembled, and a very small frightened noise emerged. It was enough. The floodgates opened. Sarah slammed the half-opened door, and burst into uncontrollable tears, smashing the glass bowl and the toffees to the floor at the feet of her husband.

'He's your son as well. You take care of him.' The veins in her neck stood out. Walter looked at the broken glass and the toffees, heard his mother's tears, caught and magnified all her rage and frustration and grief and, being unable to deal with emotion on such a scale, went into a fit, rolling about on the floor among the toffees and the broken glass. Eric came abruptly awake. He placed three fingers in Walter's mouth to prevent him from biting his tongue, and Sarah, knowing that in the matter of controlling frightened animals, her ex-farm labourer husband had more experience than she, went out into the back yard, leaned against the Pigeon Loft, and wept.

An hour later, the broken glass and toffees had been cleared away, and Walter sat where they had fallen, doing his favourite jigsaw puzzle. It was in eight large pieces, which he could now fit together and break apart in a matter of four minutes. The jigsaw was a picture of the Pied Piper of Hamelin, dancing down the road, and playing his pipe to charm the rats out of the city. The Piper wore tights and knee-high boots not unlike those worn by Robin Hood in other jigsaws, and the rats which followed him all had smiles on their faces, disarmed of their characteristic rattishness by the calming music of the pipe.

Walter completed the puzzle for the fifth time, and began to break it up, preparatory to completing it for a sixth, but Sarah leaned forward from the chair in which she was sitting, and touched his arm. 'That's enough for tonight. It's bedtime.' Walter put the pieces of jigsaw back into their box, replaced the lid, and returned the box to the cupboard in which it was kept. He came close to his mother, kissed her on the cheek, and said, 'Good night.'

'Good night, Walter. I'll be up to see you in a minute.'

I'll be up to see you in a minute. I'll be up to tuck you in bed. He was eighteen years old. Soon he would be nineteen. She was fifty.

Part Three

He becomes a Wage-Earner

Are you going to make me proud, Walter?
Are you going to do well, and make
me pleased with you?

THEY sat in Mr Richards' office, he and his mother sitting side by side. He was wearing his best suit, with a new shirt and a new tie, tied by his mother. He had cleaned his black shoes, the ones he wore only on Sundays, three times. Three times he had shown them to his mother, and three times she had sent him back into the kitchen to clean them again. Even after that, she had sighed her sigh of disappointment, and finished them off herself.

She had told him to keep his mouth closed, and to speak only when spoken to. This would not be easy; Walter's mouth was almost permanently open, owing to the size of his teeth. He had watched her sprinkling lavender water inside her blouse. He had watched her buttoning up the top of her blouse. It was her best blouse. She had told him to sit up straight and try to look alert. As he had held out her best coat for her to slip in her arms, she had said, 'Now this is important. Do you understand?' He had nodded, and said, 'Yes,' and when she was satisfied with the angle of her best hat, she had squeezed his hand, and said, 'Good boy! You do your best, and try to make me proud of you.'

As they sat side by side in the office, Sarah's hands shook with the strain of trying to make a good impression for them both. Walter noticed the shaking hands, and listened docilely while she asked Mr Richards not to be put off by his appearance. 'He's far more capable than you might think,' she said. Then she smiled at Walter, for he had remembered to sit up straight, and was doing so, as much as was humanly possible, his knees touching and his arms neatly folded.

Mr Richards asked Walter how old he was, and Walter remembered how old he was, and replied, 'Twenty-one.'

'Can you sweep the floor, Walter?' Mr Richards was speaking in a quiet and gentle voice as if he were talking to a baby. And Walter replied, 'Yes, sir,' and glanced at his mother for approbation, pleased with himself that he had remembered to call Mr Richards 'sir'.

'Just call me "Mr Richards", Walter. No need to be too formal. I haven't been knighted yet, you know.' Then he smiled, and Walter's mother smiled, and laughed the laugh she laughed when she was nervous.

Mr Richards said, 'I'm going to take you upstairs to the Stock Room, and show you a machine, and I want you to tell me truthfully if you think you can work it.'

As they moved from Mr Richards' office out into the shop, they passed the Toiletry Counter, and Walter remembered how good it smelled. He remembered that he had been in this Woolworth's before, several times with his mother. On those occasions she had held his hand with a tight grasp, but today, as they followed Mr Richards through the shop, and Walter tried to slide his hand into his mother's, she pushed him away, and gave a look which he recognized as meaning, 'Don't do that.'

Mr Richards led them into a large lift, and closed the outer door. The door looked to Walter like one side of a concertina, and the inner door looked like trelliswork, which stretched out when it was opened and slid together when closed.

'You'll have to get used to using this. Press the top button for me, please, Walter.' Mr Richards pointed to a row of three buttons on the side of the lift. Walter placed his index finger on the top button, and pressed. Nothing happened. He looked at his mother, who smiled her nervous smile. There was a silence. Mr Richards was watching him. His mother said, 'Press it hard, Walter.' He pressed the top button again, as hard as he could. Still nothing happened. Walter turned to Mr Richards, and said somewhat accusingly, 'Broke.'

'No, it's not.' Mr Richards still maintained his quiet reassuring voice. Then he asked Walter's mother, 'Has he ever been in a lift before?'

'Oh, yes, but not in one like this, I'm afraid. Only the sort where they have a disabled person to press the button for you.'

'What do you think could be wrong with it, Walter?'

Walter waited a moment, gave the matter thought, and repeated, 'Broke.'

'No, it's not broken. Open the door again, and close it.'

Walter did as he was told, sliding back first the trellis, then the concertina. 'Now shut them.' Walter did so, and looked to Mr Richards for further instructions. 'Try again.' Walter pressed the top button, and the lift began to go upwards.

'I did that on purpose, to show you how it works. The lift won't move unless both doors are closed tight. Do you understand, Walter?'

Walter nodded, and they arrived at the Stock Room. Mr Richards signalled to Walter to slide back the gates. Walter did so, and the Stock Room was revealed. A group of people who had been standing by or leaning against a large workbench in the centre of the room suddenly began to move about, picking things up or writing things down. The room had become full of activity.

A man in grey overalls came forward to greet Mr Richards. 'Good morning, sir. How are you today?' Mr Richards replied with a sound which was between a grunt and a cough, but did not contain any reminder that he had not been knighted. He said, 'This is Master Walter Williams, who would like to come and work for us, and this lady is his mother.'

The man shook hands with Walter's mother, but not with Walter. Instead he looked Walter up and down. Walter held out his hand to be shaken, having remembered his mother's telling him, 'Always give a good strong handshake. Then people know where they are with you.' But the man did not see Walter's hand, his eyes being on Mr Richards, who was scrutinizing the Stock Room to make sure that all those who were there had a right to be there, and if they had, that they were working.

'Don't let those girls stay chatting up here. Get them back down, down on the floor, behind their counters.'

'Yes, sir.'

'Want you to show Walter how to work the press. What do you think?'

'Well, at least he looks a strong lad. That's what we need.'

Mr Richards placed an arm over the shoulder of the man in grey overalls, and led him on ahead towards the press. Although he spoke in a whisper, both Walter and Sarah could hear what he said.

'Now, he's not very bright, as you can see, but if you think he can do the job, we should give him a trial. They like this sort of thing at Head Office – giving this sort of job to someone who's handicapped. It's less money gone in wages, and good public relations for the shop.' The man nodded, and Mr Richards went on, 'I'm a member of the Round Table. They're very keen on this sort of thing too. Might help in one or two places, see what I mean? Any road, I don't expect you to carry him. If he can't pull his weight, then that's that. Give him a couple of weeks, eh? Trial. What do you think?'

The man replied that he thought it was an excellent idea. Then he turned to Walter, and said, 'This here is a press. The green button starts it, like this.' He pressed the green button, and nothing happened.

Walter knew better than to suggest that the press was broken. This would be a test, like the other.

'Oh, yes, I remember now. It's jammed.' The next ten minutes were spent in watching the man in grey overalls dismantle parts of the machine, and attempt to remove some string which had got tangled in the works. Mr Richards grew tired of watching this demonstration, and excused himself by saying he had letters to write.

When the string had been untangled and the various parts replaced, the green button was pressed again, and this time Walter and his mother had the pleasure of hearing the machine make its noise, and watching the top half of it descend to compress cardboard and waste paper into a tight bale. 'Now, that's quite opportune, that happening. It means you'll know never to put string in with the waste. String we keep in a box over there. It gets used up in time.' He pointed to where a large round cardboard drum stood, overflowing with knotted string.

'The red button stops it, like this.' This time the machine obeyed its button, and stopped the pressing and the noise. 'Cardboard and waste paper have to be collected from all the bins in the shop. There are two bins behind every counter.' Walter thought about the Toiletry Counter, and of the girls who worked there, with their faces drawn on them in bright colours.

'Oh, and this floor gets very dusty. So you never put a broom to it before you've first sprinkled water on it with the watering-can you'll find in the Gents. Over here's the skip.' The man pulled at a large square basket on casters. 'You take this down in the lift you came up in, and you empty all the bins into it. Never leave the girls behind their counters without their bins. That just gives them an excuse to come up here to talk to Mike there.' The man pointed to a young man who was standing by the workbench, unpacking boxes of liquorice all-sorts, whereupon the young man grabbed a handful of all-sorts from one of the boxes, and stuffed them into his mouth, winking at Walter. 'Got that?' said the man in the grey overalls. 'Skip down in lift. Bins emptied into skip. Skip back in lift. Remove string and place in drum. Cardboard and waste paper into machine.' Sarah said she was sure that Walter had indeed got it, and would give satisfaction.

He was to be there at half past eight on the following Monday, and leave at six, after he and the trainee floor-walkers had swept out the entire shop. From the back to the front, they would sweep the aisles between every counter. Every sweet wrapper and cigarette packet, every hairpin and comb, every sticky sweet and fly-button had to be swept up and put away, ready for the women who mopped to do their mopping early the following morning.

Sarah and Walter sat side by side on the top deck of the bus going home. Sarah gave him a boiled sweet from her bag. He closed his eyes to unwrap the sweet, then placed it in his mouth, and tried to guess its colour. This was a game they often played. Walter sucked at the sweet, and said. 'Orange,' and Sarah, who had given him a red one, told him he was right. He was not allowed to remove the sweet once it was in his mouth, so he would never know she was lying.

She touched the back of his hand with her leather glove, and said, 'Two weeks' trial they're giving you. Two weeks to test you out. Are you going to make me proud, Walter? Are you going to do well, and make me pleased with you?' Walter nodded, and sucked hard on the red boiled sweet.

'There's a good boy!'

An unkind person had once said
that the sound of Walter talking was like
a fart in a bath of soapy water

WALTER was so keen to succeed at his new job that he seldom stood still even for a moment.

He could make sense. The manager of the Stock Room could understand what Walter said. Sometimes. At other times he would ask Walter to stand still, and repeat what he had said. 'Please . . . Mister . . . Hin-gall-ee . . . can some . . . someone . . . help . . . me . . . with this bale?' Walter salivated richly when he was asked to stand still and repeat a sentence out loud, and often Mr Hingley would pretend that Walter had spat in his eye, and say, 'Here, Walter! Watch where you're aiming.' At this Walter would laugh. He didn't know why he laughed, except that laughing seemed to be the safest thing to do. But laughing made him spit even more, and he would have to cover his mouth with a dirty hand.

When Walter laughed, he rocked back and forwards in an exaggerated way, to show people what he was doing. Look! He was laughing. Look! It made people feel better when they saw Walter laughing. They would smile or they themselves would laugh. To those who worked at Woolworth's it seemed that Walter was permanently in a state of good humour.

'Poor Walter! He's a lot happier the way he is, thank God,' though what God had to do with it was something Walter was never able to work out. Laughing was what Walter did best. He was good at his job, but at laughing he was even better. An unkind person had once said that the sound of Walter talking was like a fart in a bath of soapy water.

Mr Hingley had said that without Walter they would all be out of a job. If Walter didn't bale all the cardboard and waste paper, it would mount up so fast and so high that customers would have to climb over it, and crawl about on their hands and knees to find the counters they wanted, saying, ''Scuse me, could you tell me the way to Haberdashery,' and being answered, 'Just keep crawling for two more counters, and it's on your right.'

'What you laughing for?'

'Don't know.'

'Don't *know*?'

'Yes.'

'Don't know was made to know. Is this rubbish yours?' Mr Hingley would point to some straw at his feet.

'No.'

'Whose is it, then?'

'Belongs to Woolworth's.'

'Shift it!'

Walter would laugh, and do as he was told, but a moment later he would be back at Mr Hingley's side, saliva running down from his chin on to his overalls, giggling and pointing to some paper on the floor.

'Do you want this paper, Mr Hin-gall-ee?' Walter's head would nod on each syllable with the effort to get the name right. Mr Hingley would look at Walter, then back to the string he was trying to untangle. It was a game, a game they often played.

Walter would wait, his finger still pointing at the paper on the floor. Then he would make a noise, signifying that his question had not been answered.

The string in Mr Hingley's hands would seem to be even more tangled than it had been when he began to try to unravel it. He hated cutting good string. You couldn't get strong string nowadays. But to spend half an hour untangling three yards of it was not in the best interests of Woolworth's shareholders. Time was money. The string wasn't worth half his hourly rate.

The look Mr Hingley would give Walter would be one of warning. It was a game; they played it often. Walter, enjoying the danger of going too far, would persist. 'Do you want the paper, Mr Hingley? Do you?' Mr Hingley would give a sudden and violent lurch towards Walter, stamping his foot down hard and close to Walter's feet, and shouting, *'No!'* into Walter's ear. Then Walter would step back, and mumble to himself in the third person to prove that his actions belonged to the external order of things, and had very little to do with him personally.

'Sometimes he understands everything you say to him,' Walter would mumble, ducking and grabbing to pick up the waste paper and take it to his press, and Mr Hingley would shout over one shoulder to him, 'It wouldn't be lying on the floor if I wanted it, would it, Walter?' Mr Hingley had never met a Woolworth's shareholder. He unravelled string chiefly to put off writing out the Stock Sheet, since he always ordered too much or too little, and the Stock Sheet would show this up. Also his spelling was bad. Mr Hingley hated the thought that the girls in the office would giggle over the words he had spelt wrongly.

'Sometimes he's almost as intelligent as you or me,' Walter would mumble.

'Talking to yourself again, Walter?'

'No, sir.'

'Take you away for that.'

'Yes, sir.'

'Better stop doing it, then, hadn't you?'

'Stop it, then,' Walter would echo, laughing and dribbling on to the paper in his hands.

'Like a bloody parrot you are sometimes, do you know that?'

'No. Do you?' It was a game; they played it often. Walter would rock backwards and forwards on the balls of his feet, putting paper into the press and taking it out again, laughing and dribbling and talking to himself, as he tore up the paper in his hands. 'Face like a parrot too,' he would mutter, 'Wouldn't be seen dead with a hooter like yours, Walter. What a beak! Coooor!' and realizing that Walter was getting over-excited, and that his rocking was becoming faster and faster, Mr Hingley would adopt his serious voice, and say, 'Alright, Walter. Calm down. Stop being silly. Just calm down. Hey! What's on the telly tonight?' and Walter would reply, 'Fursday!' (if the day was Thursday) triumphantly, swinging round from his press and projecting his saliva the full length of the Stock Room.

Then he would go into a familiar routine, which Mr Hingley wisely encouraged, knowing that it would use up some of Walter's excess energy and distract him from being silly and self-derogatory. This was it: Walter's favourite television programme was *Sportsview*, which used for its opening credits a screen split into nine segments, in every one of which a different sporting activity was going on. The music which accompanied these pictures was a rousing tune, which grew and grew in intensity. Walter's routine was to mime all nine of these sporting activities one after another as quickly as he could, humming the rousing music and ending with a robust crescendo.

It was a game; they played it often.

'Where's my bloody Stock Sheet? And shut that row up.' Walter's crescendo was cut short by the boom of a foghorn voice. He covered his mouth with one hand, and used the other to pretend he was busy. Miss Rushden ran the Office, indeed she pretty well ran the whole store. She was a large stout woman, with a voice louder and deeper than most men's voices. Her favourite pleasure in life was to terrify people, and since she was able to do this very easily, her life was given over almost entirely to pleasure. Her feet, hands and other extremities were even larger, in proportion, than the rest of her. This assisted her to dominate anybody she met. In particular she dominated the young ladies of the General Office, to which her own office was adjacent, and which consequently had a very high turnover of staff, two of whom had left after only a week in it, and complained to their doctor of deafness. He had syringed their ears, and told them to stay away from Miss Rushden.

She stood in the doorway, her thick arms folded, and her large left foot tapping. Apart from this noise, there was silence. 'Has everybody in this bloody place gone deaf?' The women who looked after the rows and rows of shelves full of stock had disappeared to the furthest corner of the room, and were hiding behind a stack of ironing boards. The young men who, as part of their training to be floor-walkers, walked no floors, but unloaded and unpacked the merchandise, were hiding in the Gents. Mr Hingley had dropped his only partially unravelled string, and was scribbling numbers on a scrap of paper, whispering them over to himself in an attempt to convince Miss Rushden that he was in the process of working out a most difficult piece of mathematics. Finally he put the back of his hand to his brow, wiped it, and, without looking up, said, 'I haven't had time to do it yet.'

'Haven't had time to *do* it?' Miss Rushden's scornful disbelief rattled the bottles in the Co-op Dairy, ten shops further down the street. 'I can hear everything that goes on in here, you know. You've been playing silly buggers with that monkey over there.' She pointed at a cowering and silent Walter.

The only way Mr Hingley could summon up the courage to match her in volume was to keep his eyes down. His face reddened, and the veins in his neck swelled, as he shouted, 'If you've got a complaint, you know where to take it.'

'Complaint my bloody armpits! You make bloody time. Most of my girls are getting sores on their bums from sitting waiting for you lot.' With that, she stamped her way back to her office, and slammed the door.

Knowing the door to be safely shut, Mr Hingley stuck out his tongue, lifted two fingers, and blew a raspberry. Then he said, 'You'll get me the bloody sack one of these days, Walter.'

The women who looked after the shelves and the young trainee floor-walkers whose training so largely consisted of unloading and un-packing merchandise had come out of hiding, and were standing about, idling the last half hour away.

'What are you doing tonight, Mr Hin-gall-ee?'

Mr Hingley made a gesture as if to strike Walter, and said, 'Get away with you, you dirty-minded hound!' Walter knew this to be a joke, though he did not know in what the joke consisted, or why it should cause the women and the trainee floor-walkers to laugh so much. But it did. It never failed, and he, Walter, had his part in it, since it was always his question which began the joke.

'Do you want this string, Mr Hin-gall-ee?'

'No, Walter, you can keep it.'

'Oh, thank you. Thank you very much, Mr Hin-gall-ee.' Walter was play-acting, pretending that the string was of tremendous importance.

'Use it to hang yourself with.'

A joke again. Walter would extend the joke. 'Strangle you, this could. Round your neck, and pull it tight.' He had placed the string round his own neck, and was making the noises of being strangled.

The young women did not laugh; the trainee floor-walkers did not laugh; Mr Hingley did not laugh at Walter's joke. They looked at him, his head lolling to one side, his tongue protruding as he made, for their approval, the horrid noises of one who is being strangled.

'You get on my tits sometimes, Walter,' said Mr Hingley.

3

Will all members of the Pygmy Pouter Club please meet in the left-hand corner of the cafeteria?

THE Harrogate Fancy Pigeon Show was held that year in the Main Betting Hall of a Greyhound Stadium not far from Preston, owing to the discovery of faults in the electrical equipment of the Exhibition Hall at Harrogate, so Walter and his father did not have the expense and inconvenience of an overnight stay, but were able to bring Amy, their Long-Faced English Tumbler, in a basket that morning in time for judging.

Eric had taken Walter to the Fancy Pigeon Show on three previous occasions. They had taken the train to Harrogate, and stayed overnight at a bed-and-breakfast lodging house.

Walter had enjoyed the Shows, but his father had found it restricting to have Walter in tow. Eric had experienced the abrupt endings to or the tailings-off of conversations, as the people to whom he had been talking had noticed Walter standing close behind him, and had realized that Walter was his son.

Usually Eric would not strike up conversations with people he had never met before. When he had been a farm labourer, he had worked for most of the time on his own, unsupervised, and on the occasions when he had worked in company, as with the haymakers or with the stockman at lambing time, he had said very little, and very little had been said to him. Even as a porter, he was not of that sociable sort which converses with the passengers. But on one day of the year, during the eleven hours between the Opening of the Show at ten a.m. and its closing at nine p.m., Eric did more talking and more listening than he did in all the rest of the year put together. For three hundred and sixty-four days of the year (three hundred and sixty-five in leap years), he found little of importance to say, and those who spoke to him soon learned that they might rarely expect a reply. But today, the day of the Show, was different. He needed his one day of conversation a year. He thought about and looked forward to little else.

In previous years, those fanciers who could afford it would stay

83

overnight at one of the big Harrogate hotels, and the others like himself, who were less well off, would drop into the Lounge Bar of one of these hotels so as to be able to talk Pigeon Talk with their richer brethren. The wives of those fanciers who stayed in the hotels would wear cocktail dresses, or even long evening dresses, which glittered, and their hair would have been permed for the occasion. Their husbands would wear suits, with collars and ties, and the less rich fanciers who had merely dropped in would wear suits also, so that it would not be easy to tell the rich and the less rich apart. The less rich fanciers would not have brought their wives. Even Eric only brought Walter.

The first time Eric took Walter to the Harrogate Show, they had followed this ritual. Walter had stood in a corner of the Lounge Bar holding a glass of Coca Cola, while Eric had circulated amongst the fanciers. But while discussing the various merits of the Gazzi Silver or Sulphur Tri-Coloured Dragoons with a fancier who specialized in them, Eric had heard three women close by begin to giggle and choke on their drinks. One of them had said, 'I wonder who he belongs to?' and when her husband asked whom they were talking about, had made the unfortunate error of pointing to Walter.

Walter's reaction had been as it always was when anyone pointed towards him. He laughed his loud pretend-laugh so loudly that all conversation in the Lounge Bar came to a halt. Then he covered his mouth with his free hand, and pointed the hand which held the glass of Coca Cola back at the woman who had laughed at him. The liquid from his glass had run down the back of a woman in a low-necked lurex dress, who screamed. Walter had said 'Sorry.' This was another automatic reaction to any action of his own which appeared to have been construed as a fault. Unfortunately he continued to say it several times, until the silence of the other guests in the Lounge Bar had become so strong as almost to be solid, and froze the word on his lips. He had looked towards Eric for support. Eric had avoided his son's eyes until conversation had resumed, and he had been able to bring his own to a natural conclusion. Then he had edged his way round the crowded room towards the door, knowing that Walter would not have let him out of sight, and when he had reached it, allowed his glance to rest for a moment on Walter before giving a tiny cock of his head to indicate that he was going.

Eric had left the hotel, and Walter had followed him, five yards behind. He knew that he had done something wrong, and that his father would be angry. In his hand, he still carried his now empty glass.

The following year, Eric had suggested to Sarah that Walter should be left at home, since his presence disturbed people. But Sarah had replied that if Eric felt too ashamed of his own son to spend one day out of a whole year in his company, doing one of the few things from which Walter got pleasure, then she would wait until he had gone, borrow the neighbour's cat for an hour, and personally place it in the Pigeon Loft.

Since then, Walter had spent the first evening in bed at the bed-and-breakfast lodging house, and stratagems had been devised to keep him standing harmlessly in one place during the Show while his father circulated. This year he was to be in charge of Amy's safety. Security at a Show of Fancy Pigeons is negligible compared to that of a Racing Pigeon Show, where the birds are worth much more since they can win, or be parents to the winners of, large sums of money. Fancy Pigeons are more beautiful, or at least more strange, but they do not win money, and so are worth less. Anyone is allowed to open a cage, and take out a bird to examine it. It would be easy for a stranger to steal Amy, if she were not watched. Even the hands of a benevolent stranger might be germ-laden. Amy herself would become irritable if mauled and pulled about by any Tom, Dick or Harry. Therefore Walter and Eric must take it in turns to stand by her cage, and make sure she was not molested. Walter first.

Walter stood by the cage, which now bore a green ticket, denoting Third in Class. There were many Classes, some having no more than five entries, but the Class for Best Long-Faced English Tumbler, Adult Hen, Self Yellow, had included seven birds (four from the same breeder, two of them entered in his wife's name), so Third in Class was an award to be proud of. Walter was proud. He stood proudly by Amy's cage, protecting her from anyone who might wish to ruffle her feathers. He had not moved for two hours. So far nobody had attempted to open the cage. His father had brought him a pork pie, and had brought Amy some maple peas. He had sent Walter off with a plastic cup to find water, and had allowed Walter to freshen the water in Amy's drinking-bowl himself.

Eric had asked if Walter wished to visit the toilet, and Walter had shaken his head. Were his legs tired? Did he wish to sit down? Again, Walter had shaken his head. So Eric had patted his son's shoulder, and said, 'Good boy!' and walked away again, leaving Amy still in Walter's charge.

Walter looked at the green card attached to Amy's cage, and called her 'Good girl!' He did this several times, and was overheard to do so by several fanciers who were passing. They must have known that he stood in close relation to an award-winning bird.

Eric wandered about, conversing with old acquaintances without the embarrassment of having to admit that the person with him was his son. It was not that people were unkind; it was simply that they didn't know what to say. They didn't know whether to ignore Walter altogether, or to talk to him as one might talk to a small child.

Today there was no such problem. Eric wandered freely, inspecting the many other varieties of pigeons to see how keen the competition was in other classes.

He sympathized with the owner of a Mealy Muffed Tumbler, whose bird had been overlooked in the giving of awards. This owner averred that the bird chosen as First in Class had a crooked beak, and Eric agreed, though secretly he knew that the bird had no such deformity, or if it had, he could not see it.

'The mother's a better bird than the one that won.' Eric could not be sure whether the disappointed fancier was referring to the mother of his own bird or the winning bird, and whether she were better or not would hardly be at issue, since she would be entered in a Class of Adult Hens, whereas the Mealy Muffed Tumbler with (or without) the crooked beak was a Young Hen, so it seems safer to nod agreement, and move on swiftly to see the Archangels, the Jacobins, the Scandaroons, the British Nuns, the Saxon Priests, the British German Shield Owls (there being no German German Shield Owls), the Stargard Shakers, the Danzig High Fliers, and at last the Oriental Frills.

These were his favourites. Some fanciers called them 'Owls with ties', others 'Gems of the Orient': under either name they were beautiful. He longed to own a pair, and in the 'Selling Off' section of the Show there was a pair to be bought for only two pounds. But he had made Sarah a promise that not even a feather, not even one egg wrapped in cotton wool would he bring back from Harrogate. So instead he spent a whole hour just watching them, and longing.

The two main categories of colour among the Oriental Frills were Satinette and Blondinette. But these were the two main categories merely; within them were Sulphurette, Brownette, Brunette and Turbiteen. Eric gazed at the colours, and the delicate lace-like markings on the wings, and fought with his conscience, and his conscience won. Discretion won. They would be difficult to breed, just like his Turbits, their beaks being so small, almost inverted. No more than the Turbits would they be able to feed their own young; foster-parents would have to be found at the right time. Two pounds would not be the end of the expense. The Loft would need another extension, so as to separate them from the four categories he was already breeding. And of course they would eat. All pigeons eat, and in quantity. Acres of corn in Kansas, of grain ripening on the flat Silesian plain, the hemp plant and the maple pea, all find their way eventually to the fanciers of the Harrogate Show.

'Feel that bird. You tell me what's wrong with that.' A man in a flat cap handed Eric a Red Ribbon-Tailed Indian Fantail. Eric took the bird into his hands, and felt it, not quite sure what he was actually feeling for. It seemed safest to nod, wisely, and to say, 'Very nice. Yes.' The man in the flat cap took the bird from him, smiling. He was pleased. Eric had pleased him. Eric sighed with relief.

'You like it?'

Eric nodded.

'It's cost me a fortune to get a good head on them.'

Eric nodded.

'How d'jou do?' The question did not mean that the man in the flat cap wanted to know how Eric was, but whether he had won anything.

Eric shuffled his feet. 'Only entered one. She came third, though, in quite a large class. I'm well satisfied.'

The man in the flat cap gave Eric a thumbs-up sign, and turned away to place his much-handled bird back in its cage. Eric went on. On his own initiative he started conversations with various breeders who stood, as Walter was standing, before the cages of their champions, and when he was asked how he had done, he would smile modestly, and give the same reply, 'I'm well satisfied.'

And he was. He was satisfied, proud and pleased. Most important of all, he was enjoying himself. This was his one day of the year.

It was not that he knew all there was to know about fancy pigeons, and wished to enlighten the world. But he had an interest; not everyone could say that. From the moment, twenty-four years ago, that Sarah had discovered that she was pregnant, when Eric ceased to be her interest, and she refused any longer to be his, he had lacked an interest until he was adopted by a racing pigeon which had lost its way. Sarah's interest had been her baby. She had undertaken it and, even though the baby, Walter, had turned out not to be a normal baby, an interest of that sort, once undertaken, cannot be renounced. Eric's interest was a comparatively inexpensive hobby, in which he could lose himself, an activity for the most part carried out alone, but an interest shared (as Sarah's was not) by others, by the fancy among whom he moved once a year at the Harrogate Show.

'Do what men do when they're on their own,' Sarah had told him on the night she knew she was pregnant. He had searched for an activity that men do on their own. He had found pigeons.

He supposed that there were couples who got married and lived happily ever after, couples who had normal healthy children, and continued to enjoy each other's bodies, but he also knew that there were others, like himself and Sarah, who grew apart, and never healed together again. Strictly speaking, Walter belonged to them both. But Eric also had his pigeons, and Sarah had nothing. Except Walter.

'Will all members of the Pygmy Pouter Club please meet in the left-hand corner of the cafeteria?' The Tannoy, which was more accustomed to greyhound racing than the placid showing of pigeons, began its announcements with a screech, and ended them with a whistle. 'The Norwich Cropper Club and the Antwerp Smerles Club –' the whistle took over, and drowned out the location of these clubs' meeting-place, but all meetings took place in the cafeteria eventually; those who fancied Antwerp Smerles and Norwich Croppers had only to hang about there, and they would meet their fellows.

Eric returned to Amy's cage, and found Walter moving from foot to foot. He hoped he had arrived in time. 'It's by the Entrance. Go on. Hurry up! I'll look after her.' Walter dashed away in the direction of the Gents.

The Tannoy screeched. 'The Bohemian Brunner Pouter Club and the Barb, Carrier and Scandaroon Club will meet at five o'clock in the cafeteria. Please be prompt.' The Tannoy whistled.

Eric had attended the Tumbler Club meeting just before lunch. (They had met in the cafeteria.) All clubs had to meet at some time during the Show to decide how many Classes each breed of pigeon should have the following year, and to elect a judge for each Class from amongst themselves – a delicate matter, since a judge was required to be a specialist breeder of that Class, and would be debarred, by virtue of his judgeship, from entering birds in it himself. Eric's name had not been put forward as a candidate, but this was not to be expected. He was comparatively new with Tumblers. He had, however, been congratulated on Amy's success, and been bought half a pint of lager. One fellow fancier had even remembered Freda, and had asked after her. It was a day of pride.

'The Birmingham Rollers Club . . .' The Tannoy screeched. 'The Bald and Beard Club . . .' The Tannoy whistled. Walter came running back to his father and to Amy.

'It's alright. No need to run. We're not in any hurry.' Eric looked around to make sure that nobody he knew was within earshot. 'Did you get there in time?' Walter nodded and smiled. 'That's a good boy.'

Walter's legs were tired from standing on the same spot for so long, and Eric's were tired from much walking about. Eric looked at Walter's expression of pleasure at being at the Show, at Amy's success and consequently his father's, and watched it change under his gaze to the expression of one who knows he is under observation, still eager to please but with anxiety creeping into the eagerness, like a dog which waits for you to throw a ball or a piece of wood, and he thought, 'You are not my fault. Even champion pigeons are capable of bearing runts. You're not my fault. Not mine. Not your own. If anyone is to be blamed, it's my father and my sister.' And even his sister had been under age, and known no better than to do what she was told. Obedience is not a fault.

It was the first time he had ever thought in these terms. He placed an arm over Walter's shoulder. Walter grinned a grin of pleasure.

Eric said, 'Let's go an' have a sit-down, shall we? Amy'll not come to any harm.' But as they started to move, the Tannoy screeched and whistled in a particularly self-important way, preparatory to making the longest announcement made so far that day.

'Ladies and Gentlemen! Fanciers, and those unlike myself, who have the good fortune to be fancied. Our Celebrity Judge is about to choose the pigeon which will be listed in our Hall of Fame.' There was no real likelihood of any list of pigeons being hung up in the Greyhound Stadium, not even in its cafeteria, but a Tannoy is to be allowed a certain licence when it takes the trouble to be comprehensible for more than ten seconds at a stretch. 'Which fortunate bird will be chosen as this year's Best Bird of the Show? Don't wait! Don't wait! Don't hesitate! It only happens once a year. Come to the right-hand corner near the Exit, where our six hopeful beauties are waiting to be scrutinized.'

Fanciers began to drift to the right-hand corner near the Exit. Eric had one last thought about the pair of Oriental Frills, and wondered if they were still for sale. But there was always next year. Better to keep something to look forward to. His arm over Walter's shoulder, he led him towards the six best birds of the Show.

The six finalists were a Blue Gazzi Modena, a Bald Long-Faced Tumbler, a Magpie, a Red Jacobin, a Pouter, and a Double-Crested Trumpeter. 'It'll be the Blue Gazzi Modena,' said the fancier standing on Walter's left foot. 'What do you bet me?' Walter turned and grinned his special grin at the man, and wondered why the man frowned, looked worried and turned away.

The Celebrity Judge took his chrome telescopic judging-stick from his pocket, extended it, poked it between the bars of the cage housing the Blue Gazzi Modena, and touched it, first just under its beak, then on the underside of its tail. The bird responded almost flirtatiously, standing even more erect than before, with its tail stuck up vertically and its head well back. It reminded Walter of a teapot. Then the Judge touched the Pouter, which inflated its crop to such an extent, and strutted so on its long thin legs, that it appeared to have entered a Mr Universe Contest, resembling something which had been squeezed upwards from the bottom to form the shape of an icecream cornet.

The Celebrity Judge took each bird out of its cage several times, and examined it closely. This was a particularly delicate operation in the case of the Double-Crested Trumpeter, which had such long feathers sticking out from the sides of its feet that it could hardly turn round in the cage. The crowd became impatient, and pressed forward against the arms of the Stewards. But the Celebrity Judge would not be rushed into a hasty decision. Judges were not rushed at Crufts or the National Cat Show; *he* would not be rushed.

Finally he took two steps backwards, and nodded to his female Assistant to indicate that he had made up his mind, and, like a surgeon at some trepanning or appendectomy, held out his hand without looking at her, so that there might be placed within it, the coveted blue rosette with gold lettering which would announce 'Best in Show'.

The crowd became silent, remaining pressed tight against the arms of the Stewards. With all attention so concentrated elsewhere it seemed to a small boy who had taken a fancy to a Black-Lace Fantail an ideal moment to open its cage, grasp the unsuspecting bird with both hands, and begin his run towards the Exit. A Steward saw the boy running, shouted, and gave chase. The blue rosette was already within the hand of the Celebrity Judge. He remained immobile. He would not make the presentation while there were distractions. The Steward chasing the thief bumped into a woman, who was holding a Chinese Owl, which was released as she fell over, and took to the air. The woman screamed. Six other Stewards unclasped the arms which had been restraining spectators, and began to push their way through the crowd to join the chase after the small boy. The Celebrity Judge saw, without being able entirely to believe what he saw, that the crowd had actually begun to turn away from the presentation, and having turned, to move.

One bird had already been stolen. People were moving. Amy would be in danger. Walter knew his duty. He began to struggle through the crowd towards Amy's cage. Eric had been pushed on to his knees twice, and his right hand had been trampled by Stewards. Raising his bruised hand and gripping the hem of some fancier's jacket to pull himself to his feet, Eric attempted to follow Walter. In pulling himself up, he pulled the fancier down, and cries pursued him in his own pursnit.

One of the Stewards had reached the small boy, and was pulling him, almost dragging him backwards by the collar of his shirt. Choking, the boy released his grip on the Black-Lace Fantail, which broke free, and flapped clumsily upwards to join the Chinese Owl, leaving the small boy with six black-lace tail-feathers still in his hand.

The crowd gasped as the tailless Black-Lace Fantail attempted to gain height. Walter dodged agitatedly in and out among the fanciers, but made little progress. Eric had decided on a more roundabout route in an attempt to cut Walter off, and had become momentarily lost, beguiled by a row of Voorburg Shield Croppers which he had not seen on his previous tour.

All eyes, except those of Eric, Walter and the Celebrity Judge, were now scanning the high rafters of the Main Betting Hall, trying to spot the exact whereabouts of the Black-Lace Fantail and the Chinese Owl.

There was a very large man blocking Walter's way. Walter looked up at the man, and said, 'Excuse me.' The man removed his gaze for a while from the rafters, and replied, 'Sorry, mate. I don't dance,' breaking thereafter into deep-throated laughter. Walter thought it polite to join in the laughter, while attempting to squeeze past the man, but the man took exception to Walter's unconvincing laugh, and gripping him by the lapels of his jacket, said, 'Here! Watch it,' and pushed him away.

Pushed by the large man, Walter fell hard against a row of cages containing Birmingham Rollers. As the cages fell, their doors opened, and twenty-six frightened Birmingham Rollers took to the air, scattering loose feathers over the crowd like confetti. Seven people in the adjoining aisle were trapped under the fallen cages and confused by the escaping birds. Others who had seen the falling cages in time to dodge them had, in dodging, bumped into still other fanciers, who in their turn knocked over the next aisle of cages, which contained Antwerp Smerles. Fourteen Antwerp Smerles followed the twenty-six Birmingham Rollers, the Chinese Owl and the tailless Black-Lace Fantail up into the rafters above the upturned faces of the astonished crowd. Feathers of various colours drifted down.

Walter lay where he had been pushed. His back hurt, and he was not sure if he could move. Moreover there were three Birmingham Rollers trapped in their cages beneath him, and if he did move, they might escape.

Eric had found Amy, and was talking to her, trying to calm her down. The freedom of the birds which had escaped seemed to have an unsettling effect on those still behind bars. The Celebrity Judge, in an access of petulance, presented the blue rosette to the Blue Gazzi Modena, with nobody watching, and went off in a huff.

Two Stewards pulled Walter slowly to his feet, while a third attempted to right the three cages beneath him. This had the effect of un-trapping the birds, but the ascent of three more Birmingham Rollers to join the throng of birds already in the roof could only be anti-climactic. Walter made first the discovery that he could stand, then that he could walk, left the Stewards, ignoring their advice to visit the First Aid Room, and joined his father at Amy's cage, where the presence of both of the humans who belonged to her had a pronounced calming effect on that prize-winning bird.

Most of the other birds who were still confined were by no means calm. Some rushed the bars of their cages, their crops inflated, their tails down and scraping the floor, making the angry sounds which mean, 'Keep off my territory' at full volume. Others ran their beaks along the bars of their cages, like jailbirds rattling their tin mugs to gain attention. The Tannoy whistled, the Tannoy squeaked, but the sound of three thousand four hundred and thirty-seven discontented pigeons quite drowned out the announcement that the Blue Gazzi Modena had become eligible to have its name inscribed in the Hall of Fame. Even its owner was looking upwards, with the rest of the fanciers at the forty-five birds which were now circling above them, wondering how they might be reunited with their cages and whether any of the Antwerp Smerles were his.

4

You fall asleep and Jesus decides if he wants you to live with him in Paradise

WALTER walked along the back alley which separated the back yards of Bancroft Street from the back yards of Crossley Street. Three small children were racing each other from one end of the alley to the other. Walter stopped as they approached him, and pressed himself against the wall, not wishing to knock any of them down, or to spoil the chance of any one runner by being in his way. The child running along the gutter in the middle of the alley had the advantage, since the cobblestones on either side were damp and slippery.

Walter was no longer allowed to enter the house by the front door on his return from Woolworth's, because, apart from the dirt he had accumulated about himself, his mother had often found sticky things on the carpet, which he had brought in on the soles of his shoes. Toffees dropped by children, paint from a can which a careless assistant had allowed to fall from the counter, jam, honey, even glue, all these had at one time or another been innocently carried home on Walter's shoes.

Sarah had thought of supplying her son with one pair of shoes to travel in and another to work in, but her knowledge of the time it took him to tie and untie his shoe-laces and that his work-shoes would get dirtier and dirtier because he would never remember to bring them home to be cleaned, made her decide against this plan. Besides, if Walter continued to get substances of various sorts stuck to the soles of his work-shoes, and these substances accumulated, he would eventually have great difficulty in walking, and would give offence to customers by standing several feet taller than they. Or the work-shoes would be lost, or even stolen, and Walter would know no better than to tread the ever-sticky floors of Woolworth's in his stockinged feet.

Walter enjoyed the walk from the bus. He would walk briskly on his toes, with his arms swinging, and his head thrown back to study the sky. He would whistle, in a tuneless, but optimistic tone. When he reached the alley, sometimes he would jump as high as he could, so as to look over into the back yard of a neighbour. He liked entering the house from the back, because it gave him a chance to say 'Hello' to his father's pigeons, peeping at them through the slats Eric had put on to the Loft for light and ventilation.

This evening his step was particularly springy, and his lips were pursed in an extra effort to make a louder and more tuneful whistle. The day had been successful. He had helped – no, he had taken a leading part – in cleaning up four jars of raspberry jam, which had fallen from the arms of a Counter Assistant who was working out her week's notice, given for persistent lateness. The jam had slipped from her grasp right outside Mr Richards' office. Mr Richards, who had given her notice in the first place, now shouted at her, and sent her up to the General Office to collect the money owing to her, with instructions to leave the building at once.

Walter had stepped in at once to start cleaning up the mess. Under the supervision of one of the floor-walkers (Mr Sykes, whose promotion was well overdue), he had cleared away the jam and broken glass, and had washed the floor in what seemed like record time. When all this was done, all that Mr Richards had to say to Mr Sykes was that the display on Haberdashery was a disgrace to his department, but he had placed an arm round Walter's shoulder, and had thanked him warmly, and told him once more what he had often told him, and always in a loud voice so that others could hear, 'I don't know what I'd do without you, Walter. The best thing I ever did was taking you on.' The girls behind the counters within earshot had looked at one another, and smiled, and they had smiled at Walter, and Walter had grinned up into the face of Mr Richards, and had said, 'Thank you, Mr Richards.'

He was still smiling at the memory when he reached the back yard of his parents' house. He remembered to close the gate behind him. Then he peered between the slats of the Loft, and said, 'Hello, pigeons.' The birds stood side by side on their perches, almost all of them in pairs. Some stood on one leg (for whatever reason Walter did not know), some used both legs to support themselves, and some crouched in a sitting-down position. One White-Lace Fantail crouched thus, quivering one of its wings and making a low throaty noise to show approval, while its partner pecked gently and lovingly round the crouching pigeon's head and neck. Eric had explained to Walter that this is how pigeons show affection for each other. The crouching bird opened and closed its eyes, enjoying the love-making. Its eyelids came up from below to cover the eye, instead of coming down like the eyelids of human beings.

Walter watched the pigeon's eyes, fascinated. The standing bird placed its beak inside that of the crouching bird, and both rocked their heads from side to side. Walter knew that this was called 'billing'. The crouching bird quivered and cooed more strongly, and the standing bird placed first one leg and then the other on its partner's back. The bird beneath lifted its tail, and, with a flap of wings to steady itself, the bird above placed its tail sideways and under the loved one's tail. No more. They had mated. It was February, almost spring. Soon there would be eggs to look for, the days before hatching to be counted, then the tiny featherless bodies and extra food to be given to all those birds whose eggs had hatched and who were feeding them a kind of cheese produced from between their feathers in their breasts, then the featherless bodies become slowly feathered, a persistent squeaking from the nest and the young squabs fed now with digested grain pumped into voracious mouths from the crops of parent birds who would need even more food while doing so. By the time the young squabs began to pick some grain for themselves the parents would already have mated again; more eggs would be expected. It never occurred to Walter that this activity of his father's pigeons had anything to do with what had happened to him in the Park.

The White-Lace Fantails who had just mated were billing again. If they had been free, not confined in a Loft, they would have taken to the sky in a flight of mutual congratulation at having successfully passed sperm from cock to hen in spite of the difficulty caused by the shape of their tails. Forgetting to remove his jam-stained shoes, Walter rushed into the house to tell his father what he had just seen.

'Dad!' There was nobody in the kitchen. Usually at this time, his mother would be there to supervise the cleaning of shoes. Walter sensed that something was wrong. Nobody had answered his call, and there was nothing being cooked on the stove.

He opened the door to the living-room. His mother was sitting at the dining table, opposite a woman who occasionally came to the house with a catalogue from which his mother would choose things to buy. The woman would leave the catalogue with Sarah for a few days, and she would use it for Walter's lessons, pointing to pictures of objects, the names of which he had then to tell her.

Today there was no catalogue on the table. Between his mother and the woman there was a teapot, milk jug, sugar bowl and two cups and saucers. He stood by the door, holding it open, and waiting for his mother to speak. She did not speak. She turned her face to the window, and lifted the handkerchief she was clasping, so that it covered her eyes. Her face was red.

Had the woman done something bad to his mother? This woman had never looked at Walter directly, on any of the occasions when she had come with the catalogue. She had never looked into his eyes. Whenever she had spoken to Walter in the past, she had looked at the ground, or to one side of him. And now, when she turned to face him, she looked at the carpet, and said, 'Hello, Walter.'

Walter nodded. She would not see him nod. She was not looking at his head.

'What are you going to tell him?' the woman said to Walter's mother. Walter's mother kept the handkerchief over her eyes, and shook her head.

Something was wrong. Perhaps his mother had an ache in her head. The woman should not pester her. Walter wished she would go away. The clock on the mantel ticked out the seconds, and Walter listened to it. He had never noticed that it had so loud a tick before.

'Do you want me to go?'

His mother nodded. The woman drank what tea was left in her cup, and stood up. 'You know where I live, if there's . . . ?' Walter's mother nodded again. She knew where the woman lived. Who did not?

The woman was going. Whatever was wrong would soon not be wrong any more. Walter's mother said, 'Thank you,' to the woman.

'Not at all. We all need help at times like this.' The woman looked at Walter for the first time in her life. 'It won't be easy,' she said. 'I'll be off, then.'

She had gone. She had moved out of the living-room and into the hall, and Walter had heard the front door close behind her. He remembered his shoes, went quickly back into the kitchen before his mother could speak, bent down, and began to untie the laces. When the shoes were off, he placed them on a page of the previous evening's paper, and placed the paper in a corner. As he turned from doing so, he saw his mother standing by the kitchen door.

'More sticky soles?' Walter nodded. Her face was red and puffed up. She had been crying, but was not now.

'Better clean them now, then. Before you forget.' Walter took the oldest knife from the cutlery drawer, and began to scrape raspberry jam from the soles of his shoes.

'What is it? Chewing-gum again?' Walter shook his head.

'What, then?'

'Jam.'

'What sort?' She leaned against the sink for support. 'Or don't you know?' If she kept talking, she might be able to prevent herself from screaming or going mad. She might just be able to hold on long enough for the rage inside her to pass. The almost overwhelming desire to let go, to break everything in sight, to scream and cry until she was exhausted, must be contained. Words would help. If she could keep him answering questions, he wouldn't catch on yet. Not yet. She wasn't ready for that. Yet. Already he was watching her, with that frightened apprehensive look.

'Did you drop it?'

He didn't understand.

'The jam. Was it you who dropped it?'

He shook his head. 'I cleaned it . . . Cleaned it for Mr Richards.'

'Good boy!' She was biting hard on her lower lip to stop it trembling. 'Will they give you more money, do you think?'

Walter shrugged his shoulders, and shook his head. He discovered that he was no longer looking forward to telling her how Mr Richards had placed an arm around his shoulder, and praised him for all to hear.

'What's that supposed to mean?' Her voice was harder now. 'Is it because you don't know, or you don't think they'll give you more money, or you don't understand the question? Shrugging your shoulders, that's no good to anybody.' Someone had to be strong with him. Someone had to try. She would sell her mother's rings and the cultured pearls. The ear-rings wouldn't be worth much.

'It was raspberry . . . I think.' He had removed the sticky jam from his shoes. The jam was grey now, made grey by the dust from the floor of the Stock Room. In amongst the grey mess, there were tiny splinters of broken glass, sparkling.

'What shall I . . . ?' He was holding out the crumpled newspaper containing jam and splinters of glass.

'What do you usually do with it?' She must hold on. She must be strong.

'Fire!' He emphasized the word, as if she were the one in doubt.

'We don't have a fire. It's nearly spring.'

'Yes . . . Fantails mated.' His face showed pleasure. Exaggerated pleasure, the pleasure of having observed something special.

He would never mate. Not her son. And she would never. Never again. 'Bully for them.' She remembered her husband's excitement when the first eggs of the season were laid. 'Bully for them.' Mother Nature was carrying on in the Pigeon Loft as if nothing had happened. But Eric was dead.

'Tell Dad.' He screwed the newspaper tighter, building up the excitement of his discovery.

'Put that in the bin.' She watched him bend down and place it in the pedal-bin.

'Where is he?' He had completed his task, and was watching her closely, looking for some clue that would explain the difference in her manner.

'Where's he gone?' They had played a game when he was small, in short cotton trousers over nappies, played it still when he was 'just a late developer', continued to play it as he grew, might even sometimes, if she were in a good mood and prepared to allow childishness in her wage-earning son, play it now. 'Where's he gone?' She would hide her thumb or even a sweetie within her fingers to make him giggle. He sang the words to her, as once she had sung to him. 'Where's he gone?'

She turned her head away to hide the trembling lips. 'Where's he gone?' He had caught her look, and moved to face her, with an anxious searching gaze which broke her heart. She had failed, was crying inaudibly, suffering pain in her throat and chest so as not to make a noise. Her whole body shook with the effort of control. Tears dripped on to the floor from her chin. She was leaning against the back door, her face pressed into the corner, shaking, taking in gulps of breath she didn't want. Why should she breathe?

He watched her, silent now and still, feeling the darkness at the base of his stomach grow. This was the feeling he recognized as fear; his vocabulary was not yet so wide as to include the word, but he knew the feeling well; it was what you felt just before a scream burst out of you. His mother was not in control, and he was frightened. The feeling was getting worse, and she wouldn't look at him, wouldn't help him, hold him, even for a moment touch him. He pressed himself against her, clutching at her blouse, his arms around her waist. She was struggling to free herself, shouting at him to let go, protecting her face from his greasy, spotty, anxious, animal's face, fighting off a son who was taller, stronger than she, whose head was a weight on her shoulder, and whose need to be cuddled made her sick.

As she pushed him away, flaying around wildly with her arms and shouting between sobs, he started his scream. It was a long continuous earsplitting scream of terror, punctuated by the stamping of his feet. As he topped up with breath so as to make the scream persist, he bit the back of his own hand. She rounded on him, first striking him across the face, then gripping the hair at the back of his neck, pulling him towards the sink, and pushing his head under the cold-water tap.

He made no resistance after her slap across his face. The fact that she had taken control relieved much of the fear he felt. The cold water struck the back of his head; he felt it slide down the sides of his face and neck, and wet the collar of his shirt. His body relaxed. He watched the water run from the end of his nose into the sink, and circle the plug-hole, and concentrated on the feel of it. Sarah was pressing his neck to keep his head down, but since he did not resist, she loosened her grip, then removed it, and reached for a drying-up cloth.

Walter remained obediently where he was, with his head under the tap, until she turned off the water, placed the drying-up cloth over his head, and guided him into the living-room.

She sat on the settee, and Walter lay on it in the foetal position, with his wet head resting in her lap. She moved the drying-up cloth slowly and gently back and forth to dry his face and hair. After a while she said, 'Your dad's gone to sleep for a very long time. We won't see him again, until we fall asleep forever. Then we'll meet him again, where and when God wants us to. It's hard for you to understand, I know. But even though we shall miss him . . .'

She could not go on. She would not miss Eric; her tears were not for that. All through her married life until now, she had still preserved some thoughts, some hope of freedom, or at least of relief. Now Eric had found that freedom; he had relief. Her tears were for herself, not her husband. She was trapped, still trapped, forever trapped with a twenty-seven-year-old-late-developer. It was comic. Here he lay on her lap, this *thing* she had made. From now on, she was totally respon-sible for Walter. The trap had tightened; the wire round her neck was pulling. She was like a rabbit which hadn't the sense to draw back while the noose was still slack. If only she had left, run away all those years ago, used her mother's jewellery to go somewhere, anywhere at all! If! The head in her lap moved, and she must speak to it.

'Even though I know you'll miss him a lot, you've got to remember that he's happy now, where he is. He has no problems, you see. You must be glad for him. We all have to fall asleep some time, but when we do, it's a sleep of peace. Jesus calls us to him, and we are glad to be called. That's the day of Reckoning. You fall asleep, and Jesus decides if He wants you to live with Him in Paradise. Only those who have been good get to live forever with Jesus. We won't see your dad any more, but Jesus will look after him.'

Gently she began to rock Walter's head, so that his whole body moved backwards and forwards. His wet hair had left a damp patch on her dress. It would dry out. If she rocked him for long enough, she might be able to convince herself as well as her son of the truth of what she had just told him. She had to. There had to be a point to it all. There must be some compensation for life; that was only fair. She began to sing.

> 'Jesus loves me. This I know,
> For the Bible tells me so . . .'

They remained in the same position for well over an hour, Sarah singing hymns, passing from one to another without pausing, and remembering all the words as if she had written them herself. Walter was reassured by the closeness of his mother. Only one thing worried him, and that was the problem of how he was going to stay awake. He did not wish to fall asleep, as it seemed his father had done, for he did not wish to be called by Jesus yet. Not yet.

> 'Shall we gather at the river,
> The beautiful, beautiful river?
> Gather with the saints at the river,
> Which flows by the hand of God?'

5

Even the girls who had left their counters to have a quiet smoke behind the stacks of detergents would remark on his silence

THE day after Walter had been told that his father was with Jesus, his mother woke him at the usual time, and he caught the bus he always caught. The conductor joked with him, as was usual, but Walter didn't respond. He was silent.

The Walter who laughed his braying pointing laugh, the Walter who giggled, the Walter who made people feel good because they were not he, the Walter who comforted the unsure by showing them that not all madness is tragic, was having a day off.

Today the tonic and comforter of the passengers on the early morning bus sat in silence, and stared into the middle distance, and when the bus reached the stop at which Walter got off, the conductor had to shake him.

'Are you alright, lad?'

Walter didn't answer.

He walked from the bus stop to the Staff Entrance of Woolworth's. He stood, as he always stood, waiting for Mr Hingley to unlock the lift gates, and press the button for the lift which would take them up to the Stock Room, but this morning, instead of giggling and pointing when Mr Hingley dangled the keys in front of his face prior to pulling them away just as Walter made a grab for them, Walter did not grab; he did not giggle. He only stared at the concrete, and at the empty crisp bags and cigarette packets and at the silver paper which blew about the yard.

Mr Hingley ruffled Walter's Brylcreemed hair, and said, 'What's up with thee?'

Walter was silent.

'You've got a face like a month of Mondays.' Still getting no reply, he followed Walter's gaze down to the ground, and said, 'Yes, I want you to clean up this yard today. I'll get one of the other lads to help you.'

'Are you sick?' They were now in the lift. Walter shook his head.

When he had changed into his overalls, he went to his press, and started to make a bale.

Jean, who looked after the shelves of soap-powders, detergents, pan-scourers and disinfectants, arrived singing. She was always good-humoured, known for it. She said nobody would apply for a job at Woolworth's without a very odd sense of humour. She was unmarried, and looked after her mother. She had steel-grey hair, cropped short, and wore wire-rimmed spectacles, and both her chin and nose were pointed. Her shelves were the closest to Walter's press.

She skipped around the Stock Room twice, taking her overcoat off as she did so in the manner of an extremely clumsy stripper, and singing, 'I've Got a Handful of Songs to Sing You'. After a while she caught the eye of Mr Hingley, who gestured at her to be quiet, and pointed at Walter's back.

Jean frowned, not understanding the meaning of the gesture. But clearly it concerned Walter, so she tiptoed over to him, shouted, 'Got you!' and engaged him in a mock fight, pulling his neck back with one arm and holding him in a half-nelson with the other.

Usually Walter enjoyed these mock wrestling matches. He liked the attention. But today, he went limp, and gave no resistance.

Jean let him go, and moved round to look into his face. His eyes refused to meet hers. Instead he took a step back away from her, and bent down to pick up the tool he used to cut the baling-wire.

'Hey, sweetheart, what's wrong? Come on, tell me. What's the matter?' She crouched down quickly before he could get up, placing an arm around his shoulder, and talking to him as if he were a baby.

Walter said, 'S'nuffing. It's alright.' Then, after he had resumed his work, he added, without directing the statement at anybody in particular, 'Jesus wanted him,' and then, after thought, 'I'll look after the pigeons.'

There had been other times when Walter had been silent, when he had sulked, but they had always occurred after he had started work, and the cause was always known. If he had been wrongly accused of falling down in his duties, and he felt the fault was not his, he would first protest loudly, shouting the name of the real culprit, spitting as he did so, and justifying his innocence with arms flying wildly about his head. If his justification were ignored, and he were told to shut up and get on with it, then he would sulk. Walter sulking became the centre of a circle of general emotional discomfort. His shoulders were always round, and appeared to become rounder. His face and jaw were always long, and appeared to become longer. And he was quiet. This was an unnatural quietness; it was the quietness of a Walter not laughing to himself or talking in the third person or playing both parts in a duologue only imperfectly remembered from a previous evening's television programme. The heavy silence, the silence of Walter, the unnatural hang-dog silence would affect everyone else who worked in the Stock Room. Even the girls who had left their counters down below, to come visiting friends and to have a quiet smoke behind the stacks of detergents, even they would remark on the silence, and would say, 'What's up with Walter, then?'

Then someone would take his side, and talk in an exaggeratedly loud voice about what a good worker he was, and how the store could not operate without him. 'Imagine,' the someone would say, 'the piles of cardboard boxes filling the spaces between the counters.' Wonder would be expressed at the inevitable consequences to Woolworth's should Walter ever slacken, of the enormous fines the Council would impose on Mr Richards, as his rubbish swelled out into the High Street, bringing traffic to a stop and immobilizing the Town Centre.

Then Mr Hingley would place an arm around Walter's shoulder, and ask him for a special favour. The favour was always the same. It was that Walter should move some stock in the Confectionery Department. And Mr Hingley would wink at Walter, and at the very same moment, Miss Evans, who was in charge of the Confectionery, would announce in her clear gentle precise voice, 'I shall be incommunicado, Mr Hingley, for the next quarter of an hour,' and off she would go to visit the Ladies.

Everyone knew that the stock Walter was sent to move did not exist, and that he would spend fifteen minutes pretending to try to find it, while stuffing his mouth with a half-pound bar of milk chocolate or a large slice of coconut slab, and that thereafter the heavy silence would be over, and Walter himself again.

But that was not to be today. Today was different. Today a Walter they had never known before had come to work, a Walter who went about his work silently and methodically, ignoring or seeming not to hear the voices of concern.

Each in turn of those who worked in the Stock Room expressed concern; each in turn tried to find out from Walter what was wrong.

Gwyneth, whose wide domain included plants, seeds, garden tools, gents' socks, shirts, ties and underwear, asked Walter in her warm Cornish accent what had happened to upset him. Walter maintained that he was alright. 'Well, you'm don't look alright, Walter; you'm don't, really.' She pulled the bright red hair-ribbon from her long dark ringlets, shook them, and retied the knot so as to secure the ringlets from the side of her face. But Walter only looked away.

Mike, the young man whom Walter had first seen stuffing liquorice all-sorts into his mouth, when Walter had come with his mother for the interview with Mr Richards, was told to take Walter and two brooms down to the back yard, and clean it. 'What's the matter, kiddo?' he said to Walter in the lift. Walter looked at the bristles on his yard-brush, and remained silent.

In the back yard they found Lynn, one of Mike's many girl-friends. Most of Lynn's time was spent in leaning against the wall of the yard, hoping that Mike would be sent down to unload a lorry. Mike was quick, funny and energetic. Very little of this energy went into the un-loading of lorries; it was divided almost equally between sex and the attempt to create a belief in all the people whom Mike ever met that he was slick, clever, ambitious and, above all, charming. To Walter he seemed just like a whirlwind of activity. Everything Mike did was done with a flourish. Mike unpacking a case – throwing, catching, slamming down – was not a young man performing a routine job, but a paradigm of manager-material pitching in.

Since much of Mike's conversation with Lynn was conducted while catching or throwing boxes from lorry to ground or from ground to lift, and since one of the regular drivers was a Jehovah's Witness, Mike and Lynn had invented a code so as not to offend the godly. In this code, Lynn's privy member was called 'Janey', Mike's 'Big John': Mike was not one to sell himself short. Mike and Lynn believed that the sentence, 'Janey thinks it's time Big John came to visit her,' would be thought by a Jehovah's Witness or any other eavesdropping third party to refer to mutual friends, and the reply, 'Big John says he's got nothing to wear, and he's broke' (meaning that Mike was unfortunately without a condom and had no money to buy any) would only support this mis-apprehension.

Walter started in the far corner of the yard, sweeping the rubbish towards the lift. Mike left his yard-brush leaning against the wall, and pressed Lynn into a corner, where no one but Walter could see that his hands were inside her clothes.

'Is Janey better?' ('Is your period over?')

'Yes, thank you. She's getting lonely.'

'Oh, yes she is, i'nt she? I can feel that. She's saying, "Come up and see me sometime." '

'What about tonight?'

'What about right now?'

'Don't be daft.'

'There's only Walter. He wouldn't even know what we were doing.'

Walter's bowed shoulders. Walter's elongated face, were still mute signs of the pain he felt at Jesus's having taken his father, and his sense of the unfairness that a body couldn't so much as go to sleep without being removed by Jesus in this way, but Lynn could not read the signs. She said, 'What's the matter with him, anyway?'

'Dunno. He's sulking. Come on, it's months since we had a stander.'

'Not here, Mike. That Jehovah's Witness might turn up with a lorryload of John Innes Compost, and want to bless us.'

'He's not due for weeks. Here, come on, let us. We've only got to take 'em down a bit.'

'No, not with him brushing away over there. Send him upstairs, then we'll see.'

'I can't do that. They'll want to know where I am. If he tells them I'm with you, they'll all be down here, wanting to watch.'

'Cheeky buggers!'

'Come on! Just let Big John walk in, and have a look round. Just a bit of stock-taking.'

'No, he's watching. Look! He keeps turning round.'

And Walter was turning round. His sense of unfairness had increased to include the fact that Mike was not doing any of the sweeping, though that would not have bothered him on an ordinary day.

'Sod that fucking Walter! Hey, Fuck-face, keep your eyes down. There are pound notes in that rubbish.'

Usually Walter would have laughed his braying laugh at that, and pointed. But not today. He looked away, his shoulders bowed, and began to sweep again.

Mike turned back to Lynn; the lower half of him had never turned away. 'Christ!' he said, 'I think I've creamed my jeans.' He moved a little away from her, held the broad leather belt he was wearing away from his twenty-eight-inch waist, and wriggled his small tight little bottom about. 'That's better,' he said.

'Tonight.'

'Big John can't screw you tonight, darling. He's got to go to sodding Evening Class.'

By now, Walter had almost finished sweeping the yard. Lynn and Mike kissed. Mike picked up his brush again, and Lynn walked off down the alley towards the High Street.

Mike stood leaning on his brush, with the lift doors open, waiting for Walter to finish. 'You're a pain in the anus, you are, Walter,' he said. 'Do you know that?'

6

You've not been yourself today, Walter.
Now, that's not like you

THE day passed, and as always at five o'clock a loud bell sounded in the store downstairs to announce the end of trading for the day. At each cash register, the Counter Assistant rang up 'No Sale', and left the cash register open so that one of the girls from the General Office could check the money, which would be transferred to leather bags. Most of the counters were then covered with dark green sheets, except for Cosmetics, Confectionery and Groceries, which were covered with white sheets.

Each counter Assistant then stood to attention at that corner of the counter which was nearest the door to the Cloak Room.

As the Counter Girls stood to attention, and the girls from the General Office checked and emptied the tills, Mr Richards, the Manager, would make his tour of inspection. He would walk the aisles between the counters, appraising each girl's appearance, and choosing at random a counter from which he would pull the green or the white sheet like a bullfighter making a pass. Then he would inspect the display. If he should spot untidiness or a price-card upside down, he would shout to the floor-walker who had sinned, and the unfortunate man would come running to correct his error and to ask forgiveness.

On hearing the bell sound from downstairs, the four young trainee floor-walkers in the Stock Room would grab brooms from the corner where they were kept, jostling and arguing in order to attain the broom with most bristles. Then they would stand in the lift, shouting and swearing at Walter to hurry. Walter always took his time, and this evening he took even longer. Usually it was part of the ritual that he would complain of being left a broom with insufficient bristles. He would keep the others waiting while he insisted that Mr Hingley should inspect his balding broom and promise to order a new one. But not this evening. This evening, although he was slower than usual, he made no complaint, no request for a new broom. His time was taken in silence.

Finishing early meant no more to Walter than a longer wait for his bus home. To the young trainee floor-walkers, it meant sex, films, alcohol, food, the television, more food and sleep. Usually as the lift descended to the shop floor, they would crowd Walter into a corner, and tickle him until, laughing hysterically, he slid to the floor, imploring them to stop, but enjoying the attention. By doing so they hoped to disrupt the solemnity and silence of Mr Richards' inspection, but Walter had always stopped laughing by the time the lift had reached the ground floor.

Today there was silence in the lift, and no tickling. Walter leaned his back against the side of the lift, and stared down at the floor. His manner did not encourage tickling. The young trainee floor-walkers looked at each other, but said nothing.

The lift reached the shop floor, and one of the boys opened the gates. Seeing that the inspection was not yet over, they waited where they were. Finally Mr Richards nodded to the Assistant Manager, and a second bell sounded. Then the Counter Girls rushed towards the Cloak Room, elbowing each other to get out, and treading on each other's feet. The moving mass of rust-brown overalls, coming from all directions and squeezing through one narrow doorway, looked like a highly organized army of worker ants, evacuating a nest infected with DDT.

The trainee floor-walkers and Walter moved to the back of the store. Each taking an aisle, they began sweeping towards the glass doors at the front of the shop. All eyes scanned the floor for treasure. Silver, copper, even pound notes had, at one time or another, been found. These, being without identification of ownership, might safely be kept. A wallet or purse would usually be handed in, depending on who found it, and whether he thought he had been seen picking it up.

Walter moved forwards slowly, disturbed at the prospect of going home to his mother. It would be different now. She would probably cry again, and that would frighten him.

Then his thoughts moved to pigeons. He visualized the Russian High-Fliers, soaring ever onwards and upwards, higher and higher. Would he ever be able to get them down? The clouds, within which they might become lost, reminded him of Paradise, where even at this very moment his father would be standing in front of Jesus. Would his father have been asked to take off his jacket and trousers in order to wear white flowing robes like those of Jesus wore? Walter found it difficult to imagine his father in flowing robes of any colour. Unlike Jesus and the disciples. Walter's father had no beard, and his hair was far from long. It had been cut regularly once a fortnight in the style he had always asked for, which was short back and sides.

'Leave that, Walter. I want to have a word with you.'

Walter hadn't noticed Mr Richards approach him, partly because of his preoccupation with the sartorial arrangements of Jesus, and partly because Mr Richards habitually crept about, and took his staff by surprise, so that his nickname among them was 'Pussyfoot'.

Now Mr Richards first placed his hand on Walter's shoulder, then walked ahead of him to the Manager's Office. Once inside, he closed the door carefully, and placed this time, not a hand, but a whole arm round Walter's shoulder.

'I'm worried about you, Walter, Mr Hingley's worried about you; he told me so, and that means I worry too. You've not been yourself today. Now, that's not like you, Walter. Mr Hingley says you won't tell anyone why. I want to help. You're a good worker. I'd hate to have to let you go.'

Walter looked up into Mr Richards' face. His hair was short, like that of Walter's father, but he did have a small neat moustache. Walter half-closed his eyes, and tried to picture Mr Richards without his dark brown pin-striped suit, but with long white robes. Just as he had tried to imagine his father's first meeting with Jesus, he now tried to imagine Jesus faced with Mr Richards. It was difficult. He strained to do it. A picture began to form, then fell to pieces again. No matter how hard he tried, he couldn't think what Mr Richards and Jesus could possibly find to say to each other.

'What are you squinting like that for?'

Walter opened his eyes fully.

'Do you hear what I'm saying?' The white robes finally fell away, like a vampire's body turning to dust, and were replaced by the brown pin-striped suit.

'Yes, sir.'

'Well, then?' Mr Richards applied more pressure to Walter's left shoulder. This was not punishment, but encouragement. The boy needed it. Mr Richards was proud of the way he had with people. They responded to him. He could not have reached his present position without the talent for provoking such a response, which was, even at first meeting, the response of follower to leader, and not just to any leader, but to a leader who knew where he was going.

'Well come on, lad. Spit it out,' Mr Richards moved to his desk, and sat at it, commandingly, yet with warmth and friendship. This was strategy – the open hand combined with the subtle reminder of who the leader is. As Mr Richards sat in the leader's chair, Walter laughed, then quickly covered his mouth with his right hand.

'What's so funny?'

Walter moved the hand from his mouth. 'You said "spit".'

Mr Richards looked at Walter with incomprehension.

Walter explained. 'People don't like it. Me. Spitting. Tell me not to.'

Mr Richards grunted, still unconvinced that what he had said had held any humour. Then he looked at his watch, and said, 'Well, I haven't much time. You'd better get back to sweeping the floor. Do try to be more of your old self tomorrow. I can't have all my staff depressed by you. Go on, then.'

Walter said, 'Yes, sir,' and began to leave the office. At the door, he turned. 'I'm sorry, Mr Richards, sir. I've not felt very well today. My dad's went to live with Jesus yesterday. He won't be coming home any more. But I'll try to be more myself tomorrow.' Then Walter closed the office door behind him, and the manager sat for a full five seconds with his mouth open.

At the end of that time, discovering his mouth to be still open, he closed it, and swallowed. He put his hand down to the side waistband of flesh that protruded from beneath the bottom of his waistcoat and the top of his trousers, and felt it. He must get more exercise. He must take up tennis again; he really must; no need to take his turn on the Public Courts; he could afford to join a Tennis Club. Before he turned the light out and left the office, he made a hurried note on his Memo Pad, *Walter's dad dead. Tell Hingley* and then beneath it as an afterthought, *Consider small increase wages. What do we pay him now?*

By now the floor had been swept and the rubbish disposed of, and the four trainee floor-walkers were back in the lift, waiting for Walter. Mike had already entered in his pocket diary the length of time it had taken them to sweep the floor. He did this every working evening. The record stood at fifteen minutes, twelve seconds. Mike's ambition was to complete the whole operation in thirteen minutes flat, and catch an earlier bus home. Tonight, owing to Walter's sloth and his subsequent absence, the time had been twenty-one minutes, five seconds.

The trainee floor-walkers tapped their feet, and sighed with frustration. When they saw Walter come out of Mr Richard's office, they shouted to him to hurry.

Walter took his time. His thoughts were elsewhere. As he drew closer, Mike and Clifford, one of the other boys, came impatiently out of the lift, grasped Walter by the lapels of his jacket, and pulled him violently into the lift. The lift gates were slammed shut, and abuse of every kind was hurled at Walter. Questions as to why he had been taken to the manager's office went unanswered. Walter looked at the floor.

Then Ernie, who was not known for bright ideas, had one. He told

Walter that, as Mr Hingley had wanted to get away early, he had en-trusted Mike with the key, and that, since Walter had kept them all waiting, they had decided to lock him in for the night. Stanley, the fourth trainee floor-walker, offered that it could all be explained away later as a mistake. They would simply say that they had been unable to find Walter, and had assumed that he had gone home.

Though Ernie's idea had been to tease Walter, the first part of the tease was true. Mike did have the keys. Walter had seen Mr Hingley give them to him. And the boys' manner, as they elaborated the tease, was serious. Walter listened as their enthusiasm built. He looked from one to another, trying desperately to catch one of them smiling, which would tell him it was a joke. But none smiled. All were serious. They were determined, they said, to teach him a lesson.

The lift reached the Stock Room, and Clifford and Mike pushed Walter out of it in front of them, and then stood, one on either side, guarding him while Ernie and Stan went to the Wash Room to wash their hands and collect their coats.

Walter stood, flanked by his two guards, still in his overalls with the balding broom still in his hand. Minutes passed. Hours. Several years passed. Mike shouted to the boys in the Wash Room to hurry, then took Walter's broom out of his hand, and placed it in the corner with the others.

With one guard away, Walter, terrified, made a bid for freedom, by dashing back into the lift, and sliding the trellis gate shut. Unfortun-ately, Mike's reactions were quicker than Walter's. Before the gate was completely closed, he had rushed to the lift, getting his foot in the way of the gate, and preventing it from closing.

Walter kicked desperately at Mike's foot, trying to dislodge it. Mike pulled at his side of the gate, and Walter pushed as hard as he could at the other. Walter was stronger than Mike, but Mike outwitted him by relaxing his pull for a moment, so that Walter relaxed his push in order to concentrate on dislodging the foot. Then Mike applied his entire strength, taking Walter by surprise, and pulling the gate open far enough to get his whole body into the lift.

Walter backed away into the far corner, and crouched low, his arms lifted to protect his face. As Mike approached, he slid down on to the floor, making himself into as near the shape of a ball as he could, hud-dling with his knees up to protect his privates, his arms covering his head to protect his face and skull. He began to moan and whine, like a small child who has just been told it is to be punished, begging not to be kicked, not to be hurt, slobbering out a flow of words, almost indis-tinguishable, running into each other. 'Please. No. Don't. Sorry.

Don't hurt me. Got to go home tonight. Please don't. No. Good boy. I'll be a good boy.'

Mike stood still. He did not wish to approach closer, for the closer he got, the more agonized and pitiful were Walter's pleas for clemency. But Mike did not feel pity; he felt sick. Ill. His stomach gurgled, and he felt a stale taste in his mouth. He was disgusted by Walter, disgusted by what he himself was doing, something which had started out as a joke, a game, and was no longer a game. The cringing heap of humanity in the corner upset him because he knew that something in him had wanted to see it, to hold this position of power, to create fear in another. Now it had turned sour, and his stomach rejected it.

He did not know that Walter's pleas for clemency were automatic, almost rehearsed, had been learned and practised in the school play-ground, and used often in circumstances similar to the one he found himself in now.

The others were standing near the lift, waiting for Mike to do something. The pause had lasted too long. It was impossible to kick the body now. All his spite, anger, and excitement had drained away. He said, 'Get up.'

Walter made a moaning noise, covered his face with his hands, and pretended to sob. The noise convinced no one, and made Mike angry again. The others waited.

Mike tried to decide what to do. He had been forced by the lump in the corner into the role of bully. The fake sobbing continued, and Mike moved forward, lifted Walter to his feet, and brought him out of the lift and over to the bench used for unpacking.

'Don't be bloody stupid, Walter. Nobody's going to hurt you.'

Walter kept his face covered, and continued his moaning. He leaned his elbows on the bench, and Mike tried to prise Walter's hands away from his face, to see whether any real tears accompanied the disturbing noise.

By now the other boys were losing interest. Clifford and Ernie moved to the lift, and stood in it, waiting. Walter continued to moan and to resist Mike's efforts to uncover his face. Stanley tapped Mike on the shoulder, and performed an elaborate mime, indicating that the four of them should go for a drink, leaving Walter behind to cool off.

Mike got the message, and backed away from Walter to the lift. The last few feet were a scramble, and, as the lift gate was slammed and the Down button pressed, Walter took his hands from his face, and listened to the jollity from the four trainee floor-walkers as they descended to ground level, from which they would proceed to Yates' Wine Lodge.

Walter rushed to the lift, and shouted after them, pleading to be let out. There was no reply. He listened. The outer gate of the lift below was being locked. He heard a voice shout, 'Goodnight, Walter. Sweet dreams.' It was Mike's voice.

Walter shouted, 'I'll tell me dad.' No reply. He pressed his right ear against the lift gate, and listened. No sound. He turned, and looked round the empty Stock Room, which was getting darker. The long aisles, shelved at either side, ran away from him through gloom into pitch blackness. He remembered that he no longer had a dad to tell. He was alone.

He gripped the gate of the lift with both hands, and listened. He could hear scratching. It came out of the darkness from the end of the aisle he was facing. Something was scratching in the blackness, a quiet scratching; there was someone there, where no one should be. He gripped the lift tighter. The scratching noise persisted, and then a shadow moved across the floor of the Stock Room. Walter inhaled, and kept the breath inside his chest for as long as he could. Someone was in the Stock Room with him. He was not alone. But why didn't this someone wish to be seen? The scratching drew closer. He was trapped with – he did not know what with. He began to whimper. He knew that the noise would attract attention, but could not help himself. He dared not move. His coat was in the Wash Room, and he badly wanted to use the lavatory, but he dared not move. He waited.

Another shadow moved slowly over what was left of the light on the Stock Room floor. Somewhere inside Walter's head, a fact isolated itself from the frightened fishes. Shadows were made by things. They were made by people and by things. Since he could see shadows, there must be things to make them. He kept his head still, and peered into the darkness. He did not wish to see whatever was in the Stock Room with him, but to close his eyes would be even more frightening. His eye-movements took in the skylight. As he looked at it, it grew darker, then light again. The first fact was joined by another fact, and already the fishes swam less madly, as fear receded. For Walter had seen something like this before, in summer, when the Stock Room would sometimes be flooded with sunlight, then grow darker, then sunny again. Clouds were not things, but they made shadows by passing in front of the sun.

The shadows were made by clouds. It was nothing to be afraid of.

They had pretended; they had teased him; they had not locked the gate; they would not. Walter had become brave. He moved slowly, sideways, towards the Wash Room, reached it without incident, used the lavatory, collected his coat. He would press the button, and bring the lift up to the Stock Room. He would travel in it to the ground level, and find that the outer door was unlocked. They had teased him; that was all. They would be waiting to laugh at him. They would laugh, and he too, Walter, would laugh. They would never lock Walter in the store, for Mr Richards would hear of it, and he would give them all the sack.

He opened the door of the Wash Room with caution. It was darker now, and the small unexpected noise of a creaking floorboard as he crossed the Stock Room brought back his fear. The distance from the Wash Room to the lift was further than he had remembered it.

As he lifted his hand to press the lift button, the scratching began again, this time even louder and closer. *Clouds did not cause scratching.* His hand froze on the button. There was a squeal. Walter turned his head quickly. Two bright eyes were staring back at him. There was nothing else to see, just blackness, and the eyes on a level with his own. Walter lifted the hand he would have used to press the button towards his mouth instead. The eyes moved. They moved towards him. Walter bit hard at his fingers. The squealing noise began again, louder. The eyes were getting closer. Walter's mouth opened. The squealing came from just below the staring eyes. Walter squealed.

The Stock Room cat jumped from the line of shelves it had been patrolling on to the bench which was used for unpacking. It had its own unpacking to do, but not yet, not for a while. First it must tease and frighten the mouse it carried in its mouth.

Walter was shaking, and very close to tears. He watched the cat release the mouse from its mouth, and stalk it. He watched its limping run, backwards and forwards across the bench, each time easily outwitted by the cat, which cuffed it into changing direction and trying to move faster. Walter drew in breath with each blow the mouse received.

The game went on, and Walter watched, until the cat cuffed the mouse so hard that it slid across the bench, and fell off the other side on to the floor. Alive, but injured, it began to limp towards the safety of the shelves, but the cat was there first, jumping from the bench to cut off its escape, and start the game all over again. Walter turned his attention back to the lift button. After all, the cat was only doing what it was supposed to do.

The lift arrived. Walter entered it. It descended. He slid the inner gate open, and tried the outer gate. It was locked.

He was unable to believe it. They couldn't have. He listened. Perhaps they were on the other side of the gate, waiting for him. There was no sound beyond what came from the High Street at the end of the alley. He tried again to pull the outer gate open, banging at it, shouting, kicking at the gate with his foot. Someone must hear him.

He waited, knowing that no one would hear. They had gone; they had left him on his own. He would be late home.

He pressed the button that would take the lift to the level of the shop floor. Perhaps there he could attract somebody's attention.

In the store, he closed the gates of the lift behind him. It was a habit he had been made to acquire, since, if the gates were left open, the lift would go neither up nor down.

The back of the store was in darkness, but at the front there was light from the streetlamps outside. He gazed round the covered counters, and saw the head and shoulders of a woman. He moved quickly towards her. 'Please! I can't get out. They've locked me in.' The woman was made out of plaster. She was a plaster head and shoulders, wearing jewellery and a headscarf.

There was light at the front of the store light beyond the thick glass windows. He would go towards it. There would be people in the street, and they would help him.

He pressed his face against the plate glass, making signs to the passers by. Most did not notice him. Of those who did, some smiled, or waved back. They could not hear his shouts for help or understand what the the wild waving of his arms was intended to signify.

'I'll be late home.' As he shouted, his voice echoed in the empty store. 'I'll be late home.' A young man in a duffel coat stopped, and came closer to the glass. 'They've locked me in. I've got to feed the pigeons.' The young man could not make out what Walter was saying, and, having raised Walter's hopes of rescue, made a dismissive gesture, and walked on.

The heating system of the store had switched itself off and, even with his overcoat on, Walter was still cold. Spring, but still cold. Fewer of the pigeon's eggs would hatch because of it. It would be warmer away from the glass door, but back there, at the back of the shop, it was dark. He held on to the counters, feeling his way. Sweets and Cosmetics were nearest the front, then Soaps, Shampoos, Combs, Hairslides. Right at the back there would be Household Wares, and among them, some cheap rugs. He would lie down, and cover himself. His mother would come looking for him, or she would phone the police. He only need wait.

There was nothing he could do. He passed Men's Socks, Braces and Ties. There was nothing there to warm him. He could not remember what was on the next counter, nor could he see. He lifted the sheet which covered it, and felt. Lampshades. He couldn't be far from Rugs now.

From the next counter came the ticking of at least fifty alarm clocks, each with a different tick, and each (he knew, having seen them by day-light) telling a different time. Whichever was right, he should be home by now, and his mother would be worried.

He reached Household Wares, and located the rugs by feeling for them. They were stacked against the back wall of the store. He would be warmer if he sheltered behind a counter. He dragged a bundle of rugs behind the nearest counter, and lay [down on it, reserving one rug to place over himself.

He lay and listened. He could hear the ticking of the different clocks, but as if in the distance now. There were other odd noises for which he could find no reason. He had expected it to be silent here, apart from the clocks, but the small creaks and taps and scraping sounds, some at regular intervals and some sudden, worried and frightened him. Most of these noises were, in fact, due to the contraction of metal pipes and of wood as the temperature fell, but Walter could not know that. To him they were people, moving about the store. Once, he had been told, one of the women who arrived early to mop the floor had discovered an old tramp behind some cardboard boxes, where he had hidden himself the night before. He had remained in the store all night for warmth and chocolate. He must have sampled every kind of biscuit there was on sale, for all the tins were without lids.

The old tramp entered Walter's mind, and remained there. With every new sound, Walter imagined the old man's face leaning over his, and the shower of biscuit crumbs that would fall from his mouth into Walter's staring eyes.

At four minutes to eleven, Mike and the other trainee floor-walkers were urinating against the outer door of the stock-lift. They urinated with cheerful abandon, enjoying the release of pressure from bladders which had been filled in the warmth of Yates' Wine Lodge.

Clifford had announced that he was about to hand in his notice, and train to be accepted by the Meteorological Office. This announcement had reminded the other three how dissatisfied they were with the progress of their careers. It was not that, like Clifford, they wished to study the mysteries of cumulus and cirrus, but unloading lorries, unpacking, checking, sweeping out the store was not the kind of life they had dreamed of. Mike had lost four girlfriends, each of whom at different times had looked through the glass of the shop doors, and seen him sweeping the floor with Walter. 'Thought you told me you were a manager,' they had each said. Mike had explained that in order to become a manager, one had first to be a floor-walker, in order to be a floor-walker, first a trainee floor-walker, and that in Woolworth's, trainee floor-walkers swept the floor as an important part of their training. Even Mike had been unable to make this statement carry enough plausibility to convince the girls.

'Where's that bloody key? Hey! come on! The poor bugger must have shit himself by now.' Mike found the key, and, after several attempts, inserted it into the lock.

'There we are! Never been known to miss a hole.' They giggled, and held each other up. The outer gate was slid back, the button pressed, and the lift arrived. They began to argue over which of them was to go in, one or all. Since they all wanted to see Walter's face, they would all go.

The lift rose to the Stock Room, and they staggered out, looking for Walter. They called his name, but there was no answer. The cat hissed at Stanley, resenting this interruption to its work.

'Bloody spooky in here! He's probably down in the shop, stuffing himself with chocolate.' Back into the lift they all went, and the lift descended to the shop floor.

When the lift stopped, Clifford drew the gate back as quietly as he could. The other three put their index fingers vertically against their mouths, and tried not to giggle.

Clifford took a sheet from one of the counters, and draped it over his head, pretending to be a ghost. The others tiptoed out of the lift, and did the same. Their impersonation was made a little less effective by the necessity of lifting the sheets up at the front so as to be able to see where they were going, but they made a virtue of this necessity by flapping the sheet fronts about in what they reckoned to be a ghostly manner. So they began their search.

They found Walter easily. Like the old tramp, he snored. Standing over him, they began to make howling noises, as a dog is said to do when someone has died. Mike began this sound, and the others took it up, building it, harmonizing, flapping their sheets over Walter's face.

He woke to this. He screamed. Here were things, a howling noise, movement. The impersonation of ghosts was wasted on him, for he could see nothing clearly, but whatever was there was enough to inspire terror. He scrambled to this feet, tripped on the rug, fell and rose again. Wherever he turned, some *thing* was in his way. He fought with one, wrestling with it, knocking it down, and heard the sound of bone crack hard against the corner of a counter. The thing he had been fighting lay there, and didn't get up. The howling stopped. He could hear the sound of his own frightened breathing.

What had hit the corner of the counter had been Stanley's head. It was unheard of that Walter should fight anyone, inconceivable that he could win. Hampered as they were by sheets, Mike, Ernie and Clifford came at Walter, angry now, determined to punish him.

Screaming and howling the three shapes moved against Walter, who screamed also, not in anger, but in fear. One of them caught him by the belt of his overcoat, and swung him round. Another struck him across the face. Walter's nose bled copiously. Then he was on the floor, slipping in his own blood, and the things were on top of him. He struggled, bit, and kicked. He scrambled to his feet, and reached out for some support. The things tried to drag him back down.

Walter's hands gripped something on the counter, something heavy; he had found the weighing-scales on Confectionery. He gripped the scales firmly, but as he felt his feet slipping again, and the force of the *things* pulling him down, he flung them with as much strength as he had left towards the glass doors. They crashed through one of the doors. Walter let out a kick at the things which were pulling him, struggled free, and escaped through the hole and the splintered glass, falling into the arms of a policeman.

'What do you think *you're* doing?' the policeman said. Walter's nose was spurting blood and he had a long deep cut in his hand and wrist from the splintered glass of the door. He pointed back into the interior of the shop, and the blood from his wound dripped, black in the sodium lighting of the street, on to the pavement.

Walter was taken home in a police car, having had his hand and nose treated at the hospital. Stanley, who had concussion, was kept in overnight for observation. Mike and Ernie were allowed to go home after having made a statement to the police.

On seeing the glass break, Clifford had rushed to the back of the shop, and hidden behind some cardboard boxes. By the time the cleaners arrived, he had hidden himself in the Stock Room, and by the time the Stock Room staff had arrived, he had used the lift to make his escape. His resignation was sent by post. He wrote that he would rather forfeit his holiday pay than work out his two weeks' notice.

Mike and Ernie stuck to the story they had told the police. It was Mike's story, and Ernie had simply nodded, and signed a joint statement. They claimed that both of them had been trying to protect Walter against Stanley and Clifford, who had a grudge against Walter, and intended to get their own back by frightening him.

Walter was not required either to confirm or to deny this story, either by the police or Mr Richards. Stanley was instructed not to return to work, and his cards were sent to him, without the enclosure of a reference which would have helped him to get another job. Stanley at first felt some slight bitterness at the unfairness of this treatment, but being, as Mike well knew, of an equable temperament decided that, since the story was partly true (for he, as much as the others, *had* intended to frighten Walter), and since references were only of use in the getting of posh jobs, he did not greatly mind. Instead he applied for, and got, a job as a builder's labourer, removing fireplaces from posh houses, and was paid twice as much as he had been receiving as a trainee floor-walker.

Mr Richards told Mike and Ernie that he did not entirely believe their story, and stopped two pounds a week from their wages until the replacement glass for the doors had been paid for. Indeed, nobody in the Stock Room believed the account Mike had given of the affair, and all knew that the only reason Mr Richards had accepted it was because Mike was the most likely trainee floor-walker to succeed. Consequently the atmosphere in the Stock Room for the following fortnight was of cool politeness. After that, memories became blurred, and three months later Mike was told to come to work in a smart suit with a collar and tie. No longer a trainee, he was a fully fledged floor-walker.

Part Four

His mother is taken by Jesus

She had never asked him before what he was thinking

SLEEPING. He always slept well. She stood, watching him sleep, had risen earlier from her own bed than was necessary, in order to stand over him while he slept. Sleeping, she could bear him. If he slept for ever, she would be content.

Yet the face on the pillow never ceased to make her angry. She herself had been pretty, and had been told so, more than once. His father had looked – not handsome, not even passably good-looking, since his neck had been long and thin like a bird's neck, but at least *alright*: Eric had looked alright. But Walter, sleeping, Witless Walter, was a mistake made by nature, and God had chosen not to correct it. The heavy hooded eyelids, closed now over bulging eyes. The hooked nose, which resembled a joke nose one might buy at the seaside, with an elastic band to hold it over one's real nose. The large pointed jaw, and protruding teeth, yellow and green where they stuck out sharply from the gums. The oily sallow skin and tiny white-headed pimples.

Leaning over him, close to his sleeping face, she whispered, 'You must be the ugliest person in this town, and you spent nine months inside me.' His breath was foul. 'Constipated. Must be. Never thinks to tell me these things.'

She moved away, and sat against the wall on a straight-backed chair to watch him. There was plenty of time. She spoke to God, as she had spoken many times before. 'Why has my life been so ill arranged, Lord? Why allow me only one child, and that an ill-put-together, foul-smelling, dribbling lump of ugliness?' God might have replied that she had never tried to make another, that although matrimony was a holy state and sanctified for the procreation of children, she had denied her husband access to her womb after it had once been filled, so that He, God, could hardly be held responsible for any subsequent barren-ness. But God was old and wise and knew well the futility of argument with a complaining woman. He permitted her to continue.

'I won't mince words with you, Lord. Not now; I'm too old.' She never had minced words. God sighed, and wondered whether a sparrow somewhere might be falling, to distract His attention. 'I've visited Your chapel twice every Sunday, since I was taken there, at five years old, to Sunday School. Almost sixty years, multiplied by fifty-two, then doubled. I can't begin to count the hours I've sat on hard benches or knelt on a prayer-stool to Your greater glory, and tried to cast everything from my mind but Your face.' It would be the face of Christ she meant; the other two persons of the Trinity didn't have a face. The Face composed itself in patience, and continued to listen. 'I never believed those pictures with the halo. Not like that. Not You. You had to be more beautiful in my mind, more masculine than any of those. Man was made in Your likeness.' She looked across at the sleeping figure. 'Is this what You look like? Is Walter made in Your likeness? Is that Your likeness, a physically grotesque man of twenty-seven, with the brain of an infant? Why?'

Why the years of soiled blankets and sheets, the crying, shouting, screaming? Why the hope that he would improve, would learn, that with age he would change, would become at least less of an embarrassment? God had made that hope, had allowed it to persist, kept Sarah at it. Had His intention been to punish? If so, for what? 'Everybody has thoughts. Thoughts they shouldn't have. Unnatural.' Everybody must have those thoughts sometimes, the shameful, unnatural thoughts, which slipped into her mind and clung, like spiders clinging to the side of the bath. You might wish to wash them away down the dark plug-hole, and clean yourself, but there would be no hole in your mind down which to wash them, so they would persist.

But everyone would have such thoughts: it was unfair to punish her. God was unfair and heartless. She had complained to Him so often, and He never took any notice. Walter's mother wiped the tears from her face with a small lace handkerchief which smelt of lavender. She returned the handkerchief to the pocket of her apron, and went over to the bed. It was time to wake her son.

The first thing he saw every morning was her face.

Sleeping was like being dead. She would shake him out of sleep at half past seven every morning. He didn't like it. He was drowned, and she would pull him to the surface with a long rope. He would struggle, but the rope would only become tighter. The water round him would bubble, pulling him down, water up his nostrils and inside his head, hair flattened over his eyes.

He would come up slowly, gulping at the air when he reached the top. 'Come on, Walter. You can't lie there forever.'

That's what she always said, every morning. The water was warm. He liked it above his head. Not having to think. You can't ever go backwards. Even when you remember last week, you can't go there. The clock keeps ticking, moving you on. When you're in a pleasant bit of time, why can't you just stop there?'

She shook him. He nodded. Alive, there was time to pass, things to remember, other people asking questions. Rules.

She watched him all the time. All the time, his mother watching. She said they were tied together by a rope he couldn't see. He always did as he was told now, yet she got no pleasure, not even when he was good. She used to like him to remember things. Now she liked nothing. Smile, he had seen her smile. But he could no longer remember her smile.

The first thing he saw every morning was her face. It was not like his own. Her face was small, round and shiny. She did not wear make-up like the Counter Girls. It was dirty stuff; she did not hold with it. 'Come on! Out you get!' He closed his eyes, remembering the warmth of the water, and she shook him.

Her eyes were not hooded like his. 'Move, will you?' He sat up, blinking. His mother's eyes did not stick out, but fitted with the rest of her face. They were red this morning, because she cried for him.

She took his ankles, and swung them round so that his feet were off the bed and touching the cold linoleum.

Her nose was not like the top half of a parrot's beak. He did not go to school any more; he was too old now to go to school. They had called him names, 'Parrot Face' and 'Witless Walter'.

Her teeth did not stick out. They were false now, because she was old; he had seen them out of her mouth.

She stood back from the bed, and watched him. She would remain to make sure that he stood up, his body entirely leaving the bed. She would not leave the room until he had taken his pyjamas off. He could tell her he was alright now, but she would stand there; she would not go. He would whine, but she would wait.

He took of his pyjama jacket. She should know now that he had grown out of messing himself, it was a subject no longer mentioned. He dropped his pyjama trousers to the floor, and turned round on the spot. No need for words now. Looks were enough.

She left him, and went into the bathroom. He heard the sound of water running, wrapped a towel around his waist, and sat on the bed until she called for him.

He sat on the toilet, while she waited outside the door, listening. He made water, but nothing else.

'I'll give you something this morning to make your bowels move. And if you have to go while you're at work, remember to clean yourself properly. And wash your hands.'

The sound of the toilet being flushed brought her into the bathroom. He sat in the lukewarm water, while she slid the lavender-scented soap all over his body. He didn't shout now, or scream, or make any noises to stop her. He didn't struggle. He just sat there.

She slid her soapy hands all over his chest, back and legs. She never touched his willy. She would point to that, and give him the soap. 'Do it some more. Come on. More soap. Between your legs.'

She was standing now, and she had the towel ready. As he stepped, out of the bath, she turned her head away. 'You must be rotten inside, the way your breath smells.'

He stood there while she dried his back, legs and buttocks, rubbing them hard. 'If you can't do Number Twos in the morning, you must tell me. Alright?' He nodded. 'No sense in leaving it until you've got to smelling like a parrot's cage. What will they think at work?'

He didn't know what they would think.

'Don't know was made to know. If people complain about you, you'll be out of a job. Woolworth's customers don't want you breathing down their necks, not with that breath.'

She finished drying his face, neck, ears and feet. He did the rest. He had clean underwear every other day. She would watch to make sure he wore it.

As I get into my clothes, I tell myself aloud what I have to remember. 'Don't dawdle!' 'You're slouching, Walter. Stand up straight.' 'Pay attention.' 'You are a cross for my back, Walter, you really are.' All my socks are darned. She does them well. I won't wear nylon socks. I'd rather break things up than wear socks that squeak and crackle. She knows now not to buy them. I taught her. 'It's not worth the screaming fits, even though wool is more expensive.' I wear a navy-blue suit to go to work in. At work I wear an overall. Seventy-four bus, that's what I get. 'Not the Forty-seven, Walter. Silly blockhead! Seventy-four, not Forty-seven. Mill Hill, Chorlton, Flixstead. The number Six goes to Flixstead too. You don't want that.' I sit on my bed, rocking, taking time to dress. She watches. 'Number Two is a Special. Only bring it out at holiday times. Always clean, Number Two.' I laugh because she has to wait for me. No, Forty-seven's not my bus, not for going home on. Seventy-four. 'There you are, you see. You're alright, Walter. Walter's alright. Only eleven pence to the shilling, but he knows what it's about.'

'Are you ready?'

I look at her and laugh, rocking backwards and forwards as I sit on the bed. She shakes her head, and looks at the linoleum on my bedroom floor. I stop laughing, and try to see what she is looking at. But there's nothing there, only the pattern.

'Li No Lee Um. Not lino, Walter. Linoleum.'

Breakfast was on the table. She would lay it out the night before, and come down before she woke him, to cook the rest. She couldn't sleep.

She sat beside him, not facing him. She had the view out of the window to look at, and did not have to look at him. He swung his legs backwards and forwards as he ate. Whenever she heard them bang against the chair, she shouted at him to stop.

She wouldn't eat until after he had left the house.

She stared out of the window. She only looked at him to see whether he had finished.

She could feel him looking at her with those bulging eyes. The hooded lids blinked as he grinned and chortled to himself. How could she know what he was thinking?

If anyone looks at me, I point my finger at them, and start to laugh. I throw my head back, and laugh until they turn away. She taught me. At school. they would do that to me, and when I told her she said, ' Do it to them back, then,' but if I waited for them to do it first, I felt sad inside, and couldn't laugh. So I started to laugh at them before they had time to laugh at me. I put my hand over my mouth, and pointed, and laughed. It made them angry, and they called me names. Then they stopped laughing at me. They would pretend I was not there. Then I would laugh to myself. I started laughing a lot then. I keep myself ready incase somebody who doesn't know me should point at me and laugh. I'm laughing to myself now. It annoys her.

She woke me up.

Scooping food into his mouth like an animal! Dribbling as he giggled insanely, and let the cornflakes drop from his mouth back into the bowl! The noise he made! She felt like sitting at table with cotton wool stuffed in her ears.

What did he think of her? There had to be something going on inside that head. What was he thinking about that he found so funny?

'What are you thinking about, Walter?'

Walter stopped shovelling cornflakes into his mouth, and looked at her. She had never asked him such a question before. He stared at her for some time, then laughed again half-heartedly, and lowered his head to continue eating. She leaned forward, and grabbed hold of the hand which held the spoon.

'I want an answer.'

Again he looked at her, and tried to smile. Her expression told him that she was in earnest. He would have to speak.

'Thinking, Walter. I want to know what you're thinking about.' Though she said it with force, she knew the danger. He was stronger than she. Frightened, he might up-end the table.

'Thinking?' He was laughing again. It was clear that she was angry. Perhaps she thought he had been thinking of dirty things. She had warned him of what God might do if he were to allow himself to think in a dirty way. One of the boys in the Stock Room had shown him a magazine, and forced him to look at it when he would have turned his head away. Did she know? Did she think he was thinking about that? He did not know what he had been thinking about.

She used her other hand to remove the spoon from him. 'Answer me, will you? What were you thinking about?'

'No. Not them.'

'Them what?'

'I don't like mucky books. ''Look at those, Walter. What a pair of knockers, eh? Cor! You could suffocate between those, eh''?'

'What are you talking about?'

'I didn't look. Honest. Cross my heart, and hope to die.' He made the sign of the cross, somewhere in the region where he thought his heart might be. 'Mucky ladies in mucky books.'

She turned away from him, and looked again at the view outside the window. He saw that she was biting her lower lip. Her false teeth were worn down more at one side of her mouth than the other. That was the side she chewed.

'Got your bus fare?' He nodded. 'What's your kerb drill?' He told her, singing it like a television commercial.

She walked with him down the path to the gate. He preferred her not to, but she always did, unless there was snow, or it was raining hard. She stood on tiptoe to kiss him on the side of his cheek. He hated her doing this. He knew the neighbours watched. It was better when she kissed him in the hall, where nobody could see.

'Don't come out with me.'

'Why not? I want to. It's not raining.'

The neighbours felt sorry for her. He had heard them say so.

'*You're a martyr to put up with it.*'
'Nonsense. He's no trouble really.'

'*But you take such care.*'

'I have to. He is mine. Only God knows why, and He's not saying.'

'*Thank Goodness he's got a job.*'

'Yes, that's a blessing. I kiss him every morning you know.'

'*Yes, we've seen you.*'

'I think to myself, ''Would I really be sorry if God took him?'' '

'*You'd miss him, surely?*'

'God made him, so He should have to clean up, after he's messed himself all over the house.'

'*He doesn't still do that, does he?*'

'No. Not any more.'

'*What will he do when you're gone?*'

All the conductors on the Seventy-Four knew him. They knew where he'd want to get off. They knew his name; they'd say, 'Good Morning, Walter.' He would point and laugh at them. They liked him doing that. One of them would tease him about girlfriends, just like Mr Hin-gall-ee did at work. 'What were you up to last night, eh? How far did she let you go?'

I laugh. He laughs. They laugh. 'Did you get your oats, then?' They laugh. He laughs. So I laugh.

He didn't understand the question, but the passengers laughed, and seemed to like him. Sometimes the conductor (whichever it was) would pull his cap down over his eyes. His large nose would stop it going further. 'Here's our Casanova here! Here's sexy Walter!'

He would get off at Yates' Wine Lodge, and walk past Boots', Ravel's and Owen Owen's. There was an alley by the side of Woolworth's where he worked. The lorries had to back up that alley in order to deliver goods. He would walk up it, and into the back yard, and then he would wait outside the doors of the lift which would take him up to the Stock Room. Every morning, he would be early, and he would stand and wait for Mr Hin-gall-ee to unlock the gates of the lift, before he could get in it.

'Morning, Walter. Eager to get at it?' That's what he always said. And Walter would say, 'Yes, Mr Hin-gall-ee,' and rub his hands together.

He would take his jacket off, and hang it in the Gents' Wash Room. He had to wear a brown overall, so that the customers would know he worked for Woolworth's when he asked them to let him pass with the rubbish. But before he saw any customers, he had first to clear the Stock Room floor of any cardboard or waste paper. And he would put this into his press to make bales. His press was Electric; electricity made it work; he must never put his hand inside, even if it jammed. Instead he had to fetch Mr Hin-gall-ee.

'*Don't put your hands inside, Walter.*'

'*No, Mr Hin-gall-ee.*'

When the Stock Room was clean, he would push a large basket into the lift, and take it to the shop floor to collect all the rubbish from behind the counters. If the shop was full, he would have to keep shouting, 'Excuse me. Excuse me, please.' He must shout politely, not loudly. Once Mr Richards, the Manager, had told him not to shout so loudly. 'Shout quietly, Walter,' he said. Then he laughed.

'*It's a joke Walter.*'

So then I laughed. Mr Richards laughed, and then I laughed. You have to laugh at jokes, don't you?

2

If he didn't mend his ways
she would go a long way away
where he would never find her

WALTER opened his eyes slowly, and tried to focus them on the chair beside the chest-of-drawers in which his mother always sat, waiting to shake him until he woke. It took some time for him to realize that the chair was empty. Slowly he lifted his head from the pillow, and supported himself on one elbow. He looked round the room, and not finding her, closed his eyes again. It was too soon. He had woken too early.

But the amount of light coming through the summer curtains told him that it was not early. The sound of traffic from outside told him that it was not too early.

The silence inside the room worried him. There were no sounds coming from downstairs. Where was she?

Walter pushed the bedclothes back slowly. If he were to get out of bed before it was time to do so, she would be angry. He would be under her feet. He listened again for any sound which would tell him what was happening. Nothing. He swung his own feet to the floor. Usually his mother would do that. He was performing actions which were hers; that was dangerous. The lino was cold, and so was the room. It was summer, but the sun had not been strong enough this year to warm the people, some of whom still had fires. He moved to the door, listened, then went out on to the landing. He was creeping like a burglar, half-expecting his mother to jump out at him, and shout. He moved slowly to the door of his mother's bedroom, and listened. He had never been in there, at least not that he could remember.

He knocked on the door, and waited, expecting to hear her shout at him. No shout came. He waited, and knocked a little louder. No answer.

'Mother?' His voice was shaky. Something was wrong. If she had been up, she would have heard him by now, even though he had walked on his toes; she knew every creak and knock the house made. He remembered times she had looked up from the evening paper, and said, 'Subsidence!' and when he had asked what that was, she had replied, still reading the paper, 'That noise. It means the house is sinking.'

Walter trod on each of the sixteen stairs down to the hall, and studied the pattern of the carpet on each as he descended. The carpet in the hall was red, without a pattern. On the rug by the front door lay a brown envelope. Walter bent to look at the name on it, 'Mrs Sarah Williams, 23 Bancroft St, Bamber Bridge, near Preston, Lancs.' It was an address he knew well, having been made to memorize it, in case he should ever get lost.

There was nobody in the living-room, parlour or kitchen. Out in the yard, his pigeons were making their 'Why haven't we been fed?' noise. It was late, then; they never called to him like that until he had had his own breakfast. The table in the living-room had been laid ready; she always did that the night before, to save time. Once she had said, 'I don't know why I do such things to save time. I have too much of it as it is.'

Walter went back into the hall, and put on his macintosh over his pyjamas. He returned to the kitchen, and placed wellingtons on his bare feet. Then he unlocked the backdoor, and went into the yard to the Pigeon Loft.

'It's alright. You haven't been forgotten.' In the shed beside the loft, Walter used the old pair of grocery scales to weigh out the right quantities of rape, niger, linseed, hemp, millet, groats, maple peas and tares. His father had taught him to recognize the different seeds and grain, and which iron weights he should put on the scales for what. But since hemp was what they seemed to like best, picking out the small grey pellets so quickly that they seemed to be appearing in a speeded-up film, Walter cheated and gave them more than the ration, using the four-ounce weight instead of the two-ounce. As he mixed the ingredients, he talked to the birds continually as his father had done, 'Who's a pretty bird, then? Who's going to have a nice breakfast? Yes, then. There you are,' opening the door of the Loft carefully so that no bird flew out, and bending low while the tumblers and tipplers flew about his head, wing-flapping each other to get at the food. Sometimes birds landed on Walter's head, arms, and shoulders. Since in the past this had led to Walter's having to wash his hair or change his jacket before leaving for work, he now wore an old overall and one of his father's caps to do the feeding. But this morning was different.

This morning he was late. The birds showed their disapproval of his lateness by pecking at each other, and making the grunting sound which pigeons make to show they are not pleased. Walter poured the food into the feeding-trough, and changed the drinking-water. The trough was immediately covered by hungry and angry pigeons.

Before Sarah had put a stop to the hatching of any more eggs, Walter had taken down the partitions which kept each variety of bird separate, so that he could sit on his stool in the Loft, and watch all the birds at the same time. The Long-Faced English Tumblers, who were his favourites because of the long flip-flop feathers on their feet, and the silly diving, rolling and tumbling they did in the air when they were let out, had now interbred with the Russian High-Fliers, so that now their offspring tumbled high among the clouds and out of sight, and the only tumbling still to be seen was of the pure-bred birds. The cross between the White-Lace Fantails and the Russian High-Fliers was not interesting, and their cross with the Tumblers merely produced Parti-Coloured Fantails. As for the colourful Turbits, the White-Lace Fantails ignored them, and only one Turbit had attempted an alliance with a Russian High-Flier, but this was after a rigorous egg-collecting had started, so Walter would never know what a Russian High-Flying Turbit would look like.

The food for the pigeons was paid out of Walter's pocket-money, and Walter's mother had warned him that if he allowed any more eggs to be hatched and squabs to be born, she would stop his pocket money altogether, so that the pigeons would starve. Even after Freda, the prize-winner, his father's favourite, Old Reliable, even after she had found a corner of the loft and sat there facing the wall, her feathers puffed out, as dying pigeons are wont to do, even after she had, during the night, fallen dead from that last perch, and been found next morning by Walter, and buried in a tiny patch of the front garden where fire-coloured nasturtiums bloomed, even then his mother had not allowed him to hatch out any more eggs. It was a waste of good money, she told him, paying all that out for fancy food. Wild pigeons eat what they can. 'As they go, they go. Next time, take the body over to the park, or into the fields somewhere away from the house. I'm not having a pigeons' cemetery under my front window.'

This morning he was pecked and wing-flapped by two sitting birds. He exchanged the real eggs under them for plastic ones, and the unsuspecting birds returned, grumbling, to their nests and attempted to hatch the hollow eggs.

The birds fed, Walter returned to the back door of the house, where he removed his wellingtons, and left them on the step until he had laid newspaper down on the kitchen floor. Then he brought in the wellingtons, and stood them on the paper. That done, he listened. No sound. Nothing.

He went back into the hall, and stood at the bottom of the stairs, looking up. She had to be somewhere. It wasn't a Sunday, so she couldn't be at Chapel.

He climbed the stairs, and knocked on the bathroom door. No answer. The door was unlocked, so he opened it, and looked in. No one inside.

He tapped again on her bedroom door. 'Mother?' No answer. He turned the handle slowly, and pushed the door open a little.

'Mother?' No answer. He was afraid to open the door any wider, and look into a room he had never seen.

'Please!' He waited, and listened to the silence. 'I'm sorry.' He was not sure for what. 'Don't play that game,' His voice cracked. He did not wish to play that game. They had not played Hide and Seek for . . . he could not remember how long for. Strictly speaking, it had not been a game at all, however called so; his mother had used it as a punishment. If Walter had done some wrong action, she would hide herself in some place he could not discover, until he had cried, and screamed for her to come out. When she had revealed herself, she had warned him that, if he didn't mend his ways, she would go a long way away where he would never find her.

She must be punishing him for something, and he could not remember what he had done wrong.

'Won't do it again. Promise.' His hand still held the door-handle, but all he could see of the room was one side of a very large and highly polished Victorian wardrobe.

'Please come out. I'm sorry.' He waited. The only sound was a clock ticking. *'What does a clock do, Walter?' 'Tells the time, miss.' 'And what else?' 'Ticks, miss.' 'Very good. Now, what does the little hand do?'*

'Can I come in?' He waited.

'Shall I?' No answer.

Slowly he opened the door, an inch at a time. With each inch, he spoke the words, 'Mother.' At any moment she would shout at him, stop his pocket money, take his plate and make him eat his food under the stairs. *'Tells us what time it is.' 'No, I'm asking about the little hand. What does it say?'*

Finally the door was open, and she had not shouted. The room was in darkness, but for a beam of sunlight, cutting through the gap between the curtains, and dividing the room into halves. The bed was very wide, and higher than his own. The eiderdown which covered it was purple, with elaborate gold embroidery of dragons breathing out scarlet and green flames.

He turned his eyes slowly towards the pillow, and saw the outline of a head. The face was in darkness, but the beam of sunlight touched the edge of his mother's hair. He had never seen her hair let down. It was white, and spread out over the eiderdown from both sides of her face. It was so long, it must have reached her waist. Where the light caught it, it glistened like frost. Years of brushing night and morning had given it that shine.

Walter moved forward one step. 'Mother?' He could see her face clearly enough now to notice that her eyes were closed. He moved closer, and put his hand into hers, feeling the wedding and engagement rings on her fingers. The had was closed and cold. The fingers did not move in response to his own. '*Why do we need clocks, children?*' '*Yes, to tell the time, of course, but why do we need time?*'

He was frightened. Certainly something was wrong. He went to the window, and pulled back the curtains, still expecting her to wake, blinded by the light, and shout at him. But even when the whole room was flooded with daylight, her eyes remained closed.

Everything in the room seemed larger than life. He sat on a stool which was set in front of a dressing-table, which had three mirrors at different angles, so that he could see three of himself at once.

On the bedside table an alarm clock ticked away the time he had learned to tell. He was going to be late for work, since he could not leave without waking her.

Walter moved to his mother's bedside, and shook her shoulder. It was curiously stiff, like wood. He had no idea how to re-set the alarm clock, so that it would ring and waken her, so instead he shouted, 'Wake up, mother!' as loud as he could. He touched her wooden shoulder again, but found himself reluctant to shake it, so instead he shouted again, this time very close to her ear.

She remained still, her eyes closed. Walter wondered what he should do next. He returned to the kitchen, found two saucepans, brought them to his mother's bedroom, and clashed them together like cymbals. Even this had no effect.

Once she had woken him from a very deep sleep by squeezing a sponge of cold water over his face. He took one of the saucepans to the bathroom, and partially filled it with cold water. Standing over her, he held the pan as high above her face as he could, and begged her yet again to wake up so that he would not have to use the water. There was no reply.

As gently as he could, he tipped the pan. Water trickled down on to his mother's forehead. It ran over her closed eyes, on to her cheeks, down the sides of her neck and under the collar of her nightie until the pan was empty.

He remained where he was, frowning and holding out the pan, until the droplets of water which were lodged in the corners of his mother's mouth had dried.

His arm ached from holding the saucepan. It was clear that his mother did not intend to wake. He placed the pan on the bedside rug, and as he did so, remembered how his father had gone to live with Jesus in Paradise. '*When you grow old, Walter, you sometimes fall asleep for a long time, and you have to stay like that until Jesus makes up his mind whether He wants you to go and live with him.*' Jesus's eventual decision his mother had told him, would depend on how good He thought you had been up to then.

How long would he have to wait for Jesus to decide about his mother? He could not go to work until he knew. He must stay here, and wait with her until Jesus had decided. He must be here when his mother woke up.

Then there came a dreadful thought. What if Jesus did decide that Walter's mother should leave Bamber Bridge to live with him? Perhaps if Walter spoke to Jesus, and explained that he would not know what to do without his mother, that might help Jesus to come to a quick decision. 'Talk to Jesus, Walter. Don't just reel off what I've taught you as if it were a game. It's not a game. It's serious. He listens. Talk to Him as you'd talk to a friend. That's what He's there for.'

Walter knelt on the bedside rug, and placed his hands together to make the shape of a steeple. He closed his eyes, and coughed to clear his throat. He frowned, trying hard to think of what to say. The tick of the clock seemed even louder now. Time passed; nothing could stop it. Unless he spoke to Jesus quickly, he might be too late. He screwed his eyes up tighter, to help him to concentrate, and then he began:

'Gentle Jesus, meek and mild, look upon this little child. Pity my simplicity. Suffer me to . . .'

He had to stop. The prayer wasn't finished, but he had to stop. It wasn't right. What he was saying wasn't right. He didn't want Jesus to suffer him to come to Thee, if 'Thee' was Jesus. He didn't want to go to Jesus, not now, not yet. He wanted his mother back.

Walter thumped his fists on the side of the bed with temper. Why hadn't his mother taught him a prayer which would explain what he wanted? What was the point of 'Bless Mummy and Daddy and Grandma and the pigeons' when what he needed was to . . . He couldn't find the words to express exactly what was needed.

He rose to his feet, and bit at the back of his hand to stop himself bursting into tears of frustration. He rocked backwards and forwards as if ready to begin a race. He paced round the room, cursing the goldfish inside his head which wouldn't let him think. The clock ticked on, and he couldn't think of the right sort of words, the sort of words which would cause Jesus to listen. All prayers had special words in them, words you wouldn't use every day, words that you saved for only Jesus. Telling him to talk to Jesus as a friend had not meant that he should use ordinary words, but that he shouldn't singsong or gabble the prayer to get it all in while he could still remember it. He covered his ears with his hands to shut out the sound of the clock's insistent tick, and lowered himself on to his knees again, his eyes screwed up tight. He could think like this. Catch one goldfish, and keep it still. With his hands to his ears, he began:

> 'Gentle Jesus meek and mild,
> Look upon this little child.
> Pity my simplicity.
> Please send my mother back to me.'

After a moment, he added the words, 'As soon as you can,' and stood up.

The prayer had pleased him. He had made it rhyme. And since his mother had told him that Jesus could see anything he did, there was no need to go into details about why he needed her more than Jesus did. Jesus would understand. He would know that Walter had to have his mother back. All Walter had to do was to wait.

He stood watching his mother's eyelids for any sign of movement. Jesus would now be considering what he had said.

Twenty minutes later, his legs were tired, so he went to this mother's pink basketwork chair, and sat down. From here he could watch her face. She would be angry to find herself damp when she woke up, but if she gave him time to explain, she would understand the necessity.

At eleven twenty by the clock on the bedside table, his stomach began to make noises to remind him that he had had no breakfast. But if he left his mother now, she might wake, and anyway, were he to go downstairs and begin eating before Jesus had come to a decision, Jesus might be offended, and think that Walter did not really want his mother back.

At half past one, he had to go to the toilet, either that or mess himself and his mother's pink basketwork chair. He had held off as long as he could, moving himself about in the chair, and now there was no help for it. He stood quickly, whispered, 'Excuse me, Jesus,' and rushed for the bathroom.

When he had done what was necessary, and washed his hands, his mind turned once again to food. Now that he had been excused and left the room, it was better to get something to eat while he was still out, than to return to the bedroom and have to ask to be excused again.

In the kitchen, Walter filled a large cardboard box with tins from his mother's well-stocked pantry. A dish and a spoon were all he would need to eat with. He put them, with a tin-opener, into the box, and carried it upstairs.

By two forty-three, he was back in the pink basketwork chair, having consumed a late lunch of baked beans, followed by peaches and evaporated milk.

His mother's eyes remained closed, and his own had become very heavy with the concentration of looking at one thing for such a long time. He forced himself to stay awake. He was in no doubt that very soon his mother would wake up, and everything would be as it had been before. All she had told him about Jesus convinced him that Jesus was not the sort of person who would leave Walter on his own. He couldn't be left on his own. Even to think about it frightened him so much that he had to close his eyes and shake his head until the thought went away.

He remembered that she had told him once that it was no good expecting miracles to happen overnight, or prayers to be answered on demand. 'It's not "Ask, and ye shall be given," not in this world, Walter; I shan't speak for the next, but not in this one, not down here. You have to wait. Waiting your turn is all part of living. Patience is a virtue. Our Lord, Jesus, has millions and millions of other people to think about besides you.'

Walter was tired. He tried not to yawn, in case he should do so at the very moment that Jesus decided to look down, and saw him.

At five twenty, he opened a tin of corned beef, and cut bits off the lump of compressed meat with his spoon. He ate as much as he could, and wrapped what was left in a page torn from a copy of *Woman's Own*, which he had found stacked, with several hundred other copies, on the top shelf of his mother's Victorian wardrobe. He must try to remember what it was he had wrapped in the picture of a lady in her underwear, before it went bad. 'Corned beef wrapped in lady with very little on.' He said it aloud to help him remember. He must finish the corned beef. To let good food go bad was a sin.

What would have happened at Woolworth's today when they noticed he had not arrived for work? There was no way he could think of to let them know that he had to stay at home in order to wait for his mother to wake up.

His imagination toyed with visions of the waste paper and cardboard piling up higher and higher behind all the counters until the salesgirls were standing on it to keep it down. As it mounted, so did they. They towered up above the customers so high that the customers could see up their overalls. They held down the fronts of their skirts, and were unable to reach the tills; they could neither receive money from the customers, nor give it in change. 'Leave it on the counter,' they shouted down. 'If you've got the right money, leave it on the counter. I can't wrap anything for you. Wrap it yourself. Walter hasn't turned up for work.'

Groceries would be the worst hit by Walter's absence. So many cardboard boxes! The longer his mother slept, the more work there would be for him to catch up on when he returned. Nobody else would do his job. They didn't like getting themselves dirty. 'That's your job, Walter, not ours.'

His mother's face seemed to have grown paler, or was it just the light? Outside the pigeons were making their 'Why haven't we been fed?' noise again. They would have to wait, as he was waiting. He opened the window, and shouted into the back yard, 'Patience is a virtue.' Jesus would be able to hear them too. He watched over all living things, even cockroaches and worms. Perhaps if Walter were to go down and let out the Russian High-Fliers, they would be able to fly up closer to Jesus, and maybe even catch his eye and consequently his attention.

At seven thirty, when the birds had been calling to him for their food for well over an hour, he excused himself again, and went downstairs to feed them. Jesus would not approve of cruelty to animals.

After weighing the food, and placing it in the trough he left the pigeons squabbling over it, and began carrying the heavy bags of grain and seed upstairs to his mother's room.

At the door, he studied the size of the room, and considered the amount of food still to be brought up from the shed next to the Loft. He moved the bags to the bathroom, placed the bath-plug in its hole, and tipped bag after bag of seed and grain into the bath. Hemp, millet, tares, linseed, rape, niger, maple peas and ordinary corn were mixed together. Walter stirred them up, using his hands and arms, and feeling the silkiness of the linseed as it got under his fingernails. Linseed was not the pigeons' favourite food, but it was good for them, and they ate it if they were hungry.

When the birds had eaten, and settled on their perches for the night, wondering no doubt why their supper was so late, and why they had not been let out to fly, Walter lifted each one down in turn, and placed it gently into his father's travelling basket. The basket held six birds at a time. In all he made seven journeys, carrying the birds up to his mother's room.

It took him an hour and a half, and when the last bird had been released, and had fluttered, heavy and uncertain, round his mother's bedroom, trying to find a surface on which to land which was not already occupied. Walter looked again at his mother, and saw that her eyes were still closed.

The birds made a great deal of noise and fuss about this change in their routine. They fought for room. Since this was the moulting season, feathers floated down from the top of the wardrobe, the chest-of-drawers, and even from the shade of the overhead lamp, as each bird tried to stake its own claim. If his mother were to wake up now, she would scream the place down, but there was only one of Walter, and being only one he could not be in two places at once; she would have to understand that. He had given the matter thought, and he had come to a decision. Either he let the birds slowly starve, which would be cruel, or he released them so that they became wild, and would no longer return to the Loft for food, or he kept them with him, waiting for Jesus to make his mind up. And he had chosen the third of these solutions.

As Clarice, a White-Lace Fantail, landed on Walter's mother's chin, displayed her crop (by blowing it full out) and her tail (by spreading it as wide as she could), and strutted and cooed to claim his mother's chin for her home, Walter was sure his mother blinked, and his heart stopped for a moment. He waited, but she didn't blink again, so he lifted Clarice from his mother's chin, and placed her on top of one of the dressing-table mirrors. The bird peered down, and, seeing its own reflection in an upside-down position, attempted to peck at it.

Lavender-scented soap was rubbed into a warm facecloth, which was then used to wipe the chin. His mother did not seem to be stiff any more. Perhaps it was a stage towards waking. While Walter was at it, he cleaned the rest of her face. Small feathers and dust from the top of the wardrobe had settled all over the putty-coloured and wrinkled skin. Walter worked cautiously, afraid that she might wake while he was wiping her, and afraid also that she never might.

He had removed all her ornaments, combs and brushes to the safety of a drawer before letting the birds loose, and had found in that drawer a pair of glittering ear-rings shaped like Blackpool Tower. Now, noticing some pigeon droppings matted into her long white hair, he took the brush out again, and began to brush his mother's hair clean of bird-shit.

Doing so, he discovered that he liked brushing his mother's hair. It calmed him. The static electricity which the hair still contained seemed in some way to prove that she was just sleeping, and waiting, and no more than that. With each brush-stroke he laid the hair down over the colourful counterpane, and watched wisps of it rise again towards the brush, as if it were showing him that it and she were still active.

By the time he had grown tired of brushing her hair, it was dark outside and the birds had fallen quiet, some of them standing on one leg, some on two, but almost all with eyes closed. Walter drew the curtains together, and groped his way back to the bed. He did not turn on the overhead light, because Edna and William, a pair of Turbits, had managed to claim its shade as their perch. There was plenty of room beside his mother. He would sleep on top of the counterpane as he was, fully dressed. By morning Jesus would have made up his mind.

The clock continued to tick loudly, and from time to time, a pigeon would make a quiet noise of curiosity at realizing it was not where it should be at this hour. Walter lay beside his dead mother, and allowed his protuberant eyelids to come down, shutting out all but the possibility of a bad dream. He was asleep almost at once.

Something was tapping gently at the outside of his left eyelid. It had woken him. He was awake now, but his eyes remained closed. He dared not open them in case whatever it was that was tapping should tap again at his open eye.

With his eyes still closed, he slowly lifted his right arm, and brought his hands towards his nose on which, he could by now feel, the bird was standing. Then he slid his fingers under the bird, gripping its legs and using his thumb and little finger to keep its wings pinioned. He was then able to lift the pigeon away from his face, and open his eyes to see which pigeon it had been. He had decided that it would be Dora. He was right. It was Dora.

He swung his feet to the floor, wished Dora good morning, and stroked her gently. Her eyes were brighter and more alert than his. She blinked, and then cocked her head on one side as if asking for an explanation of these new living-quarters.

Walter yawned, and looked slowly round the room. From every available surface, the eyes of pigeons were watching him. He noticed that his mother's double-fronted Victorian wardrobe was now decorated with vertical black and white lines of pigeon droppings. As well as the triple mirror of the dressing-table, his mother had a full-length mirror on a stand, and this had become tilted, and at its highest point, two English Long-Faced Tumblers, Marge and Lionel, were billing and rocking in preparation for copulation. His mother's pink basketwork chair had been taken over by Norman and Marlene. Norman was a Russian High-Flier and Marlene a Birmingham Roller, originally from another Loft, who had met Norman high in the air one evening, and followed him home.

On each of the four bedposts, a single male bird was circling on the spot, its crop inflated, claiming that particular perch for his own, and daring any other male to challenge and fight him for it. A lilac-coloured Turbit ran backwards and forwards along the top of the pelmet of the curtains. Two female White-Lace Fantails on the dressing-table began fighting, but the fight was confused by the triple reflections of the mirror, so that there seemed to be eight White-Lace Fantails altogether, and neither of the two birds could be sure that what she was flapping her wings and pecking at was in any real sense an adversary.

Walter clapped his hands together, and shouted, 'Linda! Enid! Stop it!' The two birds stopped fighting for a while, but continued to make low threatening noises at each other and at the reflections in the mirror. Walter decided that he had better cover the mirror, when Linda and Enid might calm down, realizing that there was room on the dressing-table for both of them, and believing that the other six birds had been seen off.

His mother had not moved. There was a faintly musty smell in the room, which was not the smell of pigeons, but might, he supposed, be his own smell. He opened the door cautiously so that none of the pigeons could escape to another part of of the house, betook himself to the bathroom, and found the bath full of pigeon-food.

He had never taken a bath without the supervision of his mother. He must manage as best he could. He filled the wash-basin with warm water, stripped, and stood on the bathmat, soaping himself all over. He enjoyed the feeling of the slippery lavender-scented soap all over his body. But he could not reach his back.

It was a problem. The more he thought about it, the more it worried him. Would he have to stay dirty until Jesus made his mind up, and Walter's mother woke up? His arms were long, but they would only reach around him so far. As he worried at the problem, the soap which he had spread liberally on the parts he could reach began to dry. He felt itchy. This was another cause for worry. It had never happened after a bath supervised by his mother.

He removed as much of the dry soap as he could with a towel, but still he itched. As he scratched himself, he wondered what his mother would say if she could see him. Jesus was certainly taking his time about sending her back. He began to have doubts about the everlasting love Jesus had for humanity in general and for Walter in particular; his mother had told him of it, but she might have been wrong. She had taught him to sing, 'Jesus loves me. This I know, for the Bible tells me so.' If Jesus loved him, why was he leaving Walter on his own like this? Why was He taking so long to decide?

He scratched moodily at the hair in his left armpit, and felt frustrated that he could only scratch two parts of his body at the same time, when many more than two parts itched. A positive fear then entered his mind. What if his mother had seen Heaven, and walked in Paradise with Jesus, and had liked it so much that she had asked Jesus not to send her back to Walter?

Walter looked into the bathroom mirror, and named his fear aloud. 'What if it's that? What if that's what it is, then?' One of his scratching hands ceased from scratching, and was used to hold his forehead. 'It could be, couldn't it? What if it's her, Walter? If she doesn't want to come back, then, boy? He wouldn't force her, would He? Don't suppose so. No, being Jesus, He wouldn't. Forcing's not a good thing to do. No.' He moved his hand from his forehead, and began to bite at the side of his index finger. The goldfish flicked about very fast inside his head, and he closed his eyes to stop them. His body still itched. With his free hand, he scratched it where he could. What might his mother at this moment be saying to Jesus? She had asked Heaven so many times to rescue her from her evil, wilful, disappointing son. She had spoken so many times of how much better off she would be without him, of how death was all she could look forward to and the pleasure of complaining, when she should get to Heaven, of the unfairness of her life on earth.

Within his mind, his mother's conversation with Jesus became mixed up with what she would say to him, Walter, if she could observe his present condition. 'I've earned my place. Looking after such a – stop scratching boy. You're not a dog, are you? There could only be one reason, Lord, I should have been landed with such a burden, and that's to try me out for Heaven. Shan't tell you again! Look at him! Nobody can tell me that's not a penance.'

He was naked. He itched, and his back was unclean. This was the day he was supposed to change his underwear, and he had no idea where the clean ones were kept. Again, there was no help for it; he must step once more into the underpants he had just removed. He remembered the musty smell he had noticed in his mother's bedroom. She had told him that the customers at Woolworth's would notice if he did not change his underwear. But he had not gone to Woolworth's. The pigeons would not notice if he smelled; they had their own smell.

'Where's Walter, then, eh? Where's he got to? Don't know. What you mean, "Don't know"? Haven't seen him, have I? Got to get all this rubbish cleared away. Go on! Look! "Clear it right away," I said. Got to get rid of it today, not next week, boy. Now! Move yourself! Girls can't sell goods if they're up to their whatsits in sticky toffee papers. What's funny about that, eh? Go and get Walter. Go on! Fetch him here. Where is he, anyway? What's he doing in the bathroom? Where's our handsome hero? Where's the housewives' favourite choice?'

He was dressed. He was standing at the top of the stairs, listening to the pigeons in the bedroom, and staring down at the front door. What would he do if they gave him the sack for staying away? Two letters were pushed through the letterbox. He watched them land on the mat, and expected his mother to walk into the hall from the kitchen, pick them up, and shout to him to hurry.

He waited, and then, remembering where she was, ran down the stairs two at a time, opened the front door, and shouted after the postman. But the postman was too far away to understand what Walter shouted, and looking back, and seeing the silly Williams boy standing at the front door waving his arms, waved back cheerfully.

The postman went on round the corner, and continued to make his deliveries, amused by the antics of Witless Walter at Number Twenty-Three. Walter went back inside, and closed the door. If he could have made the postman hear, he would have told him about his mother, and asked him to send someone to watch her while he went to Woolworth's.

No help. He picked up the letters, which were addressed to his mother, and took them up to her.

3

How could you let her go like that,
covered in bird-droppings,
after all the years she's cared for you?

THE sound of the doorbell woke Walter, the long persistent ringing of someone who knew that the house wasn't empty, and was determined to be answered. He swung his legs off the side of his mother's bed, and felt the stickiness of fresh pigeon-droppings crushed between his stockinged feet and the bedside rug. The sticky substance clung to the wool of his socks. As he tried to scrape them clean, he collected more, and as he moved, it seeped through, and made contact with his feet. He and the pigeons and his mother had been sharing the same room for seven days, and his mother not only continued to sleep, but had begun to look far from well.

'Is your mother in?' It was the woman who came sometimes with a catalogue, and never looked at his face. Nor was she looking at it now. She had seen through the frosted glass that it was a man coming to answer the door, had known that this could only be Walter, and had directed her glance at the area where his knees would be, before the door opened.

'Yes.'

'Only, I haven't seen for for some time, and I've come to . . .' The woman's voice trailed away. The stench which was coming towards her seemed to be rushing to excuse itself from the house. It was a stench she had not encountered since childhood, when her brother had kept a lame blackbird in the outhouse for four weeks.

The woman was so surprised by the strength of the stench that she forgot her habit of never looking at Walter's face, and allowed her glance to stray from his knees, and wander slowly up his body. His shirt, shoulders, arms and hair were covered in dried black and white bird-droppings, and a streak of them had run down the side of his cheek, in front of his right ear, stopping when it had reached the sharp corner of his jawbone.

'Did you want to see her?' The woman was looking him in the face.

143

That pleased him. 'She's . . .' He wasn't sure how to explain. 'She's not been very well. I've had to stay at home with her.'

The woman's mouth, which had been open for some time, closed, then opened again just long enough to form the words, 'What's she ill with?'

'I don't know. She won't wake up.'

The expression on the woman's face changed, and informed Walter that he had said too much. He began to worry, remembering the state of his mother's bedroom.

'Can I see her?'

'She's sleeping.'

'Yes, you said.'

'She's sleeping.'

His mother would have died before opening the door to anyone without at first checking to make sure the house was tidy. Walter stood, and the woman stood, neither knowing what to say next. The silence seemed to go on forever.

Then Walter said, 'I'd better go and see to her,' Before he could close the door, the woman had her foot up on the step.

'Just a minute. I'm in a bit of a mess, you see. The Mail Order Club have sent me a nasty letter about your mother missing her payments. I wasn't going to bother her, because I know how regular she is usually, but I'm sure she'd want to know. It's a mistake, bound to be, but they do have the right to reclaim the goods if the payments fall behind.'

She was thinking fast, lying in her teeth. Somewhere in this house there was an old lady with only an idiot son to look after her. Already she was writing the newspaper report in her head, 'Kind Neighbour Saves Elderly Lady from Starving'. It would be 'elderly'; they hardly ever say 'old' – 'pensioner' perhaps or 'OAP' if they were short of space; no, 'elderly' was better; it would do well. 'Idiot Son Kept Mother Locked in Cupboard.'

While she was trying to decide what she would wear when interviewed on television, she realized Walter had spoken. He had said, 'If you like.' Not only had he spoken, he had moved to one side to let her pass. The woman hesitated. She needed time to adjust from her fantasy of overnight fame to the smell of Walter and the house. Perhaps, once he had lured her inside, he would become violent, hold her at knife point and force her to do all sorts of disgusting things.

She stepped over the threshold, and watched him carefully as he closed the front door behind her. She would let him slit her throat open rather than allow him to touch her 'in that way', or, indeed, in any way.

Walter led the way upstairs, still worrying about the state of his mother's bedroom. He said, 'I couldn't do any cleaning. I haven't been able to leave her. Excuse the mess.' He had heard his mother say that, even when she had just finished spring cleaning. On the landing, he turned to the woman and said, 'We have to go in carefully. The birds might escape.' The woman thought it best to humour him, and nodded, 'Of course.' He opened the door just enough for her get in sideways. At first, all she could see was the side of a large Victorian wardrobe. Then she moved in further, squeezing past the door.

Her entrance disturbed the pigeons. As if they had all at that moment decided to take part in an avian version of the Paul Jones, they began with great noise and flapping to change places. The room was filled with feathers and dust. The woman placed her hand over her mouth, and what started out as a stifled scream became protection against choking.

Then she turned, and saw Walter's mother, lying with her silvery white hair spread over the purple bed-cover, her face the colour of old and very used plasticine, pigeon droppings on her hair, on her forehead, and almost completely covering the headboard of the bed.

'She's . . .' The woman stopped herself; it was better not to risk provoking him. 'She's sleeping very soundly, isn't she? I'll come back some other time.' And left him, standing there, as quickly as she could.

At the front door, her hand holding it open for a quick getaway, she shouted back at Walter, 'How could you let her go like that, covered in bird-droppings, after all the years she's cared for you? She's been dead for days, you great mistake of a man. It's criminal. They'll be coming for you, don't worry! They'll know what to do to make you learn.' She slammed the front door behind her, with enough force to crack one of the panes of frosted glass.

Walter stood where he was at the top of the stairs, his head swimming with brightly-coloured goldfish. What had she meant? Perhaps she didn't believe in Jesus. Among all the other thoughts which swam in and out and darted about, was one whch at least gave him the opportunity for uncomplicated action. He remembered noticing that Helen, one of the Turbits, had diarrhoea, and since he was already out of his mother's room, he might as well go down to the Loft outside and get the pigeons' first aid box. Castor oil was what was needed.

Part Five

He Becomes a Charge on the State

He didn't suppose it would be cold in Paradise.
Otherwise they wouldn't call it 'Paradise'

A DOCTOR, a policeman and a Social Worker arrived at three fifteen
that afternoon. Walter opened the door to them, and led them upstairs
to his mother's bedroom. Each in turn squeezed round the door, so as
not to allow any pigeons to escape.

Walter watched the doctor pull the stained eiderdown over his
mother's face. The Social Worker put an arm around Walter's shoulder, and asked him to show her where the kitchen was, so that she
could make them all a cup of tea.

As they drank the tea (without milk, since it had gone off) there were
questions, some of which Walter could not answer. No, he did not know
what day it was, or remember what he had eaten for lunch. Since
moving into his mother's room, he had not kept proper mealtimes, but
had eaten something from a tin when he was hungry; the question bore
no relation to the way he had been living, but that was too difficult to
explain to these people, so he merely told them that he thought the last
food he had eaten was frankfurters and baked beans, but that he could
not swear to it.

He did remember the names of the people with whom he had worked
at Woolworth's. The Social Worker promised that she would telephone
Mr Richards to explain why Walter had not been to work.

Finally they came to the question which all three, doctor, policeman
and Social Worker, considered to be most important. It was, 'Have
you any relations, Walter? Someone you could go and stay with?'

Walter's answer caused all three servants of the public to sigh. They
sighed in turn; then they looked at each other, and sighed again. The
policeman shook his head from side to side. Walter wondered why his
having no relations should upset them so. His mother had said it was a
blessing. Every Christmas she had said, 'Thank God we've only ourselves to buy for. I don't know how some of these large families manage,
I really don't.'

It did not seem important. The doctor had said his mother would have to be taken away. He assumed that she would be taken to hospital, but surely they would bring her back. He could look after himself until then.

Now the Social Worker was speaking. 'You can't live here on your own, Walter.'

He tried to explain that he would be alright for a few days, that now he didn't have to stay with her, he could go to work, where there were Canteen Lunches, and so he would manage until she came back.

The three public servants did not seem to understand this explanation; they did not take it in. They looked again at each other. What Walter did not know was that each was unwilling to utter a word which had not so far been uttered. After a long silence, the Social Worker said, 'I think that's your department, doctor.' The doctor took out a spotlessly clean handkerchief, and wiped his hands. 'If you'd been called to her in the first place, you'd have had to tell him then.'

The doctor coughed. Walter gave him respectful attention. The doctor wiped the corners of his mouth with the handkerchief, and said, 'Now this is not going to be easy for you to understand,' and ran down. Clearly nothing about the whole business was easy for anyone. The doctor said, 'Now, look, Walter, have you ever had a pet?'

'Pigeons.'

'Apart from pigeons. Have you ever had a dog or a pussy cat that has . . . well, grown old, and . . . I suppose even the pigeons . . .'

'Never had a dog.'

'Well, you see, your mother was quite old. And what happens to people when they get old, is . . . well, after a while, they . . . they die. It's quite natural; it happens to everyone. And that's what's happened to your mother. I'm afraid she won't be coming home.'

Walter knew what it was to die. Freda, the Favourite, the White-Lace Fantail, the Prize-Winner, had looked at the wall, refused food, and died, and Walter had buried her in the garden. He had not associated death with human beings, certainly never with his mother. The goldfish in his head raced and darted about. Finally, he said, 'Jesus wanted her?'

'Yes,' the doctor replied a little too eagerly. He was thrown by the question, but grateful to find that religion had its uses. 'That's exactly it, Walter. Jesus has called her to Him.'

The Social Worker, who was a card-carrying agnostic, made a small noise of disgust. Walter wondered if she were about to be sick. The policeman was following his own train of thought, which was what would happen to all the pigeons. Beautiful, some of them were. Two, or perhaps three, would make an excellent birthday present for his eight-year-old son. He would have to construct some sort of cage or box in which they would live, but the policeman was much practised in Home Improvement, and would enjoy that.

'I'm told they breed like rabbits. Is that true?'

He had uttered his thought aloud, and the other two public servants looked at him for an explanation.

'The pigeons.' He remembered his official postion. 'I mean, they can't stay in that room; it's a health hazard. Rats, you know what I mean?' They did not know what he meant. 'Rats and pigeons, they go together. I mean they often do, but they shouldn't.' He was not getting through to them, and so broke off. None of the pigeons would fit into his pocket without being noticeable. Perhaps if he came back later after dark, that would be best.

The Social Worker leaned forward, and touched Walter on the hand. He was thinking, or trying to. His mother had told him when his father was taken by Jesus that, once Jesus had decided that He wanted you, nobody saw you on earth again. The Social Worker had to shake Walter's hand before she has his attention. 'We'll have to find you somewhere else to live, shan't we?' She spoke as if the somewhere else to live were to be a treat. Walter's brain could not accept any more information. He felt sleepy, and he yawned. That was what his brain made him do when it was full, and no more could be squeezed into it.

'Will you come upstairs, and help me pack a suitcase?' She still had hold of his hand, and was now standing. Walter did as he was bid. He rose and followed her upstairs.

He took clean clothes into the bathroom, to change in there. The bath was still full of pigeon-food. Walter contemplated washing himself all over at the sink, but when last he had done so, as he remembered, he had itched, and he did not wish to scratch in front of strangers. So he simply changed his clothes.

While he changed, he thought about the pigeons. Perhaps if he were to leave the bedroom door and the bathroom door both open, the pigeons would find their food. He could fill the wash basin with water for them to drink. It was true that they would also bathe in it, that they would foul the water and also the seed in the bath, but at least it would last them until he returned from wherever he was being taken.

He left the wash basin full of water, and presented himself to the Social Worker on the landing. She had finished packing his case. Now she bent forward to whisper in his ear, 'Is there any loose money in the house? Perhaps in a drawer somewhere? Anything at all of value – your mother's jewellery? If there is, I'd take it now if I were you, before someone else finds it.' She tapped the side of her nose with her index finger, and closed one eye slowly.

Walter remembered the ear-rings he had seen, and took them from the drawer. He also remembered that his mother kept some money in a biscuit-tin, hidden behind the rows and rows of tinned fruit in the pantry. She called it her 'Mad' money; Walter never knew why. He removed the tin, and placed the contents, nine pounds and four shillings in his jacket pocket.

During the time it took him to perform these actions, the goldfish in his head slowed down a little. He realized that he was to be taken somewhere. He had assumed that he would be returning, but something in the lady's manner, its conspiratorial quality and its urgency, now caused him to question this assumption. There were other questions which still darted about, like what would happen to his job in Woolworth's, why Jesus had kept his mother and left him on his own, and where did the lady intend to take him and why, and there was the uncomfortable and growing certainty that he himself had no choice in determining what was to be done with him, but these were secondary to what was now the most important question, was he to return or no. If he were not, there was something he had to do.

'Will I be coming back?'

She did not answer. He persisted. 'Will I?'

The Social Worker sighed. 'No, Walter, I don't think you'll ever come back here. I'm sorry.'

Walter grabbed a saucepan from the kitchen, and ran up the stairs, two at a time. He filled it full of pigeon-food from the bath, opened the bathroom window, and poured the food out to land in the back yard. When the bath was empty, even to the last handful, he rushed into his mother's bedroom, opened the windows as wide as they would go, and shooed the pigeons out.

Like aeroplanes leaving for a night mission, they took off in twos from the wardrobe, the dressing-table, the overhead light and Walter's mother's pink basketwork chair, each pair stopping for a moment on the window-ledge and looking about, before descending to the grain spread out for them in the yard beneath.

The wind came in through the window, and blew the stained purple eiderdown away from his mother's face. She was still here. The silver-white hair was caught by the wind, and rose into the air. Walter watched. His face set itself into a mask. He could not cry, not now. He closed his eyes, and remembered his mother's hair as he had always seen it, pulled tight into a roll behind her head. Why had Jesus not taken his mother's body, when He had taken the rest of her? Could she and Jesus see him now? He turned, and looked out of the window, up into the sky. He would leave the windows open. His mother's hands had been cold for some days; she wouldn't mind. He didn't suppose it was cold in Paradise. Otherwise they wouldn't call it 'Paradise'. He was leaving the window open for the pigeons. They would get frightened when it started to get dark. They needed somewhere high to perch.

The Social Worker called to Walter from the hall, asking him to hurry. He put the saucepan on the bed beside his mother's feet. He was frozen. He couldn't move. He shivered from the cold of the open window, from fear and from sadness. His knees sank to the floor, and he put his hand over his mouth to hold in a scream. His throat ached from being stretched so wide; he had to release it, and let the noise come out. With the noise came tears. He gripped his mother's feet with one large hand, and said, 'I will be alright, though, won't I? Tell me I'll be alright.'

People he couldn't see made sounds of reassurance, and pulled him to his feet. He was helped downstairs by the policeman, and he sat at the front in the Social Worker's car. But by then he had stopped screaming, stopped crying; he was quite silent.

Women with folded arms were leaning out from doorways, not wishing to be seen, but wishing to see. To Walter they looked like a spread-out hand of picture-cards. He would not scream now, even though they watched and waited. If they had not seen him fighting with the policeman, and trying to get back into his mother's house, they had missed that sight. It would not happen again. He had promised. And they in their turn, all three, the servants of the public, had made Walter a promise. They had promised him he would be alright. He had asked, and they had told him, 'You'll be alright.'

He was shaking again now, frightened and sad, but he would not scream. He had given his promise.

2

One sulky subnormal,
handed over and signed for

'WHAT'S this?' A man in a white coat was holding some of Walter's hair.

'Pigeon-shit.' The Social Worker answered without looking up from the report she was writing. 'He had about a hundred of them shut up in his mother's bedroom with him.'

'Why's that?'

The man was asking Walter. Walter didn't want to talk. He didn't answer.

They had promised him he would be alright. He had sat beside the Social Worker in the front seat of her car, and she had told him that it was a nice place she was taking him to, but she had lied.

The man in the white coat was asking him more questions. Some of them were questions the Social Worker had already asked. Did he know his date of birth? When was his birthday? How old was he? What school had he attended?

They had driven past the large double gates, and she had waved to a man in uniform, standing outside the lodge. Walter had heard the gravel of a long driveway crunching beneath the tyres of the car, and for a moment he had felt important.

Had he ever run away from school? What had he eaten for his last meal? When had he eaten last?

They were going to look after him. They had told him so; they had promised. They were going to take care of him. That is what they had said, and he had believed them.

What day was it? What time of day? Did he realize where he was?

The ride in a car, the gate with the man in uniform, the way the Social Worker had spoken to him as she drove, all this had reassured him. She had called him Walter, and asked him about the pigeons. Then the car had stopped, and he had looked out, and seen the size of the building. As she had turned off the engine, and pulled the handbrake, she had said, 'Built as a Workhouse in 1839. You wouldn't know what a Workhouse is. I expect you would have done then.'

It was grey. Grey stone, with six storeys and far too many windows for Walter to count. He had never seen so frightening a building. He had wanted to run, to hide in the bushes, to do anything but go inside.

And they had promised.

Did he always know when he wanted to use the lavatory? Did he use it properly? Could he count? Add? Subtract? Multiply?

For a while he had refused to get out of the car. The Social Worker had grown impatient. She had said, 'It's not as bad as it looks from outside.' She had pulled at his arm, and he had resisted.

Could he write his own name? His address? The man was reading the questions from a printed sheet of paper and, as Walter gave answer to none of them, the man made a stroke with his pen against each question as it went unanswered.

Finally he had realized that he could not sit in the Social Worker's car forever. He had placed one foot out of the car on to the gravel. The goldfish in his head had told him to run, but while he was still looking about, trying to decide which way he should go, two men in white jackets had come quickly from the entrance of the hospital and taken hold of his arms, pushing him forwards towards the large double doors.

Once they were inside the hospital, the Social Worker had told the two men that Walter would be alright now, and they had backed away, and then gone inside a small room. Before the door closed, Walter had heard one of them say, 'Your deal,' and seen that they sat down and resumed their game of cards.

The Social Worker had given Walter his suitcase, and told him to carry it, since she was tired, and they had almost a quarter of a mile of corridor to walk. The quarter of a mile was wide and high, as well as long. It echoed with the sound of Walter's squeaking boots and the steady measured step of the Social Worker's sensible shoes. It echoed with the sound of iron doors being banged, of large keys being turned, with shouts and screams, sobs and moans. It echoed with the sound of a voice as high and shrill as a seagull, with the conversation of old and not-so-old men, who stood at the corners where smaller corridors crossed this large one, and whose conversation was not with each other but with themselves. The voices of these old and not-so-old men had been low and confidential, but still they had echoed. Walter had passed the men, glancing nervously at them from the corners of his eyes (since it was rude to stare), and had seen that some scratched themselves, some picked their noses, and some hugged their arms to their chests, smiling or giggling at private and pleasurable thoughts. Who were these men? What was this place?

Do you know where we are? Can you tell me when you last . . . if you last . . . have you ever . . .? Do you know . . .?

One man had repeated the word, 'Hullo,' over and over again. Walter had answered, 'Hullo,' and this had caused the man to say the word more quickly, repeating it, each time using a different inflection, 'Hullo! Hullo? *Hull*-o. Hull-*o*. Huh-lo,' on and on, even when they were well past him, with the 'Hullo' slower again, sad and flat and disappointed, as if he had wanted Walter to answer each 'Hullo' with another, and had been rejected when this did not happen. Walter had turned his head, and shouted another 'Hullo' back at the man, hearing it echo more than once, but the Social Worker had said, 'Don't encourage him,' as if the man had been a dog, begging for food from a guest's plate. The only word of hers which Walter had heard echo was the word 'him', which he had heard twice, 'him, him'. She was not a woman of any great resonance.

The corridor had smelled of boiled cabbage. The walls had been painted dark green up to the height a man could reach. Above this, they were a yellowing cream.

Do you know where you are?

At the next corner, an old man had been pacing backwards and forwards, flicking his hands vigorously as if he wished them to drop off from the ends of his arms. Walter had wondered what the man's hands could have done that he wished so desperately to lose them.

All the men he had seen wore stained clothes which didn't fit them, trousers without buttons but with elasticated tops. Some had pulled the trousers high up on to their chests, leaving large gaps between their trouser turnups and the tops of their shoes or (more often) slippers. The heads of all the men had been shaved at the sides and back, with the hair on the top left short and of equal length, as though a pudding-basin had been used to support the barber's hand while he trimmed round it.

The shortness of the men's hair had reminded Walter of his father, whose own hair had never been as short as that. He wondered whether his father and mother had yet met in Paradise. If they had, and could see down to him, he begged them to ask Jesus to take him quickly from this place.

The man in the white coat was now writing on another sheet of paper. 'Religion? C of E, I suppose?'

The Social Worker said, 'I'm not sure. There was nobody to ask. Do you know your religion, Walter?'

Walter knew well enough that he was Chapel, but he would not answer; he would not speak. The man in the white coat shrugged, and wrote down 'C of E' while the Social Worker continued to scribble at her report with a ball-point pen.

As they had approached yet another thick iron door, Walter had heard a man behind it screaming the word, 'No,' over and over again, and thought he could hear also the sound of fighting, of blows being struck and heads hitting the wall and the door itself, and all the time this hysterical voice pleading, 'No ... No ... No ... Please ...' Walter had ceased walking at this point, and had said as firmly as he could, 'Can I go home?' He had stopped so suddenly that the Social Worker, deep in her own thoughts, had not noticed, and had gone on ahead.

Walter had remained where he was near the iron door. He knew that he had turned no corners. He could find his way out. If he were to run fast enough, he could get past the men who were playing cards. If it were done, it had to be done at once and quickly. Walter had half turned, and looked back the way they had come. But if he were caught, what would be done to him in this place?

The Social Worker had noticed he was no longer by her side, and had walked back to him slowly. 'What did you say?' She had made it sound as though what he had said was in some way most extraordinary.

Walter had repeated what he had said.

The Social Worker had smiled, but Walter had sensed that this was not a smile of pleasure. 'This is your home now, Walter.' She had paused, allowing time for the words to sink in. 'You need looking after, and that's what this place is for. It's what the people here are for. To look after you.'

Walter had wondered if the people who were to look after him were like the old men he had already passed in the corridor, and who had not seemed capable of looking after themselves. There was also the matter of the iron door, against which at that moment he had seemed to hear the sound of some person being thrown. So he had pointed at it, and said, 'I'm frightened.'

'Oh, you are silly, Walter. That's nothing to do with you. They're probably just playing a game. They could be kicking a ball about. You like football, don't you?'

Walter knew the difference between the sound of a ball being kicked at a door and that of a head suffering the same fate. He had said, 'I don't like it here. You told me it was nice.'

Once again the Social Worker had smiled her patient and pleasureless smile. 'How do you know what it's like until you've tried it? I happen to think that it is nice – for someone like you. What would you do out in the town, all on your own? The Corporation wouldn't let you stay in that house; you'd have to walk the streets.'

She had removed the gloves from her hands, and placed them in her handbag. She had taken Walter's free hand in hers, and once again they had begun to walk. As they had walked together along the great corridor, Walter had felt all will, all hope, all happiness and all energy drain away from him.

And so they had come to this room, where a man in a white coat asked him questions, most of which he could answer, and none of which he would, while the Social Worker wrote on an official form with a ballpoint pen.

'He's sulking. He's decided he doesn't like it here.' The Social Worker had finished her report. She took her gloves from her handbag, and began to put them on. She had done with physical contact for the day.

The man in the white coat said, 'Hey! Don't forget to sign for the hand-over.' He handed her a printed form with a carbon copy attached.

'Just like me to forget the most important bit.'

She signed, and the man tore off the top copy, and gave it to her, saying, 'One sulky subnormal, handed over and signed for.' Then they both laughed, and the Social Worker held out a gloved hand to the white-coated man, and he shook it.

Walter watched from the glass booth of an office, as the man and woman walked together to the thick iron door. The man lifted his white coat, examined a large bunch of keys which hung at his waist, chose one, and unlocked the door with it. The Social Worker stepped through into the long corridor, and the door was locked again behind her.

Walter sat in a small hip-bath. Lukewarm grey water just covered his genitals. A man in a faded beige coat scrubbed at his back with a stiff brush and carbolic soap.

Suddenly the man forced Walter's head down between his knees, so as to wet Walter's hair and the pigeon-droppings which were matted in it. Walter swallowed some of the grey water, and began to choke, and the man slapped him on the back with such force that he bit his tongue. Then the man continued his work, rubbing carbolic soap liberally into Walter's hair, pulling out the pigeon-droppings together with a little hair, and massaging Walter's scalp until it stung.

Thereafter Walter's pubic hair was given the same treatment, although it contained no pigeon-droppings. At this point of a bath,

Walter's mother had always handed the soap and flannel to him, saying, 'You can do that,' and Walter attempted to explain this to the man. 'I . . . I do that . . . I can do that,' he said, but the man in the coat of faded beige took no notice, continued with his work, and never spoke.

The man was strong. Walter was pulled from the bath as if he had no legs of his own. The man had gained this strength from years of pulling from baths patients whose legs were of no use to them.

Walter stood shivering on the cold linoleum, while the man rubbed him all over with a small rough white towel, which bore the name of the hospital as a sign that it was the hospital's property. Walter's own property, the clothes in which he had arrived and his suitcase with its contents, had been taken away from him. The money he had rescued from his mother's biscuit tin was in the pocket of his jacket with her Eiffel Tower ear-rings. He should have asked to keep them, but since he had been taking off his clothes to have a bath, there would have been nowhere he could had put them for safety. Perhaps they would be given back to him when he was allowed to wear proper clothes again.

The man held Walter's privates cupped in his hand as he combed Walter's pubic hair. Clearly he was looking for something. With each stroke, he held the comb up to the light and close to his eyes. The same process of combing and searching was applied to the hair on Walter's head.

After the combing and searching came a searching without combing. First the man turned Walter round on the spot, scanning his body for bruises. Then he forced Walter to bend over, prised his buttocks apart, and examined what he saw before him. Then he turned Walter again, grasped his penis and squeezed it, squinting at the hole for any sign of a discharge.

Walter did not know what the man was searching for. He did not know why any of this was being done. At no time did the man explain to Walter the reason for his actions.

Next the man led Walter into another room, in which there was a weighing-machine smaller than the one which stood by the door at Woolworth's, on which customers might weigh themselves by putting a penny in the slot. The man weighed Walter (the machine did not require a penny) and made a note of Walter's weight on a card; it was eleven stone, four ounces. Then he took Walter's wrist in his hand, consulted his own wristwatch for what seemed to be a long time, and made another note. He examined the teeth in Walter's mouth, holding the mouth open with his fingers, and pulled a face. Walter took the face to mean that the man was not pleased with what he saw.

A large stiff white nightshirt was placed over Walter's head, and pulled down. Walter noticed that it had been darned and patched in a great many places. To wear over it, he was given a dressing-gown, which felt greasy. Old foodstains decorated the lapels and front. It stank of stale urine. There was no belt or cord with which to tie it, and so it stayed open at the front unless held. Walter held it. If his mother and father really were looking down at him from Paradise, they would be surprised to see him dressed like this.

He was given bedroom slippers which had been fouled several times, and felt damp. His own, which his mother had bought for him, remained in his suitcase. Wherever that was.

Walter was allocated a bed in a dormitory containing sixty-nine other beds, all of them occupied. The man in the faded beige coat directed him to his bed, and gave him two pills to swallow. He then spoke to Walter for the first time, and for the first time explained an action. He told Walter that the pills were to help him get off to sleep in the strange bed, and that they were only given on the first night. After that, he told Walter with what could only be described as a twisted smile, Walter would have to use what other methods were to hand in order to get off to sleep.

The time was seven thirty. All lights except the one in the glass booth at the end of the ward, which was occupied by the Staff Nurse, were turned out.

At eight o'clock, the Night Staff arrived, and the Day Staff went home, Walter was still awake, in spite of the two pills, and heard someone say, 'We've got a new one. Might be a bit of trouble. If he kicks up give him the needle.'

The man in the bed to Walter's right was crying into his pillow. Between sobs, he whispered words. Walter thought that the words were meant for him to hear, so he leaned closer to the man, but what he heard was,

> 'Lord, who lives in everlasting light,
> I love thee ever with heart and hand,
> That has made me to see this sight,
> First out of all the people of my land.
> Here shall I be born, King of Bliss.
> I shall not want or wish for aught.
> God of all Gods, I await them to recognize me.
> Please, please, let it be soon.'

He looked up into the darkness above his head, and tried to stop himself from thinking about what might have happened to Lydia,

Stella, Lionel, the Muffed Tumblers and the Fantails, and all the other birds he had set free. Being free to them wasn't what it was to people. They had all been born in the Loft; they were used to a routine, and, as far as Walter knew, they liked it. Free, they would be frightened. There would be cats and rats. And the rats would be real rats, not those smiling rats who followed the Pied Piper in his jigsaw.

Without proper shelter and food, the pigeons would get depressed, and become ill. They were not used to being out late at night.

Anything might happen. Turbits were not practical birds.

He thought he heard something move swiftly across the floor to the left of his bed. Then he felt a tug at the bed-cover (which also bore the name of the hospital). He became still, wondering what could be tugging at his bedclothes.

A moment later something which he took to be a large hairy dog jumped up on to the bed on top of him. He was frightened of dogs. He slid further down into the bed, and covered his head, so that if the dog bit, it would only bite the blankets.

The hairy thing pulled the covers away from Walter's head, as a dog might dig to bury a bone. He felt its hair against his face. It gave off a sweet sickly smell, not just from its breath, but also from its sweat. Walter was not to know that what he smelled was digested paraldehyde. They were arms he was fighting, human arms; it was not a hairy dog but an old hairy man. The hairy man's face was touching Walter's face. He was breathing heavily. His arms were stronger than Walter's arms, thin, bony and strong. They had pulled the covers down as far as Walter's waist, and were now trying to pull the nightshirt up.

Walter was almost suffocated by the foul sickly breath and the rough beard which its owner was rubbing all over his face. With the breath came words, sibilant hissing whispers, as the old hairy man said, 'Here! You're new. Give us a bit of a feel. Give us a bit. Excite an old man. Go on, kid; let's have a bit of fun.' With these words, Walter felt sharp nails on the end of bony fingers groping between his legs. He tried to roll himself into a ball, and to protect his privates with his hands, pulling the bony fingers away.

Walter struggled in silence, not wishing to disturb the other patients and the Night Staff, who sat drinking coffee in the illuminated glass booth at the end of the ward. Then he realized that what the old hairy man was doing to him was what Elaine had done so long ago in the Park. The sticky stuff which she had drawn from him was about to burst out again. It was too late; he couldn't prevent it. He could feel it building up inside him, ready to gush forth on to the clean sheets he had only been lying between for an hour.

Then it happened. The sticky stuff shot from him into the old man's hands and into his own hands. As it did so, Walter let out a loud involuntary sound, half pleasure and half shame.

Immediately all the lights were switched on. The old hairy man jumped from Walter's bed as a dog might jump from a chair, and scuttled halfway across the ward. A window in the nurses' booth was opened, and a voice shouted, 'Go back to your own bed, Ben Gunn. He's much too young for you, you dirty old sod.'

The old hairy man crouched in the space between the two rows of disturbed patients, and growled back at the two night nurses, 'Gyah! Pig Shit! I got him first.' Then he laughed, a gurgling asthmatic laugh, and said, 'He's a virgin. Shot his bolt.' Then, still in the same crouching position, he started to make his way back to his own bed, cackling like a pantomime witch, 'I got him. I got him first.' When he had reached his own bed at the other end of the ward, and jumped into it, again very much like a dog, the lights were extinguished, the glass panel in the nurses' booth slid closed, and the coffee-drinking was resumed.

Walter's thoughts moved backwards over what had happened to him in so short a time, reliving the time when they had dragged him, screaming, from his mother's bedside to the Social Worker's car, his promise to be a good boy (which he had kept) and their promise that he would be alright (which they had not kept), and all the prolonged ceremony of his entrance to this hospital.

He pulled his nightshirt down over what his own mother had refused to touch, and closed his eyes. He wished his mother had taken him with her to be with Jesus in Paradise.

The man in the next bed was talking again:

'You sleep, brethren, yet I see.
Sleep on now, all of ye.
My time is come, to taken be;
From you I must away.
He that hath betrayed me,
This night from him will I not flee.
In a sorry time, born was he.'

In spite of the sleeping pills he had been given, Walter spent the next four hours wide awake. The sticky stuff dried on his thighs and nightshirt and on the top sheet of the bed, a patch of which now felt stiff to the touch. This worried him. In the morning, someone might notice, and make fun of him. Walter did not know exactly what had happened on this occasion any more than on the last, but the conversation at Woolworth's had taught him that anything emanating from the place his mother would not touch was bound to be a subject for ribaldry.

At two in the morning, he fell asleep.

Four hours later, he was woken up.

3

What are you staring at, Cinderella?
Lost your slipper?

THE words which woke Walter were, 'Got any bacca? Got a farthing? Bollocks!' The old man asking the questions did not wait for answers. He had asked the questions so many times, and always received a negative response, that he knew that to wait was a waste of time.

Walter's eyes had not yet focused. He assumed that the old man's words were still part of his dream. He was waking from a dream (or rather a nightmare) in which his mother had gone to join Jesus, and he had been tricked into entering a Lunatic Asylum, where he had been poked and prodded and made to stand naked while his private parts were pulled apart and squeezed.

He closed his eyes again, and then opened them, expecting his mother to rise from the chair in which she always sat, and to come towards him, reminding him to thank the Lord for safe deliverance through the night. But instead of his mother's face, there was now a large black shiny face with very white teeth, grinning not more than six inches away from the end of Walter's nose.

The mouth which contained the teeth moved, forming words. It was speaking. Talking. Talking to him, to Walter. And what it said was, 'Get out of that wanking pit, young man. It says here in your notes that you can stand, and even walk. Well, that's very lucky, 'cos that's what you're about to do.'

Walter blinked at the face, hoping it would go away, but it stayed where it was, and slowly the details of what he had thought to be a nightmare came back to him, and he realized where he was and how he had got there, and that the nightmare was real.

'Come on, man. This ain't no Health Farm you at. We got work to do.' The black face moved, and Walter's bedclothes were pulled off him.

Walter raised himself up on one elbow, and tried to take in his surroundings. There was noise. A lot of it. All kinds of noise. The black man who had woken Walter wore a white coat. A small bald-headed man with over-large hands had grabbed one arm of this white coat, and was trying to communicate with it by using a series of subdued shrieks. The bald man reminded Walter of a Toby Jug without its hat. The black nurse appeared to understand the meaning of the shrieks, for he replied, 'Yes, Harry. I will in a minute. We have a new friend. Have you not seen him?' The Toby Jug man shook his head, and approached Walter, holding out hot spongey fingers to be shaken in friendship. Walter shook the fingers. Then the Toby Jug man turned to the black nurse again, and made a further series of shrieks, pointing at Walter, and the black nurse said, 'Yes, alright then; you show him. But don't take all day.'

Walter was not sure that he wished to be shown whatever it was the Toby Jug man had been instructed to show him, but all that at first happened was that the Toby Jug man took Walter's arm, and helped him off the bed. Then he and the Toby Jug man stood side by side on the bare floorboards between Walter's bed and the bed of the man who had cried, and spoken God's name in the night. There was only just enough room for the two of them. Then the Toby Jug man stretched out his arm, and pointed all round the room, making a noise which Walter knew must have a meaning, which he was unable to guess.

A completely naked man was propelling himself along the floor in a sitting-down position. By moving his heels, then his bottom, and then his hands, he was able to travel extremely fast. This posture was also most convenient for undertaking the activity on which his heart seemed to be set, which was the gathering up of any piece of dirt he could find, and popping it into his mouth quickly like a hungry bird. Walter watched the naked man scrape up seven pieces of dirt with his thumb-nail and pop them into his mouth before he forced himself to look away.

Not all the men in the ward wore stiff white nightshirts as Walter did. Some wore pyjamas, the trousers of which were now being re-moved and thrown into a trolley. All the pyjama trousers handled in this way had been wet or soiled during the night. The trolley was almost full, and Walter realized why the windows were all being opened so hurriedly, and why it was so cold.

The window-opener used a long thick pole. He wore a coat of faded beige, like the man who had given Walter a bath, but he was not that man; his hair was red as carrots. Even when he had opened all the windows of the ward, the stench of soiled pyjamas was still over-powering.

Walter was aware that he should be doing something but did not know what, and rather than do something wrong and be either punished for it, or scorned, or both, he thought it wiser to do nothing.

The black nurse who had woken him was now at the other end of the ward, and the Toby Jug man had held out his bunch of fingers to be shaken a second time, and then moved away. Walter looked about for Ben Gunn, with the hope of not seeing him, and because there were sixty-nine other men in the room, not counting the Staff, his hope was realized.

Everyone looked physically odd in some way. Some of the men had heads too large for their bodies, and some had heads too small. Many had bodies which were twisted, with elbows permanently bent, and fingers splayed out, unable to grasp or grip. Some walked with a strutting gait on the balls of their feet, leaning forward with chests out. These men reminded Walter of a male pigeon strutting in pursuit of a hen, who must run in front of him to avoid having her tail trodden on.

A young black patient hopped around the ward, holding his left leg by the ankle.

Not all the men communicated in grunts or noises, but the only actual words Walter could understand were those spoken (or more frequently shouted) by the two men in white coats and the carrot-haired man in faded beige.

'God, it stinks like a sewer in here. What was it you had for your dinners yesterday? Was it brussels sprouts again, was it?'

Walter had not realized that he had been noticed, but now the carrot-haired Irish ward orderly was speaking to him. It seemed safer to concentrate his gaze on the floor.

'What are you staring at, Cinderella? Lost your slipper?'

Walter grinned, thinking that the safest thing to do.

'Oh, he's got a sense of humour. Well, now that's a precious thing in a place like this. Let's hope it lasts. Meanwhile, if you can stand, you can walk, and if you can walk, you can help some of these poor paraplegics to get out of their beds, and you can start ripping their filthy pants off them.'

Walter had no idea what the word 'paraplegic' meant, but the orderly had nodded towards a man in the bed opposite. This man was sitting up in his bed, shaking all over as if he were about to freeze to death.

Walter made a tentative move towards the shaking man, not at all sure what he was going to do or what had been asked of him. The carrot-haired orderly said, 'Yes, get that one. Do our Clifford first.'

The shaking man stank of excreted brussels sprouts. Walter placed a hand under each of the man's armpits, then turned and looked for guidance to the orderly.

'Well, pull the bedclothes back first, you great twopence half-farthing. How do you expect him to get his feet to the floor? He's not the Great Houdini.' Walter left the shaking man's armpits alone for the moment, and rolled the tightly tucked-in bedclothes down towards the shaking man's feet. When the man's trunk was uncovered, the full impact of the digested brussels sprouts hit Walter hard in the face. He closed his eyes in some faint hope that, by shutting off his vision, he might succeed also in impairing his sense of smell.

Slowly and with excessive care Walter pulled the bedclothes away from the man's feet, and then began the even more difficult manoeuvre of taking the feet from the bed to the floor without allowing the top half of the shaking man to fall backwards off the other side of the bed. Where the shaking man's feet landed, Walter found a pair of soiled bedroom slippers, much like the ones he himself had been made to wear. His own, he remembered, were still under his bed.

As Walter began to place the shaking man's shaking feet into his slippers, the orderly shouted, 'Pants off first, you great lump. Get his pants off, and wipe his bum clean with them.'

Walter looked up at the face of the shaking man, who was now sitting on the side of the bed. The man's mouth was so large that it covered a third of his face. His lips were thick and shiny, and they were wide open. Wide open. Walter marvelled at the size of the man's tongue, which hung out of his mouth, dripping warm saliva on to Walter's hands.

The man's eyes were small and almost closed, but they moved, and watched Walter's eyes. Walter stood, supporting the heavy shaking man, so that he too was standing. Their faces were so close that they almost touched. The shaking man belched, and Walter smelled the wind as it was released. The enormous open mouth lifted a little at each corner.

'That's right, Clifford. Start the day with a smile, and get it over with.' The carrot-haired orderly worked with amazing speed, stripping, cleaning and redressing one patient after another, operating for most of the time by touch, since his eyes were on Walter and Clifford.

Walter smiled back at the shaking man, just to show him that there was no ill feeling. The man was larger than Walter, and heavier. As he leaned against Walter, with his head hanging loosely to one side over Walter's shoulder, it became possible to untie the cord of his pyjama trousers, which, aided by the weight of what had been deposited inside them, dropped to the floor.

Walter had to strain to support the shaking man's weight, and was not at all sure how much longer he could bear the strain. He had reached the point at which he needed further instructions. Slowly he managed to turn his head in the direction of the orderly.

'It's alright; I'm watching you. Now, don't go falling in love with Clifford before breakfast. Just you get his sodding bum wiped.'

There was no way that Walter could reach the fouled pyjamas, which he had been told to use for wiping without lowering Clifford on to the bed. He began to bend down, Clifford's body bending with his, but seeing this, the orderly shouted, 'Don't you dare let his bum stain that sheet, if it hasn't already done so.' Walter managed to hold Clifford in suspension, his bottom some three inches from the sheet, while he groped for and eventually touched the pyjama trousers. Instantly he became aware of a further problem. Clifford's feet were still inside them. He lifted one foot out, rested, then lifted the other. Then he pulled Clifford a few more inches away from the bed, and managed to hold him there while he reached round with the soiled trousers and gave Clifford's bottom a perfunctory wipe. In any case, he noticed, the sheet was already stained.

'Puts you right off brussels sprouts, doesn't it?' It came to Walter that perhaps he had found, in all this place, someone whose disposition was fundamentally friendly. 'Clifford's your job every morning from now on. When you get a bit quicker, I'll give you the pleasure of Maurice and Albert. Tuesdays are worst. They've usually had cabbage the night before, and there's so much ill wind farting about in here, you have to hold on to the bedposts to retain your dignity. Now find yourself some nice pretty clothes from that pile over there, and get yourself dressed.'

In the pile of pretty clothes were trousers with elastic waistbands, no fly-buttons and no flies. (Walter remembered how long he and his mother had struggled before he had accomplished the undoing and doing up of buttons.) There were no underpants and no vests. The shirts were all stained and collarless, and the jackets were creased and rumpled, and so either too large or too small. All the clothes were slip-on clothes; their construction held no difficulties for the dresser, their appearance no pleasure for the watcher. Everything was dark brown, lovat or dark grey. He did not wish to wear anything he found. His mother would certainly have burned everything in the pile.

'Come on! Get a move on. What's your name?' This time a man in a white coat was shouting at him; the white coats seemed to be superior to the beige. Walter looked at the floor. He did not like to be shouted at when he had done nothing wrong.

'I said, "What's your name?" '

Walter told the man quietly that his name was Walter.

'Say "sir" when you speak to me, Walter. I'm the Staff Nurse on this duty, understand?'

Walter nodded, so as to avoid the necessity of saying 'sir' immediately.

'You're new.' The Staff Nurse informed Walter of this fact in a manner which suggested that Walter did not already know it.

'Yes, sir. I know, sir.' There; he had got it over. He remembered that he had not cleaned himself since handling Clifford's pyjama trousers. 'Please, sir, can I wash my hands?'

'What for?'

'They're dirty, sir.' He held them out in proof.

'Alright. In there.' The man pointed to the Wash Room. 'And don't take so long choosing your wardrobe. It's not Friday, and we're not expecting the Queen.' The beige-coloured orderly laughed at this last remark, though Walter could not tell why. And the significance of Friday was only revealed to him later.

He washed his hands, and returned to the pile of clothes. The orderly told him to bring Clifford some clothes. 'Nice big ones. He's a hell of a big man is our Clifford.' He patted Clifford under the chin. 'Aren't you, lovely?' Clifford sat on the side of his bed, wearing only his pyjama jacket, and shaking, partly from his ailment and partly from the cold. 'And don't take all day about it,' the orderly said. 'It's so cold in here with the windows open, the brass monkeys will be after knitting themselves fur-lined jockstraps.'

Walter dressed as quickly as he could in the first things that came to hand. Then he took the largest shirt, jacket and trousers he could find in the pile and helped Clifford to get into them.

'Now bring his wheelchair from the Recreation Room.' The orderly pointed to a room on the other side of the nurses' booth. 'It's got "Number Twenty-Six" painted in blue on the handlebars. Can you recognize a two and a six when you see them?' Walter nodded, 'Well, that's a blessing, I'm sure. We'll be entering you for the Brain of Britain before we're through. Go along now, and get it. Then you can push him down to breakfast. Am I not spoiling you, Walter, with all these treats?'

The Recreation Room was almost as large as the room in which Walter had slept. It was bare, except for the chairs which surrounded the room, their backs to the walls. Some of the chairs could at one time have been described as 'easy chairs' but few of them were likely to give much ease now, the kapok stuffing having been removed by patients whose condition caused them to pick and pluck. Among them were twenty-four wheelchairs, with painted numbers on the handlebars which went up to the fifties. They seemed to be haphazardly scattered among the other chairs. Walter was later to discover that the placing was not at all haphazard, but invariable, each wheelchair patient having his own favourite place to sit.

On the window-ledge there was a radio. Its knobs had been removed. Walter was later also to discover the secrets of this radio, which had long ago been tuned to the Light Programme with a pair of pliers, on which station it permanently remained, and which could only be switched off (an operation which took place on Friday afternoons and at bedtime) by pulling its plug out of the wall-socket. The orderly who had long ago tuned the set had also permanently adjusted its volume, so that only by sitting with an ear pressed against it could one make out what was being said. What the BBC said was not relevant to the lives of the men who lived in Ward C3, and the faint persistent music of the Top Ten acted as Muzak, neither demanding nor getting attention.

Breakfast was served in the Dining Room, which was used by patients from all three wards of C Wing. C1 housed fifty patients, C2 sixty, and C3, Walter's ward, seventy. The patients were graded by the hospital authorities according to their capabilities, and C3 contained the lowest grade. It was also used as a Punishment Ward. To be sent down to C3 from either of the other wards meant that a patient had been violent, or anti-social, or a persistent irritant to other patients or to the Staff, or that the patient had regressed. A small room of C3 was used to isolate very violent patients. There was nothing in this room which could be used as a weapon, the mattress was on the floor, and shutters across the windows prevented the glass from being broken or the white enamelled chamberpot from being emptied out of it on to heads below. The floorboards near the radiator were stained where isolated patients had pissed on the radiator to make steam when the chamberpot was full.

Walter had not been graded as of low capabilities by the authorities; he had not yet been graded at all. All newcomers to the hospital were first put into C3 as part of the process of assessment. This assessment was more sophisticated than might at first appear. Even if a newcomer should prove himself to be capable, if he should also prove himself helpful to the nursing staff, he might be kept in C3 nevertheless, otherwise the proportion of three Staff to seventy patients would have been unworkable.

Unaware of this, Walter was being helpful. He had wheeled Clifford to the Dining Hall, where one hundred and eighty handicapped male persons sat at twelve very long tables. Only forty of these persons were capable of using a knife and fork. Walter sat on a chair next to Clifford's wheelchair, and looked at the spoon before him. He thought again of his mother, watching from Paradise, and knew that she would wish him to ask for a knife and fork. *A good boy eats with a knife and fork, Walter, not a spoon.*

A Staff Nurse asked those gathered here today to thank God for the blessings they were about to receive. Walter wished that he were about to receive a knife and fork. Perhaps his mother would mention it to Jesus. What he did receive, as did the other hundred and seventy-nine persons gathered there that day, was a plastic bowl containing powdered egg which had been scrambled and allowed to cool, along with a thick slice of white bread, spread sparingly with margarine. This was almost thrown on to the dining tables by the Staff, there being, at each place, a round rubber placemat coloured grey, put there to stop the plastic bowls from sliding across the tables. Each of these hundred and eighty grey rubber placemats had a pattern of raised rubber circles on the top intended not for ornament but as a further precaution against sliding bowls. In the grooves between the raised circles were reminders of meals long past.

Walter looked across at the long line of faces at the other side of the table. Some of the men held the plastic bowls up to their mouths, almost drinking the scrambled egg. Others shovelled it into their mouths with their spoons, and if it fell on to the front of their clothes, they rubbed at the wasted egg with their sleeves.

There were eleven men at Walter's table who wore plastic bibs, each having a trough at the bottom of the bib to catch spilled food, so as to give it a second chance of reaching its target. Most of them could not achieve the physical action of spooning the egg from its bowl and getting it to a mouth, not even their own. Six of the eleven sat like Clifford, not even trying to eat, but shaking and staring at the food in front of them. These men seemed to have bent and twisted hands and bodies, as if their bones were the wrong shape or size. One of them leaned forward above his bowl, opening and shutting his mouth as if willing the egg up into it.

Walter saw a nurse spoon–feed a man who could not feed himself, and when he had finished his own meal, which did not take long, he got up from his chair, and began to feed Clifford. Clifford, who was used to waiting his turn to be fed, dropped his head back as far as it would go, and watched Walter through the narrow slits behind which were his eyes.

Automatically, without even thinking about it, Walter fed Clifford in the way in which his own mother had taught him to feed himself. The nurse, who was now feeding his third patient, merely used his own hands, and spooned each spoonful into the patient's mouth, but Walter placed Clifford's right hand on the spoon, and pressing his own fingers around it, guided Clifford's hand to Clifford's mouth.

Feeding Clifford in this way was exhausting, since it required much of Walter's strength to prevent Clifford's hand from shaking and spilling the food, and it took much longer than the method of feeding practised by the Staff, but Walter thought that, if he were to show the Staff what he was capable of, they would realize that they had made a mistake and allow him to go home. The Indian nurse meanwhile had begun feeding his fifth patient. He observed Walter's novel and exhausting method of feeding Clifford, but let him get on with it.

Those of the patients who could both walk and be trusted with cups, left the table after finishing their egg and bread, and were given watered milk to take back to their places and drink. Watered milk was brought to others by the Staff in cups with spouts, and they were assisted to drink. Walter had been used to tea with his breakfast, but in its absence, even watered milk would have been welcome. However, just as Clifford swallowed his last spoonful, the same Staff Nurse who had asked him to thank God for what he was to receive, lifted a handbell, and shook it. Those patients who could stand, did. Others waited in the wheelchairs for someone to push them back to the ward. A few chairbound patients used their own arms to turn the wheels. As swiftly as breakfast had been given, its remains were cleared away. There could be no doubt that it was over.

Walter assumed that it was now his job to push Clifford back to the ward. As he turned the wheelchair, he felt a hand on his shoulder, and the Indian nurse said, 'Are you going to feed Clifford from now on?' Walter, not being sure what the right answer to that question might be, decided that a nod was the reply which would commit him least. To his relief, the Indian nurse said, 'Good boy! That will be very nice. Save me trouble.' Walter, prodded to it by a sudden mental picture of his mother's disapproval at seeing so much of her teaching (on buttons . . . on spoons) destroyed in this place, seized his chance, and asked the nurse if he might have a knife and fork next time.

'Yes, certainly. What you do is to go see that man over there.' He pointed to a beige-coated man standing behind a food-trolley, scraping left-over scrambled egg into a bucket. 'Ask him for a knife and fork before each meal. Then remember to take it back to him when you are finished. They all have to be counted, see? Knives and forks can be dangerous. You understand? Someone I once saw a fork pushed right into his eye. Blinded. Very dangerous. You understand?'

Walter nodded.

Back at Ward C3, Walter and Clifford were counted in, just as, when the door had been unlocked for them to go down to the Dining Hall, they had been counted out. This happened at every mealtime.

No patient was permitted to leave the ward without being escorted by a member of Staff, and since there were rarely more than three members of Staff on duty in Ward C3, a reason for leaving the ward had to be important.

Visitors were not encouraged. They caused work. Visiting was allowed on Wednesday and Saturday afternoons, and anyone wishing to visit had to apply in writing at least one full week before arriving. It was extremely inconvenient for Staff to take time out from their other duties in order to make sure that a patient being visited was given a special shave and put into his own clothes. Then, since visitors were not, of course, permitted to visit the ward (which could never have been brought into any condition which visitors might regard as being even minimally suited for human habitation), more time had to be taken in escorting the patient to the Visitors' Room. Fortunately for the Staff on Ward C3, very few patients ever had visitors. Walter himself did not expect anyone to come and see him. Nobody except the doctor, policeman and Social Worker knew where he was, and although the Social Worker had promised to inform Mr Richards, the manager of Woolworth's, he was in no doubt that she had broken that promise as she had the promise that he would be alright. Besides, Mr Richards was a busy man. It was unlikely that he would take half a day off work to visit Walter.

Occasionally a patient from C3 would have to be escorted to the hospital dentist. But very few of the patients had their own teeth. Most had dentures. They owned dentures, but seldom wore them, since most, at sometime or other, had had their teeth confiscated, either for biting other patients or for forgetting to take the teeth out at night and falling into the danger of swallowing them, or even for simply leaving the teeth around, by which they might become lost or misused, when confiscating them was safer, since at least the Staff (if not the patient) then knew where the teeth were.

Where they were would be in a large bowl. Whenever a nurse saw a patient sleeping with his teeth in, those teeth would be removed, rinsed meticulously in water and Milton, and placed in that bowl, which already contained more than a hundred pairs of National

Health dentures, most of them belonging to patients who had died. Then if later the relatives of that patient were to write (allowing a full week) that they wished to visit, a simple process of trial and error would provide that patient with teeth, perhaps as many as a hundred and thirty pairs from the bowl being tried before a pair was found which would fit, was not too stained, and would not fall out when he smiled. If he smiled.

It was altogether more convenient for the Staff if the patients were without teeth. One of the patients in Ward C3, whose teeth had been in such excellent condition that they drew blood every time they met in a white-coated arm, had been escorted to the dentist and spent much of one day there, emerging with nothing in his mouth but his tongue, some raw and badly cut gums, and a great deal of blood. National Health teeth had thereafter been provided for him, and were kept in the large bowl.

The red-haired orderly showed Walter where, in the Recreation Room, to place Clifford's chair. There was a straight hardbacked chair against the wall next to where Clifford liked his chair to be, and Walter sat on that.

'Now, don't you be getting yourself too comfortable there, me boy. You'll be standing in line for your shave any minute now. Harold will sort you out.'

Walter looked at the Irish orderly with absolute incomprehension.

'You'll soon pick up these little rituals we have.'

Walter, who had never heard the word 'ritual' in his life before, became convinced that it meant something unpleasant and almost certainly painful. In this he was not very far from the truth.

It seemed that the men in the beds on the lefthand side of the ward were shaved on Mondays, Wednesdays and Fridays, the others on Tuesdays, Thursdays and Fridays. The reason why everyone had to be shaved on a Friday was because that was the day when the Chief Staff Nurse made his weekly inspection. No shaving was done on Saturdays or Sundays unless one of the patients should be inconsiderate enough to have a Saturday afternoon visitor.

Walter looked round at the other patients. He was now in a different world from the one which had contained his father, mother and the pigeons. It seemed very close to what his mother had told him of Hell, except that it manifestly lacked heat. Deformed demons, half man, half animal, moved around him, some looking at him, some through him. All seemed to be waiting for something, but he could not even guess at what it was. This was their ward, not his. Some of them must have been born here, sent as children, been here so long that they had forgotten the world outside. Why were they all waiting? What were they expecting?

Ben Gunn stood in the centre of the room, shouting obscenities at anyone who brushed or touched him. In the lefthand pocket of his jacket, there was an unused toilet roll, in the right a plastic cup. The cup was of dual use. It was an ashtray (for the hospital was not a prison; the patients were given a small amount of pocket money for cigarettes or sweets, and were allowed to smoke in the Recreation Room) and also a spittoon. Sometimes it was emptied.

When Walter saw Ben Gunn, he turned to Clifford, and pretended to be talking to him. Too late! Ben Gunn had spotted him, and although he had seen Walter only briefly the night before when Walter had been brought into the ward and put to bed, and not at all during the sexual assault because the lights had been out, Ben knew all the patients of C3 by sight and, knowing Walter's to be a fresh face, realized that this was the person he had attacked. He came to Walter, and stood close to him, his short legs almost touching Walter's knees.

Walter had stopped pretending to talk to Clifford and was looking down at the polished floor. The sweet sickly stench of paraldehyde, which Ben Gunn always carried about with him, just as he carried his toilet roll and plastic cup, filled the little space there was between them, and grew even stronger as he opened his mouth, and cackled, 'Gawd, you're ugly! An ugly virgin! Cor!' Then he walked away, and the stench went with him.

Walter sat up straight, as his mother had taught him, in a hard-backed chair next to a man whose body he had handled as intimately as if it were his own. It was a different world. Hairy stinky old men touched him in the dark, and laughed at him before others. Walter looked at the screwed-up faces of the men about him. Jesus had made these men, as he had made all men. These were Jesus's mistakes, and for each He would get a cross. In the world Walter had left, there were people who could dance, sing, play musical instruments, paint, be leaders of men, like Mr Richards. There were people who looked nice, like Mrs Silver on Cosmetics or the filmstars he had seen in the papers. All those people were Jesus's successes, and for each of them He would get a tick. But if Jesus were perfect, as Walter's mother had insisted that He was, why had He not got ten out of ten? Why had He made so many mistakes?

And what were they waiting for, these mistakes, who paced up and down, or leaned against the wall, or shook, or dangled to one side over the arms of their wheelchairs, like marionettes whose strings have been cut? What did they want, these mistakes, who hugged themselves and

175

made wordless noises – screams, gasps, screeches, grunts, mumbles, moans, whines? Some of the sounds the mistakes made seemed to be sounds of pleasure. How could they enjoy themselves in here, when all their bits had been so badly put together by Jesus?

As Walter looked at the other men in the Recreation Room, and saw how many different mistakes had been made by Jesus, a hand gripped his upper arm, and pulled him to his feet. Walter let out a small cry of surprise, but when he saw the face that went with the hands, he gave no resistance to the man's pull. The man's head was too big, and his eyes seemed unfocused and were directed either to the ground or to the sky, so that the pupils almost totally disappeared under the slanted eyelids. And the man mumbled, asking questions without waiting for answers, since he himself provided both question and answer.

'Which side you sleep? Right, innit? Yes, right. That'll be it. Must be right. Jack's bed, that was. Died last week, dinnee? Tuesday, wossit? Think it was. Might not, though. Might been after that.'

During all this, the man maintained a tight grip on Walter's arm, and pulled him towards a queue he was organizing. Starting at the entrance to the Wash Room, it curled into the Recreation Room, and ran along one wall.

'Get shaved today, see? Jack got shaved Tuesday. Thassit. I remember. Tuesday Jack died; he'd had a shave. Here, you! You stand there and don't move. Got to learn. Learn you, when you're new. I learn you. Me. I'm Harold. How d'you do?'

Harold held his hand to be shaken, and Walter shook it. Then he patted Walter on the shoulder, his eyes squinting upwards, and said, 'There's a good lad. Got to learn.' It seemed to Walter that there was a great deal of shaking hands in this hospital. He wondered if it were a practice in all hospitals. Meanwhile, he was in for a wait. There were sixteen men in the queue before him and others round the corner whom he could not see. Harold had also disappeared round the corner into the Wash Room, and later Walter was to find out why.

The queue moved forward slowly, and Harold returned from the direction of the Wash Room to make hurried trips round the Recreation Room, each time bringing back a patient whose day this was for shaving, and placing him in the line behind Walter. Then he would move up and down the line, pushing at the waiting men, demanding that they keep the line straight, and pulling at the shoulders of those who stooped.

With ten men before him and twelve behind him, Walter's feeling of aloneness became absolute. He had carried it around all morning. For moments when he had been helping Clifford, it had been pushed into the background, but it was still there. Now it was full, complete, all there was. This was their world, not his. When his father and mother had been alive, he had never thought about the future. Now there seemed not to be one, no point in it, not here, not in here, not in this place, not like this. Not queueing for a shave, not cleaning and feeding Clifford, not being attacked and then laughed at by Ben Gunn. Not here in this room, not locked up, not in here, not as a helpless watcher of pacing, hearer of screaming, of shouting, of anger. Not as a smeller of perpetual stenches . . . Not as an unwilling witness of the mistakes, the smelly angry mistakes that Jesus had made. His crosses. Walter wouldn't be a cross. He wouldn't wait for Paradise here, not as a cross, not as a mistake; he wouldn't be that. His mother had taught him to be good, to do things; he could do things. He had a job. She had said to him, 'Are you going to do well, and make me proud of you?' and he had. They had liked his work at Woolworth's, and his mother had received a letter from Mr Richards. She had read it out aloud to Walter and his father. Mr Richards had written, 'Dear Mrs Williams, Your son, Walter, is working so hard, and doing his job so well as any normal person could do it. I am very pleased to inform you that we wish to keep him on, at a wage of three pounds and ten shillings per week. Walter is a good boy, whom we here think you should be proud of. Sincerely R. H. Richards, Manager.'

His mother had cried, and hugged him. He had made her proud. She had looked at him with tears on her face, and said, 'Now there's nothing wrong with you. Don't let anyone ever say there is. Anyone who has a letter like this to show has nothing to worry about. Three pounds ten! They're not exactly putting a strain on the Woolworth millions, but it could be a lot worse. You have a job. A job for life, I should think, if you want it. Good boy! I'm very very proud of you. So is your dad.'

And his father had put his paper down, and said, 'Aye, lad. Keep up the good work.'

Walter could remember that.

4

It was impossible to give every patient a straight parting without the application of a great deal of lavender-scented brilliantine

Six months later, when Harold was moved to Ward C2, and Walter had proved to the Staff what he was capable of, Walter was given the responsibility of Harold's old job.

Six chairs had to be placed in a line before the six wash basins in the Wash Room. A patient had to be placed in each of the six chairs, and each patient had to have lather applied to the area of his face which was to be shaved. This enabled the nurses to move from one patient to the next with a razor containing an extremely blunt Seven O'Clock blade, and scrape off the lather without stopping or putting down the razor.

The nurse worked quickly, and Walter had to dash about, as Harold had done, to keep up with him. Having now lived in Ward C3 for six months, he knew which patients were on which side of the ward. He rushed from the Wash Room to the Recreation Room, picking out the men whose days it was to be shaved, as Harold had done, and then back into the Wash Room to use the shaving brush and stick of shaving soap to make a lather and apply it to the faces of the waiting patients.

Unlike Harold, Walter did not insist that the line of men be straight, nor did he pull back stooping shoulders, nor did he lather all six faces one after the other, since his own experience of Harold's method had taught him that, by the time the nurse reached the third face, the soap on the remaining three would have dried and be beginning to itch, which taken with the bluntness of the razorblade, had caused several of the patients to develop rashes. The bluntness of the blade was not due to any intention of causing pain by the nurses. They themselves suspected that the hospital administration, for reasons of economy, bought razorblades in bulk, and that these blades were 'seconds' – rejects which were sold off cheaply. Also they were bound by Standing Orders which laid down that one blade should be made to last for fifty shaves.

Walter watched the nurse carefully and calculated the speed at which each nurse worked. By spending less time in forming the men into line, which, under his regime, was no longer as long or as straight as it had been, he was able always to keep two chins ahead.

However, in spite of Walter's improvements in the routine of shaving, there was one incident of violence, caused by the tender and painful rash of an extremely large patient, and the bluntness of the razorblade in use on that particular morning.

Walter was working up a creamy foam on a patient whose head always had to be held while the nurse shaved him, since the usual state of that head was to be in perpetual motion. Meanwhile the nurse applied his razor to the chin of the very large man in the next chair.

At the moment of contact between razor and chin, the large patient shot his arms up into the air, and stood. His sudden movement sent the nurse staggering backwards and the razor flying through the air. The chair was overturned, as the large patient made for the door, and the bristles of Walter's shaving brush blocked the shaking-headed patient's nasal passages.

Before Walter and the nurse had time to collect their thoughts, the large patient was back in the Wash Room, blood dripping from his chin, and a heavy chair held above his head. It seemed both to Walter and the nurse that the intentions of this patient were not peaceable. It took the nurse only the fraction of a second to come to this conclusion, and only another fraction of a second to get himself inside one of the toilet cubicles, where (the cublicles having, of course, no locks) he place his back against the door, his feet against the base of the WC, leaned at a thirty-degree angle. There he would be safe, at least for a short while, and if the large patient should attempt to climb over the door, he must relinquish his hold on the chair to do so.

Unwilling to be parties to what might happen, the other patients in the Wash Room ran quickly out of it, leaving Walter and the shaking-headed man, who alone among them all was unaware of what was happening.

Thwarted by the speed of the nurse, the large patient turned his attention towards Walter, who backed away, shaving brush in one hand, stick of shaving soap in the other. Neither seemed to be an adequate weapon with which to take on a man of six foot three, holding a chair over his head. The large patient advanced and Walter retreated. Then the shaking-headed man, who had soap up his nose, sneezed. The sneeze was so loud that it sounded like a threat, and the large man turned sharply to see who was attacking him from the rear.

It was only a moment, but Walter used it to its full advantage, and dashed out of the Wash Room, disappearing into the crowd outside, to find the other nurses on duty and tell them what had happened.

But the nurses made excuses. They were busy. It was up to the nurse doing the shaving to control his patient.

Walter gave up trying to persuade the other nurses to do anything. He stood at a distance from the Wash Room at a point where he could observe both the entrance and the exit.

He stood listening, surrounded by noise and chatter. The constant background buzz of jabbering and gibberish continued, but inside his head there was silence. He was waiting for a sound which he knew would come, which would cut through both the silence inside his head and the jabber outside.

When it came, it was not as he had imagined it. He had not thought that it would sound like an animal, like the breathless pathetic scream of a rabbit. Four seconds. Four animal noises, and then nothing.

The buzz of chatter did not stop. The patients of Ward C3 were well used to the noises caused by pain and to the meaningless sounds of hysteria. Only Walter knew. Only Walter waited and watched. But not for long.

The large patient reappeared from the Wash Room, looked about him, puzzled, and then moved into the crowd of jabbering voices. He was no longer holding a chair.

Walter went into the Wash Room.

The man up whose nose he had inadvertently applied shaving soap, now had no nose. He had no skull or teeth; he had no longer a chin to be shaved. His ears remained. Between them there was a concave of the different kinds of matter which had, a few minutes earlier, made up a face, lathered with shaving soap.

Three weeks later, there was an Inquiry, at which Walter was asked to identify the large man who had held the chair.

Walter did so. He told the Inquiry what all three nurses who had been on duty at the time of the incident had instructed him to say. He said that the patient who had been killed had been irritating the larger man, who had rushed out and come back with a chair. He said that he and the nurse in charge had tried to disarm the large man, but had been pushed aside.

Nobody cross-examined Walter; he was not subjected to harsh questioning. What he said was written down. Nobody asked him whether either he or the nurse had sustained cuts or bruises while struggling with the violent patient. The Inquiry did not inquire how the shaking-headed patient, who had never spoken one word to anybody during his sixteen years in the hospital, had been able to irritate the large man into such extreme and passionate violence.

The large man was not asked for his own version of what had happened. He was sent to another hospital.

Walter was thanked, and praised for his bravery.

A word much used by the nurses and orderlies was the word 'condemned'. They would say, 'I'm condemning these trousers,' and proceed to tear them into two halves. Or they might say, 'This jacket needs condemning,' and pull a sleeve off it. The only way their requests for new clothes, bedding, shoes, or any article of necessary equipment could be met, was if they had first 'condemned' the article in such a way as to render it unusable.

Once a month, 'condemned' articles were replaced. (Most condemnations took place at the end of the month.) Brooms, buckets, shoe-brushes, facecloths, soap, toilet rolls, all had to be accounted for, and the accounts audited.

Every Friday was a day of pomp and ceremony. Much work and speed were necessary if all were to be made ready for the Chief Staff Nurses' Friday afternoon inspection.

The open ends of all pillowslips had to face away from the door of the ward so that the Chief Staff Nurse would not see a pillow (grey and white striped, usually stained) protruding from its slip. All the taps had to be polished, and a responsible patient set to stand guard over them to make sure that nobody used them after they had been made to shine.

The bare boards of both Recreation Room and Dormitory had to be polished. One patient would carry a large tin of wax polish and a stick, with which to scoop it out and dollop in on to the floorboards at regular intervals. Four other patients would work with bumpers, pushing and pulling them to work the polish into the wood until the floor had a shine which would gain the approval of the Chief Staff Nurse. These bumpers were like doormats with bristles, which faced down, and which had on top a heavy cast-iron square, the same size as the mat. Attached to the square was a large and heavy pole with which to push the bumper backwards and forwards. Polishing the floor was tiring, and required strength. No patient liked doing it, and those who were picked had to be strictly supervised.

Since mentally handicapped patients come, like the human beings whom they in certain respects resemble, in different sizes (these sizes being, if anything, even more varied than the sizes of the human beings whom, etc, some being abnormally large, both wide and high, and some abnormally childlike), the beds in which they were to spend most of their lives were also of different sizes. Such differences would not do for the Chief Staff Nurse. Whatever size the bed might be, on Friday afternoons the iron rail at its foot had to be in line with all the other beds, so that some of the smaller beds, and the lockers beside them, might be anything up to two feet away from the wall, with consequent discomfort to the smaller patients and inconvenience for the orderlies. After the inspection, they would all be pushed back.

Since seventy chins had to be shaved on Friday mornings, Walter was excused from any of the cleaning jobs, but during the six months before Harold had left the ward, Walter had pushed and pulled the heavy bumpers back and forwards, had polished the taps, helped to make beds and re-site lockers, applied Cardinal Red Polish to the tiled window-ledges, dusted the bedside lockers, cleaned the toilet bowls, scrubbed the Wash Room floor, applied brilliantine smelling of lavender to the heads of the non-ambulant patients, and combed their ill-cut hair so that every patient had a parting on the correct side of his head, and each parting was as straight as the footrails of all the beds.

The barber, who visited the ward once a week to cut thirty-five heads of hair in under two hours, referred to his work as 'sheep-shearing'. It was impossible, therefore, to give every patient a straight parting without the application of a great deal of brilliantine, the stench of which was as overpowering and even more sickly than the smell of paraldehyde. The Chief Staff Nurse never seemed to notice that several of the patients had red and sore eyes, caused by the lavender-scented brilliantine which had run down their foreheads. If the taps and the floor shone, and all the pillowslips were facing the right way, he was happy. And his happiness was what everyone hoped for.

Once a week, there was a film show, always a comedy, sometimes silent – the Keystone Kops, W. C. Fields, Chaplin, Abbott and Costello, Laurel and Hardy; since most of the patients had poor memories, often the same film was shown two weeks running. Everyone was obliged to go to church on Sunday, which was easily arranged, since the church was inside the grounds of the hospital. Both church and hospital had been built in 1839, the hospital then being a workhouse, and its paupers had been held to be as much in need of the consolations of religion as of food and creature comforts. Religion had in those days frequently replaced both food and comforts and that it did not still do so may be accounted some form of progress.

Those patients who were allowed out for walks outside the grounds did so in an orderly crocodile, two by two like Noah's animals, except that the male patients turned right outside the hospital gates, and the female patients left; there was no intention, as Noah had, that they should increase and multiply. Neither the male nor the female patients were on wet days allowed to go out at all. This would never have done for Noah, but the drying of wet hair, clothes, and feet would have meant more work for the hospital Staff.

The days passed, and Walter gave up counting them. He knew that 'they' would never realize that they had made a mistake, and send him home. His life had become submerged within the routine of the hospital. He became a 'trusty', a friend, to the nurses and orderlies. From the day he had lied for them, they had begun to treat him as someone who was neither a patient nor a member of Staff, but as some-one who just happened to be there, someone on whom they could rely to help them. Ward C3 was, of course, where they needed help most.

More and more of his time was spent in helping others, and less and less in looking back, or expecting his mother to leave Jesus in order to come and collect him.

There were moments when he heard himself sighing, or caught himself thinking about Woolworth's. Someone else would be collecting the rubbish now. That someone else would be operating his, Walter's press. That someone else would be using Walter's wirecutters to make the bales, and would be patted on the back and praised by Mr Richards. He wondered whether anyone at Woolworth's had asked what had happened to him, whether anyone had tried to find out where he was.

There were other moments when he thought of the pigeons, usually at night, as he lay awake, listening to the man in the bed beside him talking to God. He would silently mouth their names, and see each one in flight. But as time passes, the list of names he could remember grew shorter, and the number of times he thought either of the pigeons or Woolworth's grew fewer. The natural life of a pigeon is not long, and cats may shorten it.

He was neither happy nor unhappy; he just was. His birthdays came and went, and so did Jesus's. Jesus's birthdays were celebrated with balloons, trimmings and roast chicken. Paper hats were worn by Staff and patients, and a bottle of brown ale was issued to everyone. One year a Children's Brass Band from a local school arrived (an hour later than they were expected), and the seven hundred and thirty-four male patients sang those bits of Christmas carols that they could remember, and hummed the rest. Some rocked, more excited than the children, and some cried, perhaps because they remembered happier Christ-mases, shared long ago with mothers, fathers, brothers, perhaps merely because of a generalized surfeit of emotion. The memories of such patients being, as is known, poor, the second explanation for their tears may be considered more likely.

Walter remembered all the words of all the carols, and sang them in a flat, tuneless, but loud and purposeful manner. He tried not to think of Christmases past; he tried not to upset himself. He sat, as always, beside Clifford, and held Clifford's hand, and if he found his thoughts drifting away out of his control towards the memory of his mother's voice singing, 'Away in a Manger', 'Silent Night', or 'Unto Us a Child is Born, Unto Us a Son is Given', he would squeeze Clifford's hand tighter, shake his own head from side to side, and try to laugh. Then he would turn to Clifford, and sing the words of the carol into Clifford's ear, as if he were trying to explain to Clifford the wonderful miracle of the Nativity.

Clifford gave no outward sign of hearing Walter or the carols or the Children's Brass Band. If Jesus existed for Clifford, He had not provided for His creation any way by which Clifford could join in the celebration of his Maker's birth.

Later a paper hat would be placed on Clifford's head, and the food Walter would put into his mouth would be special food. Brown ale would be held to his lips to drink, and he would drink it. But it might as well have been the vinegar Christ was given; it might as well have been medicine, champagne, or even bleach. Clifford was unable to take part in the joy of Christmas. He was unable to exhibit any pleasure in or gratitude for the fact that, thanks to Jesus, he, Clifford, had been saved.

5

People didn't laugh at the leader
of the crocodile

'I WANT to go home, and be a joy to my mother. I'll be self-contented then.'

It was ten past eleven, and the man in the next bed to Walter was talking to himself.

'Even though she's over sixty, she's the most true and honest woman in the whole of Banstead or any other area to those who know her.' (The man in the next bed was himself over sixty.) 'If I had a pound note for every lie these legal and medical people have told me, I'd be a very rich man. The worst one has moved to Dorking now, but that won't help him, don't let him think so; it'd do well for them to be more honest. They'll all be crossed off the Legal Register ... Pills for internal tension!' He made a noise of derision. 'Trying to break my mind down.'

'Pains in my head, doctor. Are you a Jew? It's as well to know. They want me in here until the land returns to certain owners. I'm not allowed to say their names. They've taken out a court order to stop me naming them.' A cry, 'I'll not be silenced.'

'There's none so chilly as our poor Willy, and he's now dead, poor thing. One worm said to his friend, "Let's go and have a piece in dead Ernest." Even a so-called madman can tell jokes, did you not know that?'

'You have your mother's eyes, Billy. That's what they always said to me. Always. Wasn't that funny? They're blue, you see, like hers. This is just a temporary assignment, being in here. Being a waiter's not a job you'd choose, now, is it? It's very depressing when you can't find the right job. I get awfully sad some days, mother. Being in here, it's not good for my health. I know you think I'm a perfectionist, but this really is not the place to spend too much time. I'm not perfect; nobody is. But I do try; it's just that I have my sad days. I can't get out of bed for being so depressed. It's the people in here depress me. I know I shouldn't say this, but there's some of them in here are more than a little odd.'

'If you come to collect me at the end of term, could you bring my cricket pads? I can't bat very well, but my knees are sore from kneeling so often to pray. If God is good, I may sleep tonight, without crying for you to touch me. I miss you so much, mummy. Please come and fetch me home.'

Muttering. 'From forth thy barren womb, shall come a child . . . Here shall I be born, King of Bliss.' The man cried, and fell asleep, and Walter fell asleep also.

Later Walter was woken by the sound of heavy snoring. Low, deep, guttural and unusual noises were coming from the man in the next bed. They sounded like snores, but in all the years he had slept next to him, Walter had never heard him snore. After considering for some time what he should do, he got out of bed, and fetched the nurse on duty.

At four a.m. on 12 July 1967 the man in the next bed to Walter's died of a heart attack.

Ten years had passed. He was a 'trusty'. They trusted him.

He had put on weight; the hospital food was mainly stodge. He was allowed to wear his own clothes, except that now they were too tight. The orderlies gave him good second-hand clothes, and he was allowed the use of an iron to keep them pressed. It was in the Staff's own interest to keep Walter happy. They found him a beige overall to do the dirtier jobs, such as the changing of Clifford, Albert and Maurice. It was a sign that he was one of them.

While others did hand-exercises, to teach them to co-ordinate eye and hand (ten years had passed; the treatment of the mentally ill progresses), while others made a man with five matchsticks, threaded beads, wove indifferent baskets, counted with buttons, played with plasticine (which was thought to lower the incidence of masturbation), scribbled drawings which, viewed by a sympathetic eye, were really quite like those of Dubuffet, and which they carried about with them all day, made round shapes of cardboard, painted shells to be stuck on the sides of plant-pots, began (but seldom completed) rugs, worked with raffia to make brightly coloured tablemats, Walter undertook no such remedial or creative occupations, but merely assisted the Staff.

While others were herded like sheep, counted in and out of the ward, made to stand naked and shivering, holding on to the wallbar in the Wash Room while Walter or one of the Staff gave them stripped washes known as 'Under the Arches', and were allowed baths only once a month, while they had to ask for sweets and cigarettes bought with their

186

own pocket money, but kept locked away in the office, Walter drank beer in the office, sitting down with the nurses, and chatting. Except that Walter himself did not chat; he was attentive, but silent. One of the reasons that this position of privilege was permitted to continue was that he never boasted of it, or overstepped the mark.

As long as his duties were done, he was allowed outside the ward whenever he desired to be, allowed to walk the grounds of the hospital. Had he asked, he would probably even have been allowed outside the Main Gate on his own. They knew he would return. He was a 'trusty'. They trusted him.

Many times, while leading his crocodile of twelve mistakes, mis-shaped by Jesus, he could have run away, darted up the nearest alley and hidden, or jumped on to a passing bus before anyone could catch him. But where would he go? How would he live? What would he do to get money? The money from his mother's biscuit tin, which he had brought to the hospital with him, had of course disappeared. Only her diamanté Eiffel Tower ear-rings had been left in his jacket pocket.

And if he were to run away, who would look after Clifford?

While leading the crocodile, he had noticed that those who lived in the real world, the world to which he had once belonged, wore clothes dissimilar to those he remembered. The women, in particular, looked very different. They wore more make-up on their faces, and had shorter hair. Some even showed their knees.

Walter found himself trying to remember what the naked women in the mucky books he had been shown in Woolworth's looked like. If he concentrated hard enough, he could bring into his mind a picture of Mike pressing his girlfriend against the lift gate in the yard at the back of Woolworth's, and he could perform in his mind that process known by cameramen as 'tracking' (though he had never met a cameraman, and did not know the word), by which a part of the picture is made to grow, pushing the rest out of the frame, and the part which grew would be Mike's hand as it lifted the girl's skirt until her knickers were showing, and then moved inside the knickers, so that the hand itself would be lost to sight, and only its outline could be seen, moving up and down. By this time, the outline of the hand would have in-creased considerably in size; it would be occupying the whole of the picture.

He looked at the women and young girls whom he saw outside the hospital grounds, and imagined for a moment that he was Mike, and that women liked him and would allow him to lift up their skirts. These thoughts worried and excited him, and he would place a hand inside his trouser pocket, and hold himself until the thoughts went away.

The men who walked behind him, holding on to one another's hands, were not interested in what they saw on their walks. They did not notice the people who stood and stared at them, or those in passing vehicles, who pointed and laughed. Walter had ceased his old habit of pointing and laughing back. It was the other men, the men behind him, at whom such people were pointing. They were the ones who were laughed at, not he. He was at the front; the people would believe him to be a member of Staff. People did not laugh at those who spent their lives looking after the sick. They did not laugh at the nurse who followed the crocodile, and would not laugh at the man who led.

Sometimes, if the weather were fine and the nurse on duty indulgent, Walter would be allowed to take Clifford on these walks, pushing his wheelchair at the front of the crocodile. Clifford liked walks. When left behind, he moved his foot up and down on the footrest of his wheelchair. It was too lethargic to be called stamping but Walter knew what it meant. Every time he was not able to take Clifford with him, he would go and sit with Clifford on his return, hold his hand, and tell him what he had seen.

His own interest in the real world, which he saw on these walks, had diminished over the years. He noticed the changes in fashion, buildings being knocked down; none of it concerned him. Some of the buildings stood, half-demolished, for years, and reminded him of houses his mother had taken him to look at during the war, with exposed wallpaper fading, fireplaces crumbling. As one year followed another, the walks outside became more and more like the film shown in the hospital on Wednesday evenings. They could distract him for a few moments, but as he returned to the hospital and entered the Lodge Gates, it was as if a hand had been held up between projector and screen to remind him that what he had been watching was only make-believe. What was real for him now was the hospital and the routine. This was his real world. It had to be. He would never get out of it.

MORE ABOUT PENGUINS
AND PELICANS

For further information about books available from Penguins please write to Dept EP, Penguin Books Ltd, Harmondsworth, Middlesex UB7 0DA.

In the U.S.A.: For a complete list of books available from Penguins in the United States write to Dept CS, Penguin Books, 625 Madison Avenue, New York, New York 10022.

In Canada: For a complete list of books available from Penguins in Canada write to Penguin Books Canada Ltd, 2801 John Street, Markham, Ontario L3R 1B4.

In Australia: For a complete list of books available from Penguins in Australia write to the Marketing Department, Penguin Books Australia Ltd, P.O. Box 257, Ringwood, Victoria 3134.

In New Zealand: For a complete list of books available from Penguins in New Zealand write to the Marketing Department, Penguin Books (N.Z.) Ltd, P.O. Box 4019, Auckland 10.

Also by David Cook

Winter Doves

'One of the few first-class writers to have emerged in recent years', said Auberon Waugh, reviewing this sequel to David Cook's outstanding prize-winning novel, *Walter*.

Walter has built a life in the mental hospital when he meets June, a short-stay patient recovering from a suicide attempt. She is bitter, attractive and corrosively articulate, she belongs, almost, in the world outside – yet she needs Walter. 'I arrived in Hell, and found a soulmate.' Comically and unexpectedly happy together, they run away from the hospital and consummate their love in a church.

Journeying south, to the underworld of London's poor and homeless in Her Majesty's Jubilee Year, their love blossoms; as generous and tender as it is acutely vulnerable.

'David Cook's style is so achieved that it can accommodate Walter, June, and the author's own passionate concern for the lost, the derided, the deprived in a seamless garment' – *Observer*

'I was caught from the start ... it demands to be re-read' – Kingsley Amis